ROYAL REVENGE

"Die! Die! Die!" a woman's voice screamed from the entrance.

Spur put a shot down the tunnel aiming it at the far speck of light. He had no idea if it would reach the light or not.

When the roaring of the shot inside the cave died down, Spur heard the woman's laugh again.

"It's all your fault, Princess, you and the jailers at Mantuco. They killed my brother, and now you're going to die to avenge his death. Too bad about the rest of you."

Spur could hear it all now clearly. He raced forward. The tunnel had all the makings of a trap, a deadly trap. A hundred angry strides later he was close enough to the entrance to see someone moving. He fired his six-gun again and saw the person drop and move sideways.

"Won't do no good, McCoy. I'm going to seal up this tunnel for good. You won't die for hours yet. But you'll die."

Other Spur Giants from *Leisure Books:*

DENVER DARLIN'
MINT-PERFECT MADAM
TALL TIMBER TROLLOP
PHOENIX FILLY

SPUR

HIGH PLAINS PRINCESS

DIRK FLETCHER

LEISURE BOOKS   NEW YORK CITY

A LEISURE BOOK®

April 1992

Published by

Dorchester Publishing Co., Inc.
276 Fifth Avenue
New York, NY 10001

Printed in the United States of America.

Chapter 1

The raw, gut-wrenching blast of a hand gun sounded close by and Spur McCoy pushed the Princess to the floor of the carriage and pulled his Colt .45 at the same time.

To the right. He looked that way and saw a man with both hands on a short gun getting ready to fire again. Spur snapped a shot at the figure, heard a groan of pain from the man sitting at his right in the carriage, then leaped out of the moving rig and ran for the assailant.

The attacker scampered around a corner and down a side street in the river city of St. Louis, Missouri. Spur charged after him, his Colt up ready to do business.

Spur went around the corner slowly, saw the man wasn't waiting for him. He was half a block ahead running hard. Spur pulled in the weapon and sprinted after the attacker. He gained slowly.

The shooter darted into an open door. It was closed when Spur got there. He saw that it was the back door of some business. He blasted it with his heavy boot and the lock broke and the door smashed open. Inside it was half light. A man breathed hard somewhere inside the big storage room. Spur jolted out of the light of the doorway just as a shot roared in the closed space. The hot lead zapped through the open door where he had been standing. He rolled behind some heavy wooden boxes.

The sound of the shot inside the closed room was like a roaring crack of thunder. He had no idea where the round originated. As the sound died out, Spur listened. He heard a scraping to his right. He saw a door there. He could see only the top half of it. Slowly the panel moved outward.

Spur lifted up and fired one shot at the bottom front of the door hoping the man was trying to slip through it. He heard a a cry of pain, then the door opened and shut in a heartbeat.

Spur McCoy, United States Secret Service Agent, surged across the room to the door and tried the knob. It was unlocked. He pulled the door open but was careful to stay on the wall side of the doorway out of danger.

Two shots jolted through the opening. Spur knelt and peered around the opening from the floor level. Two windows lighted the next room. It was some kind of a shop or fabric store or dressmaker's.

"Hold it right there, whoever you are." The voice came from the room ahead, a man's voice, heavy with some accent but understandable. "No move or this lady gets her head blown off. You want that?"

Spur kept quiet. He could see about half of the room. It was no more than 15 feet square, with a cutting table, a sewing machine, two tailor's dummies of women, two chairs and two big lamps.

"I said don't move or this woman dies," the voice said again. Spur waited. A moment later he saw a woman held around the waist by a man's arm edge out from behind a partition. The door out of the room was to the left and Spur could see it. The man behind the woman was almost hidden by her large form. He held a six-gun to the woman's head.

Slowly the pair moved toward the door. Spur saw the woman's right hand. It held a pair of cutting scissors, with long blades and a sharp point. She held it like a dagger waiting her chance.

The two moved another step. Spur could see the side of the man's face, but not enough to get off a safe shot. The woman was chunky, wide enough to shield the man.

He took another step and his hold around the woman's waist loosened a little. She bent forward and her right hand stabbed with the sharp scissors around her left side. Her first stroke brought a screech of pain from the captor. Her second a wail and as she stabbed him in the side the third time he fired the six-gun. In his agony he had dropped the muzzle of the weapon and the round slammed into the woman's right shoulder.

The force of the heavy .44 slug jolted the woman out of the assassin's grasp and knocked her sideways and to the floor. As soon as she fell, Spur McCoy fired three times as fast as he could. Two of the slugs hit the man in the chest, blasting him backward and downward. The third shot caught him under the chin as he fell, penetrating through his open screaming mouth upward into his brain and on out the top of his head. A red, sticky spray splattered the ceiling and far wall with blood and brain tissue and bits of his skull.

Spur ran to the fallen woman. She looked up and grinned through her pain.

"I guess I stabbed the bastard good!" she said, then she fainted. Spur used some clean cloth from the dress shop and bound up the woman's shoulder until it stopped bleeding. Then he went out the front of the shop to the street and asked the first reliable looking man to walk by to bring the closest doctor fast, a woman had been shot.

Back inside the store, he ushered one customer and three gawkers out the front door, then checked on the assassin. He had no papers or identification on him of any type. Spur had never seen the man before. He looked over his face and neck, but found no distinguishing marks. Then he tried the man's hands and arms. On his forearm he found a small tattoo. It was a triangle formed by three small diamond shapes. Curious.

The doctor ran in then and looked at the woman. He was short and slender with a moustache. He nodded at the work Spur had done on the shoulder. The woman came back to consciousness with a wail and a scream of pain.

The doctor looked at the dead man and shrugged. He went back to the woman.

"Mrs. Berthwaite, can you walk?"

She nodded, her bottom lip held by her upper teeth. Tears squeezed from her eyes.

"We'll get you to my office and I can fix up that shoulder. Gunshot, right?"

"Yes, but I stabbed him good."

The doctor looked at Spur who nodded. The big agent helped the woman to get to her feet and went with them to the front door. At the door, a St. Louis uniformed policeman hurried up.

"Been a shooting here, Doc?" he asked.

"One alive, one dead. Ask this gent about it."

Spur waved the officer to the rear of the store and showed him the body.

"Dead enough. Your round?"

Spur explained what had happened. He took out his wallet and extracted a thin oblong of cardboard. On it was a small picture of Spur McCoy and a statement signed by President Grant that Spur McCoy was a member of the United States Secret Service, a law officer of the federal government, and should be shown all cooperation and assistance when requested.

The policeman looked at the card, read it and stared at the small picture.

"You'll need to come down to the office and fill out a paper about the death and sign it. My Captain will need to talk to you."

"Tell me where and when. First I have to check on the Princess and her party." Before the policeman could object, Spur ran out the back door of the shop, down the side street and to where he had left the carriage. It was parked at the side of the street.

A small crowd had gathered around it, and a medical man was putting a bandage on the shoulder of Pierre Dupont, who had been riding in the carriage with Spur and the two ladies. Both the women remained in the back of the carriage.

One was Her Royal Highness Princess Alexandria, heir to the throne of the Principality of Mantuco, a small sovereign nation on the shores of southern France. She was 22 years old and on her first visit to the United States. Beside her sat

Francine Miller, the chaperon and confidant of the princess.

Spur walked up and nodded at the ladies. The doctor looked at him and frowned.

"You with these people?"

"Yes sir. Mr. Dupont here got shot from ambush and I chased down the assailant. How is Mr. Dupont's arm?"

"Oh, good shape, not much damage. The round went through the fleshy part. He'll be fine in a week or two."

"Can we go now?"

"I'll have to report this to the police."

"Good, you can come with me and show me where the police station is. I need to fill out a form myself."

"Mr. McCoy," a slightly agitated Princess Alexandria commanded from the rear seat.

"Yes, Your Highness." He turned toward her.

"Can we finish this quickly? You promised me a tour of the city and so far we have seen nothing."

Princess Alexandria's English was perfect. She had studied in London for three years. She wore an elaborate dress and a fancy hat and was sure to attract attention wherever they went. Spur had mentioned it once before; now he would demand that she and her lady in waiting dress more conservatively.

They drove to the police station with the doctor and Spur talked with the captain, filled out the forms.

"Yes, Captain. I am aware of this dissident group from France that is harassing the princess. I didn't think they would go so far as to try to harm her. From that distance the gunman could have aimed at the princess and hit the diplomat. He was not seriously wounded."

"I could arrange a police guard outside your hotel, and give you an armed escort around town," the policeman said.

"No, that's exactly what we don't need. We want to blend into the city rather than make a spectacle and a target of the lady. We won't be in town long." He thanked the officer and went back to the carriage.

Spur had worried about this; he had talked for two hours with his boss in Washington, D.C. trying to get the Mantuco Embassy to cancel this Wild West tour for the princess. He got the answer that killed all questions.

"Whatever the princess wants to do, the Mantuco Embassy is more than happy to insist that she be allowed to do it."

This was an assignment that he begged to get out of, but his boss at the Secret Service, General Wilton D. Halleck, said he was the only one who could handle it.

"McCoy, you have been assigned to the Western region. The lady wants a tour of the Wild Wild West, so you're the man. It won't be that bad. It isn't like she's seventy years old and weighs two hundred pounds."

At last he had caved in and taken the train to St. Louis. The princess was furious.

"You people promised me a tour of the Wild West! So far all I've seen is the inside of a railroad compartment. I can see those all over Europe. I want to see what the West is like."

Spur arrived last night and arranged this carriage tour for her first real outing. Now he cut it short and hurried them back to the hotel.

Upstairs in the Royal Suite, named for the occasion, he talked with all three of the visitors.

"Princess, I understand your wishes. I also didn't realize that these nationalists were so violent. If you want to make this tour, there are several things that I insist that we do. This will be for your safety, and to insure that you will see the real Wild, Wild West."

"What are these conditions?" the princess demanded.

"First, you'll need new wardrobes. As long as you dress like a princess you'll be a target. It makes you too easy to find. No fancy clothes, simple American dresses will do fine. I'll arrange to have one of the women's wear stores bring around a dozen or so outfits for you to choose from. Will that be satisfactory?"

The princess frowned, sighed. Then she brightened. "Yes. If I am to see the real Wild West, then I shouldn't attract attention to myself. Yes. I quite agree. What else?"

"We will travel with no notice or fanfare. No one will know where we are going. That way, if there are more of the nationalists around, it will be harder for them to find you."

"Yes, that's reasonable."

"My only other suggestion is that I might change plans or outings quickly sometimes, in order to throw off anyone trying to find you."

"Quite fine, I understand. What I simply will not stand for is being bored. I can be bored in my house on the Mediterranean. Oh, Francine should go with you when you talk to the shop owners to bring back dresses. She has excellent taste and knows exactly what I like."

During this whole time Pierre Dupont had not made a sound. Now he stood and smiled.

"Young man, I thank you for defending the Princess today when I was unable to do so. You undoubtedly saved her life. The crown is grateful to you. I quite agree with your suggestions so far. We will endeavor to assist at all times possible. I'll notify my embassy of the change in procedures."

Spur McCoy shook his head. "Mr. Dupont. I'd appreciate your not doing that. It is possible that there could be an informant high in your embassy in Washington. That would account for the nationalists knowing where we were today. Let's not tell them right away."

"Mmmmmmm, yes I see what you mean. Very well. I'll be in my room resting. Where will we be going next?"

"The Princess has asked for a river boat ride. Since we're here on the Mississippi River, now is the best time to take the ride. We'll go down to Memphis, Tennessee, and get off, then come back on another steam boat the next day."

"Yes, sounds good." He nodded to the princess in a kind of small bow and left the room.

"Francine is ready, Mr. McCoy," the princess said.

He opened the hotel suite's door and let the Lady in Waiting to go out first.

Francine was twenty-three years old, she had told him when they first met. She was English and had met the princess in their English school in London and they had been best friends for five years. Francine was an inch taller than the princess at five-four, and now Spur watched her as they walked. Her blonde hair came almost to her waist. She had blue eyes and a happy little face that seldom frowned. He guessed she didn't weigh more than a hundred pounds.

"I like the idea of blending in with the masses," Francine said. "It's so. . . . so democratic somehow."

"Besides that it's far less dangerous."

She watched him and then reached out and held his arm as they went down the steps to the street. She held on when they were on the sidewalk pressing close so her breast touched his arm.

"I hope you don't mind my holding your arm. Sometimes I stumble."

Spur grinned. "You're as nimble as a cat, but I don't mind in the least."

"Good," she said with a hint of a secret.

They stopped at the first women's dress store they found and went in. Spur showed them his credentials and told them what he wanted. The manager came out and with Francine's help, picked out ten dresses for each of the women. The manager had a workman take the garments to the hotel. She went back with Spur and Francine.

In short time, the princess approved all 20 dresses and snapped her fingers at Pierre, who had come back from his nap. He hastily wrote out a bank draft on the embassy's account in Washington, D.C., and the woman manager left with it tucked safely in her bosom.

Spur checked his watch. "Slightly past four o'clock. Princess, I suggest you have dinner in your room tonight for the sake of safety. We'll leave tomorrow morning from here at six A.M. to catch the morning boat heading downstream. I'll have a carriage waiting at the main entrance. Please wear some of your new clothes. I suggest your usual clothing be sent back to the embassy. I'm sure that

Mr. Dupont can take care of that for you."

The princess nodded.

"I have some arrangements to make for tomorrow. By your leave, Princess?"

She nodded once more and Spur left the room. He booked passage on the morning steamer, the *Mission Belle*, out of New Orleans, and obtained a cabin for the ladies in case they wanted to lie down. He had a sandwich and returned to his hotel room about seven.

Five minutes after he closed his door, a knock sounded on it. When he opened it, Francine stood there in one of the new dresses. It cinched tightly around her small waist.

"Oh, Mr. McCoy. The Princess wanted to tell you she's pleased with the dresses and your guiding her vacation so far. She said we all will be at the front door in the morning at six."

He held the door and smiled. "Good, if we miss the boat there isn't another one until noon."

Francine's usually happy face showed a frown. "Could I come in, I'm worried about something."

He opened the door and she stepped inside. He left the door open six inches. When he turned back toward her she stepped close to him and put her arms up and locked her fingers behind his neck.

"Spur McCoy, what I am worried about is that you haven't once tried to kiss me yet. I'm disappointed. I heard that all American men, especially Western men, were wild, wonderful lovers." She reached up and kissed his lips gently, came away from him, and when she saw no objection she pressed her body firmly against his and kissed him again, this time hard with her lips open and her tongue washing against his lips.

He had left his hands at his sides through the kiss, now he put them on her hips and eased her down from her tip toes.

"Miss Miller, I had heard that all English women were cold and unemotional and usually flat chested."

Francine giggled. "Good. I'll prove you wrong. Now kiss me again."

He did. This time his mouth came open and he crushed her to his chest until her big breasts flattened and she gave a soft sigh as he eased his lips off hers.

"That was . . . was much better," Francine said as she slowly opened her eyes. "Oh, my, just ever so much better." She smiled. "You know that the Princess and I have separate rooms."

"Yes."

"And you know that I have no great need to go back to my room tonight."

"I thought that might have entered that pretty little head of yours. Will the Princess mind?"

"Not if I tell her all about it. I've told her stories before about my. . . friends."

"Will this one be worth telling?"

She reached between them and felt his crotch and found the growing lump behind his town pants. Francine rubbed it tenderly and nodded. "Oh, yes, Spur McCoy, I think once I've felt this spur of yours, I'm going to have a fine tale to tell the Princess."

She stepped back from him, caught his hand, pushed the door shut and turned the key in the lock, then pulled him toward the big bed.

She urged him to sit on the bed, then posed in front of him. "I like this new dress. It shows off my small waist. About English women being flat chested, I'll do what I can to dispel that myth."

16

Francine did a little dance for him. Each movement caused another button to open on the one-piece dress, and the belt to open, and then in one swift move she pulled the blue dress off over her head. The chemise went next and she stood there proudly bare to the waist, wearing only thin silk bloomers of pink.

Her breasts were much larger than he had expected, with a softly brown hue to the areolas and the pinkest nipples he had ever seen. As he watched they began to fill with hot blood and to rise to the situation.

"There now, nothing flat about me. Do you agree?" She walked forward until she stood in front of him and bent slightly so he could kiss her breasts.

"Francine, you're positive you want to do this?"

She looked up and smiled. "With you, yes, more than I have wanted to for a long time. Don't make me beg."

He kissed her breasts, nibbled at the throbbing nipples, let the hot blood of her breasts feed his own desire. He felt it building and building.

Spur sucked one breast into his mouth, biting her, chewing on the tender flesh all the way to her nipple. As he chewed, he brought one hand up to her crotch and rubbed. Her legs parted and she moaned, sagging against him. His fingers found her very heartland and as he stroked across it, he could feel the wetness.

"Oh, god but that feels good, Spur McCoy. So damn good! Please don't stop."

He chewed a moment more, then hooked his thumbs over the silk bloomers and worked them down slowly. Spur came away from her breasts and kissed down her flat little stomach past her

17

navel to the beginning of the mound.

Francine gasped, and then gasped again. Her hands found his head and played with his hair and urged him lower. Soon the pink silk had pushed down so the beginnings of her blonde thatch showed.

"Oh, god, don't stop. Keep going, keep going!"

His lips moved across the thatch and lower and his fingers parted the soft blonde hairs to reveal her treasure. He kissed her pink nether lips and Francine wailed and dove onto the bed pulling him with her. Her thighs closed around his head pinning his mouth to her vagina as she trembled and rumbled and brayed softly as the tremors tore through her slender body. Her hips bucked and bucked, releasing his head, and she pounded her hips hard on the bed until the last of the spasms shook her body and then moved on.

Francine lay there moaning and panting. She turned and looked at him once, then sighed again and closed her eyes. It was five minutes before she stirred.

Spur sat beside her on the bed where he had been. She turned and sat up beside him.

"Damn me, but that was fine! So fine. I've never had one like that before. Haven't popped my cork like that without having a big one inside me since I was a young girl back in London. I was thirteen, I think."

She frowned. "See here, ain't fitting and proper and all, you still dressed and me with my twat all exposed this way. You best come off with the clothes."

She did it slowly, opening his fly first.

"Got to look at the good parts," she said. When she undid his pants fly and pulled them down and his short underwear, she nearly fell off the bed.

"What a big whanger! Lord George in the morning. He's too big to fit into little me. Way too big." She bent and kissed his erection, smiled at him and pulled the rest of his clothes off in record time.

Francine pushed him to his back and dropped on top of him.

"I like it up here. Always have. Then some bloke ain't crushing me into the floor, or a bed if'n I'm lucky. You like to talk while you doing the poking? I don't mind one way or the other. Just as long as I get it inside. You ready?"

Spur rolled her over, lifted her parted knees and drove into her in one swift hard stroke. Francine gasped and yelped, then gave a cry like a wounded sea gull and tore into another series of climaxes.

Spur went with her and just as she finished hers, he drove her round bottom a foot into the mattress and shot the last of his load before he fell down and closed his eyes and let the pent-up breath out in a series of long deep pantings.

"Glory be," Francine said. "Now that was another good one. I just may never get out of your bed, what about that big cock? I might just stay here and be your love slave forever. Damn but you make my old cunny feel good!"

"You were plenty marvelous yourself, little lady. You are a sex trap ready to spring. So sexy it makes me want to start again."

"No rush, luv, wait until you're good and ready, like a whole half hour. We've got all night." She turned his face so she could see it. "We have at least until five A.M. to make wild, wild, love, right, luv?"

It wasn't quite that late when they both relaxed on the bed.

"Damn, five times," Francine cooed. "Been a year and to hell since I been done five times. Not ever don't think." She kissed him gently then they both shut their eyes and dropped off at once to sleep.

Chapter 2

Darlene Benoit paced her hotel room in St. Louis. She was less than a mile from her mortal enemy and she could not touch her. Darlene had set up the strike on Princess Alexandria of Mantuco on the street. She and her three men had ridden ahead of the carriage and positioned themselves for possible routes the princess might take.

Unfortunately Eduard had missed her with his shot, been chased and killed. That was one more death she laid to the hands of the Prince of Mantuco. She stopped pacing and looked out the window. It was not a pretty scene from this third-rate hotel, but it was all she could afford. She had followed the princess here from Europe hoping to have an easy mark, to kill her quickly and be back in France before she was missed. Both the governments were watching her and her friends.

Now a try had been made on the princess's life, so security would be tightened. It would be harder now.

Poor Eduard. He was the worst shot of the four of them. He had been told to run right up to the carriage and then to fire two or three times. He must have panicked, fired too quickly and missed.

So they would try again. She would find out where the princess was going next. She would find out and take her revenge.

Darlene dropped on the bed and let the tears come. Mostly tears for her brother, her Didier. He had been only 19 when the gendarmes of the Principality of Mantuco had arrested him for drug smuggling. He was just a boy on a quick vacation to the gambling casinos in the seaside resort.

He might have had some opium, that did not make him a drug trafficker. He was tried and sentenced to ten years in prison. Mantuco had the worst prisons in all of Europe. In six months Didier was dead. The official cause of death was listed as a fight between two groups of prisoners. She found out the guards had beat Didier to death.

Poor Didier! She would make them pay. She would take away from the Prince what he treasured most, his darling daughter, Princess Alexandria. If Darlene could do it while the princess was here in America, that would hurt the diplomacy going on between Mantuco and the United States. She wasn't sure what it was about, but anything that strengthened Mantuco, hurt France's chances of reclaiming the land as part of France.

A knock came on the door and she got up, wiped the tears away and welcomed her two friends, Bernard and Jacques. They both came and kissed her cheek.

"Sorry about Eduard," Bernard said. "Something went wrong. I wished the rig would have come down the main street as we guessed."

"I've been guessing badly lately," Darlene said. "Maybe tomorrow. We must follow them. I saw the new man, the tall one with six-gun and the brown hair, go to the steamship office. That will be a ruse. They will not go on the boat tomorrow, they will go somewhere else.

"Bernard, I want you to watch the hotel starting at 5 A.M. If you see them leave follow them. Try for the princess only if you have a sure shot. Tomorrow I am buying a shot gun and have the barrels sawed off. I'll tell the gun store man I need it for rats and I'm not a good shot. I will wear the blouse that falls open in front and he will cut off the weapon and ask no questions."

"You must be careful," Bernard said. "These men are animals. They rape women right on the street."

Darlene smiled. "I can handle them. I have my favorite little one-shot .45 derringer. No man will ever rape me. Oh, Bernard, better have a horse handy in the morning in case they use a carriage. Find out where they are going and come here to the hotel and tell me.

"Jacques and I will be here with horses waiting for your report."

"What if they get on the steamship?"

"Don't worry, they won't. It's a feint, a ruse. They will try this since they are frightened. It's good to have them scared, it helps us figure out what they will do."

She looked at the two. "Clear on what we are to do? Jacques, you be here at seven for breakfast so we can be ready."

The men both nodded.

"I'm sorry about Eduard," Jacques said. "I know he was your friend of long standing and knew Didier. We'll all miss Eduard."

She nodded at Jacques and the men left the room. Darlene locked the door behind them and looked out the window again. Tomorrow. Perhaps tomorrow they would find the princess and blow her into hell.

Darlene rubbed her wrist. It still hurt, where they had the small tattoos affixed. She looked at it again. Three small diamonds in the rough shape of a triangle. Liberty, Equality, Fraternity, the three diamonds in the French crown of democratic government. They would prevail over the prehistoric Prince Stephan of Mantuco. They must. She had bet her very life that they would.

When the sun came up the next morning, Spur McCoy had a covered carriage waiting at the side entrance to the hotel. McCoy was 32 years old, six feet two inches tall when most men averaged less than 5–9. He kept his weight at a heavily muscled two hundred pounds.

From his extensive outdoor work, he was well tanned, wore his dark hair a little longer than most men did and was clean shaven. His green eyes missed little.

He had extensive on the job training on the prairie and mountains and could ride and hunt and track through the woods or desert. He was an excellent horseman and an expert shot with rifle or pistol. Spur had graduated from Harvard University in Boston with a special studies in government and for two years was an aide in Washington, D.C., to the U.S. Senator from New York.

His father had numerous businesses in New York

City. When the Secret Service was established by Congress to protect the currency, Spur applied for and was accepted as an agent. Since then he'd done dozens of assignments for the government, some directly for the president, but he had never had any that came close to this one. He was a nursemaid to a young girl; no, he was a nanny to a difficult little hellion. He had heard tales about this princess. She'd been dubbed the Wild, Wild Princess. He would have her well tamed before the 30-day vacation trip was over.

The diplomat came first. He carried his own bag, a brown leather one with straps and buckles around it. The ladies arrived five minutes later accompanied by two house boys with their two large bags each. The porters loaded them in the back of the carriage and Spur drove the rig away. He would leave it at the docks.

Spur had plenty of time to watch the immediate area. A half block down he had seen a bay horse tied to a rail. It was saddled but there was no rider. Five minutes later a man came from the shadows and settled down the horse, then vanished again.

Now, as Spur drove the carriage along the St. Louis street, he saw the same bay horse and rider half a block behind them. Spur took two turns and watched to see if the rider tailed them. He did. Spur put on a spurt of speed, mixed in with a dozen other carriages beginning to crowd the early morning street and ducked down an alley.

Three blocks later he could not see the rider and the bay behind him. He watched the rest of the way to the dock and hurried his three charges along. The rider did not show up by the time they were safely on the docks.

Five minutes later they walked up the gangplank

of the *Mission Belle* and watched their luggage brought on board and all put in the ladies' stateroom on the cabin deck level.

Spur was pleased with the dresses the women wore. Francine had left his room about four A.M. to go to her room to get dressed. She had on a soft brown one-piece dress that swept the floor and fitted snugly around the waist and breasts.

The Princess wore a light green dress with a small jacket and a modest little hat that partly covered her long brown hair.

The princess was almost a beauty. She was interesting, attractive, and when she smiled it was easy to see why so many people liked her. She was five feet three inches, and shapely with slightly larger hips and waist than Francine's but with just as much bosom.

She smiled at him now and he nodded.

"Your Highness?"

"I have a request. If we're to fade in with the general population, no more, 'your highness'. Please call me Alexandria, and I shall call you Spur, and this is Francine." The princess smiled softly and then grinned and Francine touched her shoulder and she sobered. "Our diplomatic friend is Pierre, so all will be on a first name basis, and I'll feel more at ease. Is that acceptable?"

"Of course. . . Alexandria," Spur said. "Oh, I would caution the three of you to stay in the cabin until we cast off. Someone tried to follow us when we left the hotel, but I think I lost him in the traffic. Still, no sense taking chances."

Pierre frowned. "The chap on the bay horse, you mean? Yes, you did lose him. I had him pegged about when you did. He wasn't terribly good at shadowing us, was he?"

Spur agreed and left the cabin for the deck. He stayed away from the rail, walked back near the big stern wheel that would propel them down the river much faster than the current, and watched the dock for the man on the bay horse. As far as he could tell, the man didn't arrive.

Soon the whistle blasted and the ropes were undone and the big river steamboat pulled slowly away from the dock. Her stern wheel began to move and they angled into the river and then the current caught them and they moved quickly downstream.

Spur returned to the ladies' cabin and found them ready to tour the ship. He took them along the walkways and through the passageways and into the casino where dozens of men and women sat around tables and wheels in a gambling wonderland.

"Oh, yes, we have gambling in our casinos in Mantuco," Alexandria said. She looked at Pierre. "I need a hundred dollars to gamble with," she demanded politely.

The diplomat frowned for a moment, then reached in his pocket and removed a purse. He handed her a crisp, new $100 U.S. federal greenback note. She nodded, caught Francine's hand and hurried toward the poker tables.

Morgan stood beside Pierre. "Sir, you must have done something extremely bad to be saddled with a rugged assignment such as this."

Pierre chuckled. "I asked for it, actually. A chance to see your country. No, I can handle her, most of the time. Known her since she was an infant. But how did you get the job?"

"Ordered to do it over my protests. I don't like

27

being a nursemaid and nanny. I just hope it isn't my last job with the Agency."

Pierre eyed Spur for a moment. He smiled and chuckled. "No, Mr. Spur McCoy, I don't think it will be. You will be able to handle the princess quite nicely. Look what you've done already in one day. Gone are the courtly dress and the big display. Yes, I think you'll do quite well."

"I'll be looking to you for help, Pierre. I'm sure I'll need it. Which means right now I better check out the gambling. It can get downright nasty on board these boats." He headed for the casino lounge.

The *Mission Belle* wasn't the biggest steamer on the Mississippi. She would never get into races with the larger, faster boats, but she was a favorite of some of the best gamblers on the river. The captain was sympathetic to them, and for a small fee from the professionals let them gamble all they wanted to, whether they cheated or not. If a player was found to be cheating he was often tossed over the side to test his skill in the Mississippi currents.

Spur found the gambling tables and at once saw Princess Alexandria. She sat at a table of six men and had a stack of chips in front of her. Francine stood beside her watching the cards. The princess lost the first two hands, getting out quickly, smartly. Then she bet $50 and all but one of the gamblers dropped out. The one who stayed was obvious to Spur as a seasoned veteran of the gambling wars.

He was in his mid thirties, dressed well, with a handsome face and well trimmed hair and a moustache. His flinty blue eyes challenged Alexandria and she called his additional $20 bet. He had a pair of aces and sixes. She had three fives.

Spur moved around the tables but watched her. She won the next two pots and then lost a big one. When he came up behind her the next time she had only $20 worth of chips left.

The gambler looked at her. "Miss, the bet is to you. I met your twenty and bumped it fifty dollars. You going to call me or fold?"

He said it matter of factly, with no more emotion than a man would talking about the price of a horse. She flared, eyes angry.

"You can see I have only twenty dollars left."

"True, little lady. Part of the game. You calling me or what?"

"I can get more money."

"Table stakes. You play only with what you have on the table."

She shrugged. "Then I can't match your bet, can I?" She smiled at him and the gambler lost his poker face. He grinned and moved his legs under the table.

"Well, now, little lady. I'd say table stakes can be interpreted several ways. Your arms are on the table, right? I'd say that if you want to call my fifty dollar raise, all you have to do is give me your marker promising that I can take you to dinner. You do that and the bet is covered and you can call me."

Alexandria looked at Francine. "Marker, what does he mean?" she asked softly in French. Francine answered in French.

"Your marker, your guarantee, your promise to go to dinner with him."

She looked up. "My marker, yes, my promise to go to dinner with you. It is done." She slid the chips into the pot. The other four men at the table grinned.

"If you lose, little lady, that dinner will be in my cabin."

Alexandria raised her brows. "For my sister and me?" She pointed at Francine.

"Nope, just you, sweet thing. It still a bet?"

"Yes, still a bet. I call you."

The gambler turned over his cards. In the five card draw game he had a straight. He reached for the pot.

"Wait!" Alexandria said sharply. She laid down her cards one at a time so he could see them. She had a heart flush.

"I'll be damned," the gambler said. "You win. This time." He stood. "My name is Kristopher Harding. You'll find out I'm not a good loser. Perhaps later today we can play again."

"Perhaps, Mr. Harding. Perhaps not. I like to win, too." He turned and walked away and Alexandria smiled.

Spur swooped down on them and suggested that they take a turn at the lunch tables.

On the *Mission Belle* the main dining saloon was over 200 feet long with a table down the center and waiters standing at attention every few feet. They dined on pheasant and oysters and various dishes of vegetables and mixed fruit. When they were through they went back to the upper deck where their cabin was and walked the deck for a few moments.

Because of numerous stops along the way, the trip from St. Louis to Memphis would take longer than Spur expected. There were delays at some stops to take on passengers and freight on the lower deck.

Alexandria went to her cabin to rest and Spur toured the boat again, watching the professional gamblers turning the unsuspecting "marks" inside out and stripping them of their cash.

He watched a three card monte game. This was a variation of the old three shells and the pea sleight of hand trick that men have gambled on for centuries. Spur knew that the three card monte dealers or "throwers" as they were often called, usually worked with a partner. He settled in against a pillar and watched a thrower working up a crowd of 15 or 20 men in the main saloon.

"Good afternoon gentlemen. Here we are ready to offer you a little entertainment, perhaps some excitement by way of a game of chance. It's simple. Three cards. The winning card is the ace of hearts. Be sure to watch it closely as I move the three face down cards from place to place.

"All you have to do is pick out the ace of hearts when I stop moving the cards. Now, remember, many say the hand is quicker than the eye, but is that true?"

The thrower then moved the cards around but fumbled and did it slowly and seemed to be a beginner at his work.

"Follow the ace as I shuffle. Quickly now." He moved the cards three or four times and turned over the ace. "Here it is, did you follow it? See, not a hard game at all." He moved the cards again, not quickly and fumbling a little.

"Now where is the card? Anyone willing to bet ten dollars to find out? Pick out the ace and win ten off my dwindling bankroll."

Nobody came forward. "Come now, gentlemen. Are none of you quick of the eye? It's a simple game. You have one chance out of three of winning. If you watch carefully and find the ace, you beat me and I pay you. If you miss the ace, I beat you and you pay me. Who will try it with a ten spot?"

He shifted the cards again, this time clumsily knocked one off the small table, and two men laughed. He picked up the card, the ace of hearts, winced, and tried again.

By this time, even Spur thought the man was a rank beginner or a fool or maybe drunk. Why shouldn't someone risk a ten dollar wager against this inept fool?

Only Spur McCoy knew the dodge. The dealer had been putting on a show for the betters. Soon someone would take the risk, only the risk taker would be the partner, the "capper" as he was called in the trade. He would make a bet. Nothing happened for a moment, then a young man came up. He was well dressed and held two ten dollar bills in his hand.

"Sir, I'll risk a tenner. I'm quick with my eyes."

"Fine, fine. Let me rub my hands just a' moment. Rheumatiz I guess. Now, here we go." The thrower moved the cards, and at a slower rate than before. Every man watching knew where the ace of hearts was, the winner.

The young man strung out the suspense, then picked out the right-hand card. It was the winner.

"Damn me, you caught me that time," the thrower said showing a touch of anger at himself. "I thought for sure I could fool you. You can't be that good. Bet me fifty dollars the next time. I don't think you're that good."

The shill frowned, looked at his won ten dollar bill and dug a twenty out of his pocket and dropped the $50 on the small table. The thrower went through an elaborate but easy to follow shuffling of the three cards, stopped and then did three more moves, then laughed wickedly and looked at his shill.

"Now by damn! Try and find the winner."

The shill didn't hesitate this time. He pointed to the middle card of the three. Sure enough it was the winner.

The thrower looked in amazement. "I'll never. Twice you beat me. I shouldn't let you play anymore." The thrower stared away out a window for a moment. Then looked upward as if praying. "I really shouldn't let you play again. You're too good."

As the thrower did this, the young capper reached for the ace and turned up a quarter inch on the corner of the card leaving a plainly visible line there. He pulled his hand back.

"Give you a chance to get even," the capper said. "Bet you a hundred dollars on the next throw."

The thrower paused. "A hundred dollars? It would let me get back some of my money. You've won sixty from me so far, right. I shouldn't." He slid the cards around on the linen tablecloth and let one almost fall off the table. He shook his head, as if trying to make up his mind. At last he turned the ace of hearts face up and put it on one side of the three.

"Very well, one time only at $100. You still want to try?"

"Yes," the young shill said. He laid his $100 on the table. He looked axiously at the thrower.

"You're not backing out on our bet?"

The thrower began to sweat. He wiped his brow, patted his cheeks with his handkerchief.

"Guess I can't now that I offered." He counted out five $20 bills and put them on the table. Then he turned over the ace of hearts and moved the cards. This time he did it faster but not so fast that the men watching couldn't follow them.

The onlookers knew where the card was. It was the one with the turned up corner! How could the young man lose? The thrower did one final flourish and looked up with his face expectant.

"Now, by Christopher, not a chance you know where the winning ace of hearts is."

The young man hesitated, put on a little show of indecision, then at last turned over the far card with the crease line on the corner. It was the ace of hearts.

The crowd roared in approval. The young capper scooped up the won money. He had turned a ten dollar bet into a profit of $160. He quickly left the table and walked out of the room.

Spur could almost smell the scent of greed in the air as the 15 men around the table surged forward.

"I'll bet," one shouted.

"No, me!" another called.

The thrower looked in his purse. "I'm low on money. I have only fifteen hundred dollars left. I need it to get even for the day. Will anyone bet me fifteen hundred?"

The first two men shook their heads and backed off. A tall man with a fine suit and a diamond stick pin in his tie stepped forward.

"You say fifteen hundred, in cash?"

"Yes sir."

The man looked at the cards. The bent over corner of the winning ace of hearts card still showed plainly. It was robbery this way with the winning card marked, but evidently the well dressed man did not mind in the least. He'd probably heard that these card sharks always robbed their victims. This was a chance to get back at one of them.

"Same winning card, the ace of hearts?" the man asked. He looked like a wealthy planter and talked with a slight Southern accent.

"Indeed. My run of bad luck must change soon."

"Done," the big man said. He laid out 15 $100 bills along the edge of the table. The thrower took all the money from his wallet and matched the amount. Then he rubbed his hands together and stared at the cards. He wiped his hands on his coat tails and began to move the cards.

Spur watched closely the man's right hand. It was done so swiftly, so neatly that no one in the crowd saw. The thrower had palmed the ace of hearts and substituted another card in its place. It also had a crease mark across one corner just the way the ace of hearts had.

The thrower made several attempts to stop before he was satisfied this time. He took his hands off the cards, then shook his head and made one more move.

The big man stared down at the cards a moment, then grinned. The bent over edge showed plainly on the card nearest him. He jabbed a thick finger at the card and flipped it over.

The card was a queen of spades, a loser.

"Well, finally the game turns my way," the thrower said. He looked at the planter who had just lost. "Sorry my good man, that's the luck of the cards. Sometimes you win, sometimes you lose." The thrower now looked around at the other men, who seemed shocked by the sudden turn.

"Anyone else want to try? Just a matter of watching the cards, a matter of your eye being as quick as my hand."

The men shook their heads and wandered away. Soon all were gone. The thrower looked at Spur, who had said nothing. He quickly pocketed the money from the table, picked up his cards and walked through the far door. He would meet the shill outside somewhere. They would set up at another table down the boat. Both would probably change their clothes. They had just made $1500. That was as much money as a working man would earn at $35 a month and $420 a year for three and a half years.

Spur left and went back to the women's cabin. They weren't there.

He scowled and hurried down to the main saloon rooms where the high stakes gamblers worked. He saw her at once. She was standing at a table where four men sat. She had cards in her hand and stared at the men. Only one other man held cards.

"All right, I understand, table stakes," Alexandria whispered.

Spur looked closer at the gambler with the cards. It was the same man she had beaten before, Kristopher Harding, and he had a strange smile now.

"Miss Alexandria, it's up to you. I bet two hundred dollars. You have only a hundred dollars left in front of you. Table stakes. So?"

Alexandria frowned, looked at her cards, then shrugged. She put her hands on the table and slid up on it sitting near the pile of chips.

"I call you, Mr. Harding. My hundred dollars and what you see sitting on the table in front of you." She dropped her voice so only the men at the table and Spur nearby could hear.

"One night in your stateroom if I lose, agreed?"

Kristopher Harding chuckled. "Just what I hoped

36

that you were going to bet. Probably tremendously overpriced, but worth taking a chance on. You ready to show your hand?"

"I called you, Mr. Harding. Let's see your hand."

Spur started to step forward to break up the game but the gambler grinned and laid down his hand face up.

Chapter 3

Spur McCoy stared at the hand of cards the gambler laid on the table. It was a good one, three aces and a pair of queens. Spur walked behind Princess Alexandria, who looked down at the hand. Her shoulders slumped. Slowly she folded her cards and began to put them on the pot.

Spur stopped her and took the cards and looked at them.

"Well, do I win the hand and what's sitting on the table or not?" Kristopher Harding asked.

Spur held up a finger at him to gain some time and looked at Alexandria's cards. She had a pair of kings and three aces. That meant there were six aces showing. Spur smiled. So both of them had cheated, but the princess was ready to give up.

She grabbed the cards from Spur and put them face down on the stack of chips and paper money.

"You win, Mr. Harding. My cabin number is 22. I expect you to take me to dinner about eight, then I shall make good on the other part of the bet."

Harding raked the chips to his side of the table and stood. He made a short bow and smiled. "It will be a pleasure. The first seating is seven. I shall be at your cabin at ten minutes until seven. Will that be satisfactory?"

"Agreed," Princess Alexandria said. She held her chin high as she nodded briefly, turned and walked away. Francine was beside her talking frantically. The Princess only smiled. McCoy scowled at the gambler a moment, then hurried after the princess. He caught them at the rail, where they watched as the craft came into some small town port. The heir to the throne of the Principality of Mantuco turned and smiled at McCoy.

"I know, you don't approve."

"Approve. You could have showed that he cheated in getting the full house with his three aces and won the bet."

The princess smiled and shook her head. "I know that he cheated. I'd figured that out the second hand he won. I didn't know exactly how he did it when he wasn't dealing. Then I knew. The fact is I was the one who cheated on that hand. My three aces were from a different deck I had palmed. It wouldn't have been hard to prove. So I couldn't challenge him."

McCoy laughed and watched the hands get ready to tie up the ship at the dock. There was a delay and the big craft drifted 20 feet back into the river.

The engines ground and big stern paddle wheel worked again and soon the craft edged back to the dock and the black men threw ropes to the wharf and she was tied up securely.

"Alexandria, why did you agree to the seven o'clock time for dinner?"

"I knew that we would be docked and get off the boat at Memphis an hour before that," the princess said. "So you see, I had nothing to lose by trying for the win."

"Cutting it a little close," McCoy said. "We were scheduled to arrive at Memphis at six, but now we're over an hour late, and from the looks of our stop here we could lose another half hour."

The princess shrugged. "So I'll let him buy me dinner, then slip out when we dock in Memphis."

"I'll keep a watch on you. If things get going badly I'll come and plead a case of life and death with Francine. Something about a coughing spell and she can't get her breath. That will mean be ready for anything."

"Even shooting?"

"No, not on this crowded boat. Somebody would get killed."

"Oh. I want to see you use that gun of yours before the tour is over."

McCoy chuckled. "Princess Alexandria, you can count on that. We'll soon be out in the Wild, Wild West where almost anything can happen."

"Even wild, wild women, Spur McCoy?"

She looked at him evenly with that interesting little tilt of her head to one side and he wasn't sure if she were teasing him or being serious.

"Yes, there are some wild women out there. Some of them can even shoot a six-gun good as a man. But we probably won't run into any of them."

Francine took it seriously. "Alexandria, this is not some bit of whimsy, this betting your bottom in a card game. These men would as soon shoot

41

a cheater as they would rake in a pot. If you bet something and don't deliver, they'll consider that welshing. For a man that would bring a quick gunfight."

"Oh, dear, these local customs. I was just trying to have a little fun."

McCoy rubbed his chin. "Next time think about it first. This little bit of fun of yours could wind up getting me killed. I'll think of something. For starters go to your cabin and change clothes. Put on something different and a bonnet that almost completely covers your face. Something with a veil."

"I don't know. . . ."

Francine took over. "We'll find something, Spur," Francine said. "Come on, Alexandria."

The princess went first. Francine hesitated beside Spur. "Tonight?" she whispered.

"We'll see. Francine. After you change clothes, meet me back here on the deck. We'll need to find somewhere else for you besides your cabin. This gambler Harding will surely be watching it. He looks like a man who doesn't like to let a better get off without paying in full."

"Oh, dear. The Prince would be furious."

Spur watched them walk away. Francine had the better figure, and her tight little bottom swayed more than the royal one. He grinned, then tried to figure out what to do. He took a walk up to the small bridge to find out how their schedule was.

The first mate scowled as he checked his watch.

"Was an hour late. Got to wait here another fifteen minutes, which will make us near to god another half hour late. It might be nine o'clock instead of six when we get to Memphis."

Spur thanked him and went back to the rail to find the two ladies.

They arrived five minutes later and he told them to stay there while he checked something. He walked quickly toward the gangplank and while 50 feet away he stopped. Kristopher Harding, the gambler himself, leaned against the ship's rail right beside the gangplank smoking a long, thin cigar.

Spur knew he would be there until the *Mission Belle* sailed. There was no chance to get off now with their luggage, or even without the luggage.

When Spur rejoined the ladies, Pierre Dupont was with them. He took the man aside.

"You know what happened in the gambling saloon?"

"Yes, it's all over the ship. It will be dinner time long before we get to Memphis, right?"

"That's true. We have to get off before then. If this Harding gets insistent, the Princess and I may have to make a jump for it. I don't know. Can the lady swim?"

Pierre looked up quickly. "Now see here, going overboard would be out of the question. This river is huge, dangerous, a mile wide in spots. I don't. . . ."

"Don't worry what we do or how we do it. If I can't get her down the gangplank at the next little port, we'll have to improvise. I want you and Francine to get off at the next stop. He won't recognize either of you. Take all of our luggage, The next stop is River City. Put up at the best hotel in the village. It's a small place. We'll meet you there. It might take us a day or two to find you, but don't worry. Understand?"

The diplomat knew when he was outmanned. He hurried up to the women, took Francine by the elbow and guided her toward the cabin. A moment later Spur eased to the rail beside Alexandria.

"I got us in trouble, didn't I?"

"Yes. Our friends will get off at the next port, without us. Harding is watching the gangplank. We'll try to get off by some other method."

The princess grinned. "Yes, now this is an adventure. You mean like swimming? How far do we have to dive to the side to clear the big rear paddle wheel?"

"You can swim?"

"I lived in the water one whole summer. We have a pool in the palace with heated water."

"Good, but I hope it won't come to swimming. We'll see."

The big ship's steam whistle bellowed out its call, and slowly backed away from the landing. It had nosed up to the dock that was built high enough to accommodate the ship's first deck level.

Spur saw the gambler leave his lookout position and head back to the top deck. He'd get in some more poker before claiming his prize. Spur checked his watch. It was a little after two in the afternoon. Plenty of time.

He looked at the deck below them. The ship was built high and wide, with almost no hold space because there was little draft on these boats. Some of the paddle wheelers on the upper Missouri needed only 20 inches of water to stay afloat. That meant the first deck was less than two feet from the muddy waters of the Mississippi. There would be no great danger jumping into the water if they needed to. Spur knew at once that they wouldn't do that in the middle of the river.

He and the girl leaned against the wooden railing on the middle deck watching the river. They were a dozen feet apart, so the gambler would have more trouble finding them, if he tried.

Princess Alexandria wore a brown print dress that covered her from neck to wrists and dragged on the deck. On her head she wore a bonnet to keep the sun off with a floppy front that nearly closed at times.

Spur waited for the next river stop, It was nearly an hour. At last he saw it. River City was a small town, a village. He and Alexandria worked slowly toward the front of the ship and went down the main stairs to the bottom deck. About 20 others went the same way and lined up near the bow where the gangplank evidently would be laid between the boat and a dock the *Mission Belle* would pull alongside.

Near the front of the group, Spur saw Pierre and Francine. He checked, but could not find the gambler watching. As the boat eased up to a long dock, the gambler came from behind some bales of freight and lit his cigar.

He talked with the First Mate, who now was standing near the gangplank as well. As soon as the plank was down and the people moved toward it, the First Mate said something and people nodded.

The line moved along. Pierre and Francine hurried off the boat without attracting Harding's notice. Just as Spur and the princess came within 20 feet of the First Mate, Spur saw the gambler looking directly at Alexandria. He grinned and began working his way toward the pair.

He came straight to them and caught Alexandria's hand.

"Well now, Miss Alexandria, this is no way to treat a man you owe something to, is it?"

Spur moved forward.

Harding whipped out a gambler's best friend, a small two-shot .45 derringer, and grinned. "Didn't think I'd be watchful of my property for the night, did you sweetheart?"

Spur started past the man as the line kept moving. Only Alexandria and the gambler had stopped. Harding gave Spur a wicked look as Spur jostled him as he moved past. A moment later, Spur's right fist crashed down on Harding's right wrist, bringing a wail of surprise and pain.

Spur heard the man's wrist break, and the gun drop to the wooden deck. Spur grabbed Alexandria and hurried around the gambler.

"Stop them!" Harding roared. "Those two right there. They're the ones who stole my wallet."

The line of people had walked off the gangplank. The workers hauled it on board and Spur and Alexandria rushed to the far side of the boat away from the dock. Behind them, Spur saw the First Mate running toward them. Harding hurried behind him, his left hand holding his right wrist tenderly.

"Get them!" Harding bellowed. "There's fifty dollars reward if you get them!"

That was two months pay for the First Mate. He ran faster, cutting off Spur's retreat. He looked at the muddy water, then back at the ship's officer. The *Mission Belle* was picking up speed. She couldn't be stopped now, not with her running late.

"Swim time," Spur said softly. There was a three foot wooden railing along the side of the ship. The Princess grinned, looked at the man behind them. She ran three steps toward the stern, then dove neatly over the railing, knifing into the water six feet beyond the side of the ship.

Spur took two steps and dove over the side. He came up and stroked hard four times directly away from the side of the ship. He heard the big paddle wheel grinding around. The eighteen foot wheel with blades that dipped into the Mississippi river 260 times a minute was well away from him.

He looked for the girl. She only then came to the surface, having stroked out 20 feet from the ship underwater. She surfaced, waved to him and began a racing stroke back toward him.

They heard shouts from the ship and then it swept past them and they saw that they were less than 50 feet from the dock. Spur treaded water a minute and pointed to the dock.

"Can you make it that far?" he called.

She was still ten feet behind him.

"Race you!" she challenged and they swam for the dock.

Alexandria sliced through the water like a harbor seal. She caught Spur and passed him and his clumsy overhand stroke with a dozen feet to go. Under the pier they found a platform and steps upward. They stood there a moment shivering and wiping the water from their clothes. Both were still fully dressed.

"What a wonderful way to cool off," Alexandria said. "Only next time, let's find a lake that isn't quite so dark and dirty. I couldn't see two feet underwater."

They climbed the steps and found Pierre waiting for them.

"You make quite an entrance," Pierre said. "Are you two with the traveling river boat show that I've heard about?"

Francine came running up and hugged Alexandria. "I thought I would never see you again!" she exclaimed.

"There's a quite respectable hotel a block from here," Pierre said. "I inquired. Our luggage is being guarded by a particularly rough-looking chap. I tore a dollar bill in half, so he'll be there. Shall we go?"

Pierre walked beside Spur on the way up the steps to the street and on toward the hotel. The man carrying four pieces of luggage followed them closely.

"This gambler, Harding, will he get off the boat and come looking for us?"

Spur considered it a moment, then shook his head. "Not a chance. He took a gamble and eventually lost. He was probably back at a poker game before we got out of the Mississippi. He's a gambler. He'll figure he's money ahead by being able to gamble tonight instead of spending it with the princess."

The diplomat stared at Spur for a few seconds, then nodded. "I daresay you're right. So what will it be for us, the hotel?"

Spur rubbed his chin and looked around at the town. Not much of a hotel here. Not many places to look. Harding could be a sore loser, not want to be welshed on by a woman.

"On the other hand, this Harding might be another kind of gambler. He probably would guess that we would think that he would give up the princess's bet, forget it and go on gambling. With us thinking that way, we could have a good night's sleep in the hotel and proceed on our way tomorrow. By that time he would have lost us.

"But if he figured we would do that, he might get off at the next port, hire a horse and race back here, broken arm and all, and demand satisfaction. Come to think of it, I do believe I broke his wrist, which would make him a poor gambler at best."

"I agree. There's a livery of sorts over there."

Spur nodded. "You keep the ladies here and I'll hire the rig and come around and collect you and our baggage."

Twenty minutes later they were on their way up the rough road to the north. It followed the river except on sweeping curves and they passed many farms and a few larger operations.

"Are those plantations with black slaves?" Alexandria asked.

"There are no more slaves," Spur said. "Not after the Civil War, which ended in 1865."

It slowly turned to dusk and Spur eyed the country ahead. He had no plan to drive all night. Perhaps an Inn. But there were no such accommodations on a road so little traveled.

It was full dark by that time and no moon showed. The horses moved along warily, not used to the road, not pleased about still being on it.

Lights showed ahead and Spur watched them with anticipation. It turned out to be a farm with a large house, two barns and a herd of dairy cows. A lantern hung over the front porch and Spur turned the horses in.

"Thank the Lord!" Francine whispered from the rear of the carriage.

Spur came to a halt near the back porch and tied the reins. "They might not have room," he said softly. "Stay here until I find out how the land lies."

As Spur left the buggy, a shadow came out of the darkness near the porch.

"Evening," the man in the shadows said.

"Good evening to you, sir," Spur said. "Wondering if you had a spare bed or two for some weary travelers?"

"Might, then again, might not."

"We'd need two rooms and beds," Spur said walking closer to the man in the shadows. Spur kept his right hand near the butt of his .45. He'd dried it out on the drive. Nice thing about solid cartridges over the percussion. A solid cartridge would fire even underwater.

"Might be able to do that. Four of you?"

"Yes, two women and two men."

"Good enough. Step down and come in. Reckon you'll want some supper."

"Be mighty kind of you. We can pay."

"Sounds fair. We be a little short on cash."

Spur helped the ladies out of the carriage and they walked into the house. It was a frame structure with no wallboard or decorations inside. A basic shelter.

When Spur saw the man he frowned. He had stringy hair and three teeth missing in front. But he smiled.

"Reckon this ain't some fancy town hotel, but we got beds and blankets. Better than sleeping out there in the carriage all night."

They sat at a plank table without a cloth on it and met the woman of the house. She was small and had stringy hair as well and black eyes that seemed to watch everything at once. She never smiled while they were there.

She banged pots around as she stoked the wood stove and soon brought them hot stew with lots of carrots and potatoes and string beans and some meat that Spur couldn't recognize. He didn't want to take the chance of finding out what it was.

A half hour after the meal, they were shown two rooms on the second floor of the house. Each had a double bed and blankets and a door but no locks on them.

Morgan shrugged. He'd keep his six-gun handy. He and Percy took one bed and the women the other. Percy undressed down to his underwear, but Spur didn't even take off his boots. He'd dried out completely and lay down on top of the quilt and blew out the coal oil lamp.

He heard the women talking through the thin wall to the other room for a few minutes, then silence. Spur could hear no more sounds from below. The bed felt good after the wild day. He hoped all would be quiet until morning. Then they'd have some coffee and maybe hot cakes and be on their way.

Spur dozed. He awoke when he heard some noise, but it didn't come again and he let his eyes close on the blackness and drifted off again.

He had no idea how much later he came awake and sat up on the bed, his six-gun fisted in his right hand as one of the women's screams daggered through the darkness.

Spur hit the floor and jolted to the door. He jerked it open and saw a lamp in the hall. It sat on a chair and beside the chair on the floor sat the mistress of the house with a shotgun aimed right at him.

"Easy, young feller. He won't hurt them none. Just use them once or twice. Figure it's our right, you busting in on us and all."

Spur's shot from the .44 blasted through the lamp plunging the hallway into total darkness.

The sound of the revolver going off in the hallway was as loud as a dynamite explosion. Spur lunged back into the bedroom just as the shotgun blasted. The screeching roaring sound came as the shotgun went off and from the buckshot that rattled into the doorframe and down the hall.

The sound deafened Spur. He had jolted back into the room the instant before the shotgun fired. In the second of light, he had seen that the woman had a single-barrelled weapon. He lunged out the door and down the hall in the total darkness until he smashed into the woman. He kicked away the shotgun and grabbed the woman in the dark. He got one leg and one arm. Spur picked her up and carried her another three steps to the door to the room where Francine and Alexandria were.

Spur felt the old woman try to bite him. He banged her head against the wall and kept going. At the door, he kicked it open and saw a lamp burning on a small table.

The man with the stringy hair and missing teeth knelt over one of the women on the bed. Spur dropped the old woman, drew his six-gun and shot the farmer in the shoulder, slamming him off the bed into a screaming mass on the floor. The sound of the six-gun firing filled the room with a roaring thunder that blocked out the man's screams, then gradually faded until Spur could hear the man bellowing on the floor. He was naked to the waist and his trousers were around his knees.

In the lamplight, Spur saw the two woman leap from the bed and hold each other on the other side of the room.

Spur stopped the old woman from crawling for the door and caught her wrist and dragged her over to the man on the floor.

"Better stop the bleeding on his shoulder or he won't be much good to you around here dead. Is this the way you treat all of your overnight guests?"

Francine began to cry and slumped to the floor. The Princess moved up so she could see the wounded man.

"I saw you use your gun," she said, her eyes bright. The nightgown she wore had been ripped down the front and she held it together modestly but the side of one breast showed.

"Are you all right?" Spur asked.

"Yes, he was after Francine. He said she had bigger . . ." She stopped.

"Did he hurt Francine?"

"Just scared her." Alexandria edged forward. "He's bleeding a lot isn't he?"

"A gunshot tends to do that."

"You're good with that weapon."

"Good enough tonight. I'll take these two downstairs and tie them up. Then we can get some sleep. We'll leave just after daylight."

He went over to Francine. She had stopped crying and wiped the tears from her pretty eyes.

"You're all right?"

She stood, then nodded, leaned forward and he held her close. He was aware of her breasts pressing through the soft white fabric of her nightdress against his chest. She snuggled against him for a moment, then gasped twice as the crying jag ended completely and she eased away from him.

"He . . . he . . ."

"It's all over now. He can't hurt you. I'm here. Alexandria is here. Get some sleep."

Pierre slipped into the room with a derringer in his right hand. He saw the situation under control.

53

He wore only his pants and his undershirt. "Looks like you have things in hand. Anything I can do?"

"Watch the old lady, she's nasty-mean."

Spur looked back at the farmers. The old woman had the man's shoulder tied up with a piece of the bed sheet. She got him to his feet and Spur motioned to them and the woman picked up the lighted lamp and they walked out of the room and down the stairs. Pierre brought up the rear with his derringer ready.

In the bedroom on the first floor, Spur told the couple to lie down on the bed, then he tied them hand and foot with some thin, strong cord. They would both still be bound when he came back down in the morning. He took the lamp and he and Pierre went up the stairs to the women's room. He knocked, then went in and set the light on the small dresser and turned it down.

Both women were under the covers. He watched them a moment. Alexandria's eyes were still bright with excitement. Francine had her eyes closed.

"We'll be fine," the princess said. She nodded and Spur and Pierre slipped out of the room.

Spur closed the door and sat on the floor leaning against the panel. "I'll stay here to morning, Pierre. You get some sleep. You get to drive tomorrow." Pierre nodded and went into the other bedroom.

If anyone put a foot on the stairs, Spur would hear them. He pushed out the spent rounds from his .44 and loaded fresh ones in the dark working from memory and habit. He checked the empty chamber and turned the cylinder so it was aligned with the barrel, then let down the hammer gently.

Spur stayed awake for an hour, then he dozed. Once the Colt .44 touched the floor when his hand let it sag. He came awake at once, saw the weapon low and lifted it.

He dozed twice more before he saw the sky lighten in the east. He was up and opened his carpetbag, changed into clean clothes, then went down to check on the host family.

Spur left them tied. Both were still sleeping. He made a fire, then heated some water, letting it come to a running boil before dropping in the ground coffee he found in a fruit jar. It was bitter strong and would wake them all up.

He took a cup full up to the diplomat, and two more to the women. Both were up and dressed in clean clothes.

In the kitchen, they all had a second cup of coffee, then Spur brought the carriage around and loaded in the luggage. He helped the women in and then went and untied the old woman.

"Don't try to do anything with that rifle over the mantle. I took the firing pin out of it. You try anything and I'll come back here and burn your place to the ground, you understand me?"

She glared at him with her one good eye. "Bastard!" she shrilled. "You hurt my Lester!"

"He's lucky I didn't kill him. I hit him in the shoulder on purpose."

Spur stepped to the door, watching the old woman rubbing her wrists where the cord had been. When she looked away, he ran out of the room, out of the house and to the wagon. He had the rig fifty yards down the road before he heard the back screen door slam and the old woman shrilling a string of curses at them.

Princess Alexandria, heir to the crown of the principality of Mantuco, leaned forward and tapped Spur on the shoulder.

"This is the most exciting trip I've ever been on. What a wonderful time I'm having. Can you guarantee that the rest of the tour will be as interesting and wonderful as the past day and night?"

Spur looked at Pierre, the diplomat, who only lifted his eyebrows skyward.

Spur glanced back at the princess. "Alexandria, if it gets any more exciting, I'm taking you back to Washington, D.C., dressed as a nun. Now settle back, we have a long ride to St. Louis."

Chapter 4

The trip back to St. Louis took them two days by carriage. The roads were bad and the food they ate at small towns was less than princely. They came into St. Louis to a good hotel and registered under assumed names and slept the clock around.

The second morning after they arrived, Francine knocked on Spur's door. He was shaving. He let her in and she grinned at his body bare to the waist.

"I like you that way," she said with a small smile. One hand came up and rubbed her breast. Spur went on shaving in the wavy mirror. He nicked himself when she came up behind him and fitted her body to his like a glove, her breasts burning into his bare back.

"Woman, you trying to get me in trouble?" Spur asked.

She put her arms around his torso and hugged him tightly. "Not trying, just doing what comes naturally when I see a gorgeous half-naked man. We've got time."

"We don't have time. The princess said she wants to get started out West today. I have to make arrangements."

"We still have time." Her hands moved down to his belt, then to his fly and found the start of a hardness there. He spun around and kissed her, shaving cream and all.

Francine giggled. "That was different," she said. She caught his hand but he shook his head.

Spur washed the soap off his face and dried it, then put on a shirt and watched Francine unbuttoning her blouse.

"Not now, Francine, beautiful lady. Later."

"When later?"

"Tonight. We'll arrange it."

She stepped forward and kissed him on the lips, then rubbed her breast again and backed away. "A promise is a promise." She frowned. "We leaving on the train today?"

"Yes."

"I better get packed."

"Tell the princess to pack up as well. About noon we'll be heading out, if I remember the train schedule."

Francine looked at him with desire still showing on her face, but went to the door and stepped into the hall.

He put a kerchief around his throat, added a soft leather vest in light brown and settled his low-crowned black hat firmly on his head. It had a row of silver Mexican peso coins around the headband and had been his favorite style hat for years.

Outside the hotel, Spur went to the depot and checked the railroad schedule. The first train left for the west at twelve-thirty. Plenty of time. He stood in the depot for five minutes watching the people around him. No one seemed to be paying him any attention.

He was still worried about the man who shot at the princess here in St. Louis before. If there was one, there probably would be more. When Spur left the depot, he watched behind him, doubled back twice but could find no one following him. He went into a store, out the back door and quickly jogged back to the hotel.

They had an early dinner about eleven in the hotel eatery, then went out the side door of the hotel where Spur had a rig waiting.

An hour later they were on the train with no problems. Spur hoped that they would lose the assassins, whoever they were. The princess would give him enough trouble all by herself, if the first two days were any measure.

It took them most of the afternoon and part of the evening to travel the 225 miles to Kansas City all the way across the state of Missouri.

Spur had obtained one of the new compartments for the princess and Francine. The four of them played the new game of bridge for two hours. Spur had tried his hand at it before but didn't understand it. The other three were good players and helped him.

At Kansas City they swung southwest on the tracks heading for Dodge City. The princess had heard so much about it she wanted to see it; experience it was the way she put it.

They had a three hour wait in Kansas City while the tracks were being repaired. A cloudburst had washed out the rails 20 miles out of town.

It was nearly midnight when they got moving.

Spur made sure that the women were safely in their compartment; then he went to the one he and Pierre had ticketed and started to get ready for a long sleep. Pierre dropped off at once, but Spur opened the curtains and looked outside. It was mostly black, but here and there he could see a few lights in small towns.

A light knock on the door brought him off the bed with his Colt in his hand.

At the door, he opened it a crack and saw Francine standing there.

"Now?" Francine said.

Spur chuckled.

"You said tonight. There's a vacant compartment right beside us. I checked. Come on."

A minute later the two of them slipped into the compartment and locked the door. A faint gas lamp gave a soft glow to the small bedroom. Francine reached up and kissed him.

"I've been looking forward to this," she said softly. Spur kissed her, then pulled her hard against him and made the kiss more insistent.

He could feel the heat of her through their clothes. Her breathing increased and her hands fumbled at his crotch. Her lips pulled away from his.

"Right now! With all our clothes on! Almost like you were forcing me." She pulled him down on the bed with him on top of her and spread her legs. Spur's hand discovered that she wore nothing under the long skirt. She pulled the skirt up high around her waist and smiled.

"Yes, I'm ready. I've been dreaming about this all afternoon."

She unbuttoned the fly of his pants and dug inside to find his hardness. She struggled for a minute, then undid his belt and let his town pants fall and pulled down his short underwear.

"Oh, damn! Look at him. So big and beautiful!" She kissed the purple tip of him and then drew him down between her raised knees. "Right now, Spur McCoy. Fuck me right now or I'll never speak to you again!"

For a moment, Spur felt like he was the one being raped; then she stroked his lance and his hot blood surged and he lowered his hips and angled toward her heartland. She guided him and a moment later his dry skin slid against her lubricated tunnel and he plunged into her in one driving stroke.

"Oh, god!" she crooned. "I don't see how there was room!" She put her arms around his neck and pulled him down. "Just lie here a minute. I want to feel him inside me, to dream about it a minute. I don't want you to be too fast."

They lay there that way a while, then slowly he began to move. He felt her hot blood surging and the heat of her chest and torso flowed through his clothes into him.

He moved again and then began a gentle stroking. Francine moaned and moved her hips countering his thrusts, making them deeper and longer.

They built slowly.

She crooned and yelped. He could feel her tiny node, and with each stroke he massaged it and now she grew more excited with each touching.

Her hips pounded up now to heighten the touch on her clit and then the spell overflowed and she broke and Francine wailed a long, wild, animal sound that grew thinner and higher as she continued.

Her body shattered into a thousand pieces as a

long series of spasms shook her and rattled her bones and made her gasp for breath.

"Oh, god! Oh, god! Oh, god! I'm going to die!" She humped at him and her hips writhed with the climaxes that ripped through her again and again.

He tapered off his thrusting, letting her revel in her own satisfaction. Gradually the tremors eased and left her body and she opened her eyes. Her keening had died out and she grinned and shook her head.

"Never one so good before. Not even one, anytime. That was fantastic. Now it's your turn."

She countered his thrusting and their pelvic bones smashed together. He thrust and held, thrust and held and in 20 repetitions he felt the giant gates open and the whole Mississippi flood downstream through his tubes. His hips pounded her like a battering ram against a castle gate. The gate came crashing down and Spur moaned as the fluids flashed out of his body.

He soared over the stars, blinded by their light, circled around the galaxy and jetted in and out of the comets and moons and vast clouds of floating dust. At last he came soaring back into our solar system and to planet earth. He gasped and shuddered and drove one last time against her willing body before he collapsed against her and she wrapped her arms around his back and her legs lifted high over his back and wrapped him again as she locked her ankles.

They lay that way for ten minutes before he moved. She unlatched him and he sat up. She came up beside him and kissed his cheek.

"You get my vote for the best lover in the world," Francine said softly. She brushed her lips over his and snuggled against him. Her eyes watched his every move.

"Spur McCoy, you can be so forceful, so commanding and tough, but then just now you were so tender, so considerate, so thoughtful. Amazing to find both qualities in the same man."

"Not so strange. It just takes an amazing woman to bring out the best in a man. You are a marvelous lady with fantastic big breasts that men will die over. A sleek, delicious body and a pair of pile-driving hips that will satisfy any man for as long as he can get it hard."

"Five times tonight?" Francine asked.

"Not tonight. It can't get any better than this. Let's save something for the next time."

His hands found her breasts and he fondled them gently. "So beautiful, a woman's second greatest asset."

"The first?"

He stroked between her legs and she laughed. "I think you're right. I knew a man once who said he didn't care if a girl was pretty or not. He could always put a sack over her head. He wasn't going to poke her head."

Spur laughed and kissed her. "We better get some sleep. I don't know quite what to expect in Dodge. I wired the sheriff there asking him for some suggestions for a ranch to visit. I told him we'd check in with him after the train arrived."

She pouted. "That's all for tonight?"

He bent and kissed her breasts through the fabric, breathing his hot breath on each one. She moaned in delight.

"All for tonight. You trying to wear me out?"

"I'd like to. Soon."

They arranged their clothes, blew out the gas

63

light and slipped back into their respective compartments.

Spur settled on the bed. There were a lot of miles left before they got to Dodge. He wondered what the town would be like now. He hadn't been there for four or five years.

When Spur woke up the next morning the train was stopped. He looked out the window. They weren't in a town. He pulled on his boots and strapped on his .44 and went to see what the trouble was.

The conductor met him as he stepped down to the right of way.

"Prairie fire ahead. Don't think it will damage the tracks but we got to wait for it to burn across. Figure about a half hour yet."

"Where are we now?"

"About twenty miles outside of Wilsonville, Kansas."

"Looks like cow country."

"Getting to be more and more."

Spur walked to the back of the car, climbed up the steps and went into the compartment unit and knocked on the women's door. Alexandria opened the door. She wore a bright blue dress that clung to her figure delightfully.

"Why are we stopped? Are we being robbed?"

Spur shook his head and told her.

"Oh. How long will it be? I want to get to some real ranches with cowboys and horses and everything."

"We're in cattle country. Just keep watching outside your window. Oh, the dining car is open if you would like some breakfast."

The train lurched into motion as they ate and soon came into the small Kansas town. There were stockyards near the tracks and in one pen hundreds of cattle waiting to be loaded on box cars and shipped to the east.

Alexandria watched them with wonder. "When will we get to Dodge City?" she asked.

"Sometime today, depending on the delays. You can rest up tonight and we'll take a tour of a ranch in the morning."

The princess nodded and Spur excused himself from the small table and went back to the compartment. The porter had been there and made up the bed. He sat and watched out the window as the train moved out from Wilsonville.

Spur went back to find the ladies and Francine answered the door. She looked surprised.

"I thought Alexandria was with you. She said she had some questions to ask you."

Spur frowned. "When was that?"

"After we finished breakfast, before we left that last little town."

Spur saw the conductor at the end of the car and he ran toward him.

"Did anyone get off at the last stop?"

"Yes," the conductor said. "Three women and a man.

"The women, did one of them wear a bright blue dress and a blue hat, about five-three or so, quite pretty?"

The conductor frowned. "Seems to me she did. Yes, she stumbled getting down the step and I caught her before she fell. She seemed to have the faintest trace of an accent."

"Oh, damn! How far to the next stop?"

"Thirty miles."

"How far are we from Wilsonville?"

"Maybe five miles. A long walk. I take it you

didn't want the lady to leave the train."

"Pull the cord, Conductor. Three of us need to get off."

Ten minutes later, Spur, Pierre and Francine stood on the railroad right of way and looked eastward as the train vanished down the tracks to the west. They couldn't quite see the small town that lay five or six miles on the rails east.

A wagon road of sorts followed along the railroad, but when they walked out to it, Spur could see no traffic going either way. There wasn't a tree or a bit of shade anywhere around.

"Damn!" Spur said for the tenth time. "I had no idea she would pull a stunt like this."

Francine nodded. "Exactly what I would have expected. I should have warned you. She does whatever she wants to, usually on the spur of the moment. Like betting her bottom on that card game."

"You two stay here with the luggage. I'll trot into town and send back a carriage for you. When it comes, get to the hotel in town and stay there. I'll be trying to find the princess."

Spur took off the leather vest and left it with Francine. He took off his gunbelt and pushed his .44 into his waistband. Then he waved and began jogging down the hint of a road to the east.

He had learned how to do an Indian trot from the Comanches. They could cover the ground on foot doing a mile in eight minutes, and run that way for 20 miles without stopping. The bad part was they were ready to fight at the end of the 20 miles.

Spur wasn't in that good a shape, but he could do six miles with no problem. He carried the Colt in his right hand as he jogged, and soon set up a pace and a rhythm that worked well for him. He checked his pocket watch. A little after ten o'clock. He should be in town by eleven, send the rig back and find the princess. They would stay there overnight and get on the Dodge City the next morning.

That had been the plan.

Spur wasn't in condition. He had covered what he figured were three miles when he took a breather by walking. The six-gun got heavier with each step. He changed it to his left hand and after a quarter of a mile, jogged again.

When he got into the edge of the small town, he slowed to a walk. It was nearly eleven-thirty. Alexandria had been in town for two hours, alone. It would be interesting to see what kind of trouble she got herself into.

The livery stable was on the near side of town. Spur gave a boy there two dollars to go out six miles and bring in a man and a woman and their luggage. The kid jumped at the chance and hitched up a light rig. Spur waited until he took off at a smart trot with the one-horse outfit.

Spur walked the two-block-long town. He didn't see the bright blue dress. He stopped at the city marshal's office and explained his problem.

"Have my two deputies on it right away, Mr. McCoy," the marshal said. He'd stared wide-eyed at Spur's identification papers and President U.S. Grant's signature.

"Appreciate it, Marshal. This woman is a foreigner, but she speaks good English. About five-three and wearing a bright blue dress and matching hat. I'll check the saloons. The lady likes to gamble."

Spur changed his mind when he remembered her wide-eyed expression when she saw the small stock pens near the railroad. He jogged through town to the far side and circled the stock pens.

She wasn't there. Two cowboys said they hadn't seen a woman out that way at all.

Spur jogged back to the first business and began checking out every saloon and gambling hall on both sides of the street. It took him nearly an hour and he didn't find any sign of Alexandria. He questioned each barkeep and none of them remembered such a woman coming in that morning.

When he came out of the last saloon next to the general store, he saw the rig come into town he had sent for Francine and Pierre.

"Find her?" Pierre asked as the buggy came up to Spur.

"No, not a trace. She has to be here somewhere." Spur got his gunbelt and strapped it on and pushed his Colt into it.

Pierre turned to the boy, handed him a dollar. "Check Miss Miller in at the hotel, and have her sign me in too. That's a good lad."

The rig moved toward the hotel and the two men stared at each other.

"Where could she be?"

Spur shook his head. "You check in each store and see if she's been in. Her bright blue dress will be remembered. Someone has to have seen her. I want to look around those stock yards again. She seemed entranced by all the cattle."

Just as Spur arrived at the stock pens, a man on a big bay rode up and tied his animal to the first fence. He stared at the cattle.

Spur approached him.

"Sir, you been around the pens this morning?"

"Yep."

"I'm wondering if you saw a woman out here.

She had on a bright blue dress and a blue hat. About five-three."

"Yep, I seen her. Little thing. Talked with a kind of accent. Looked out of place. Then Walt Urick drove up in his wagon and checked his steers. The little lady knew him and they talked, and a couple of minutes later she got into his wagon and they drove toward town."

"You sure it was a small woman in a blue dress. Young, maybe 22 or so?"

"Yep, that was her. Walt has a small spread outside of town about ten miles north on the Pawnee River. He usually stops at the general store for victuals. He didn't have no supplies, so I'd bet he stopped there."

Spur thanked him and ran for the general store. He was within half a block when a man stepped into the street 40 feet in front of him. The man drew his six-gun and watched Spur. He lifted it to cover the Secret Service Agent.

Spur stopped twenty feet from him.

"Yeah, I figured it was you, McCoy. Seen you run by one way, then talk to the barkeeps, then run the other way. Never knew you could move so fast. You never moved that quick in Wyoming two years ago."

Spur frowned. As a Secret Service Agent he'd made his share of enemies in his time. He couldn't remember this one.

"You have me confused with somebody else, sir," Spur said starting to move forward.

"Easy, McCoy. You don't have your weapon out and I do. I can gun you down with no trouble. But I'm willing to give you a fair chance. You always said how fast you were. You didn't give my brother a chance in Wyoming. Just blew two holes in his heart before he could draw."

"I don't know what you're talking about. I've got important business."

"Bet you do, McCoy. I found out all about you. By then you was on the train and out of the state. But I'll never forget your face. Thinking it over, I won't give you a fair chance. Give you about the same chance you gave Billy. I'll lower my muzzle arm's length, point it at the ground and you go for your iron. Best man wins."

McCoy watched as the man lowered his six-gun until it pointed at the ground.

"Look, let's go over and talk to the marshal. He's a good man. We can work this out."

"Never thought you was a yellow-livered coward, too, McCoy. But it figures. Anybody who would gun down a twenty-one-year-old kid's got to be yellow clean through."

The clues were piling up, but McCoy couldn't remember who the man was or what happened. He'd worked a lot in Wyoming in the past several years.

"Anytime, big man. Anytime you want to draw you go right ahead. I figure I'm giving you more chance than Billy had at that."

Spur figured the odds. All the other man had to do was lift his muzzle and fire. Spur had to draw, aim and fire. He had to count on the man missing his first shot so Spur could get off one. His hand trembled beside his holster.

It was time. If he didn't draw the other man would lift his six-gun first. Spur McCoy knew he had to draw, now!

Chapter 5

Spur McCoy's hand jolted upward, the butt of his hand hitting the butt of the Colt .44 and lifting it out of leather. His big right hand closed around the walnut grips and raised it higher continuing its movement out of its leather home. During this fraction of a second, his trigger finger slid in the trigger guard and his right thumb pulled back on the hammer, rotating the cylinder to a live round and cocking the hammer ready to fire.

As soon as the Colt .44 barrel cleared leather, Spur brought the Colt up in a point-and-shoot movement. It was different this time because he began his dive for the ground as soon as he started the draw. The dive was designed to throw off the other man's aim, give him something different to look at, hopefully confuse him and make him miss that first shot.

Spur heard the report of the other man's six-gun as he was still in mid air on the way to the ground. He heard it but felt no pain.

The gunman had missed!

Spur flopped hard belly down in the dirt, his left hand out to help cushion the fall and his right arm out with the deadly .44 spitting fire and lead. The round raced on an upward angle from the diving Spur McCoy. It hit the gunman just below his right ribs and dug upward through his torso and lodged somewhere between two ribs in his back.

The man slammed backwards from the force of the heavy bullet and his six-gun spun out of his hand. He lay on his back in the Wilsonville street and a dozen people rushed out to him.

Spur lifted from the dirt, his right thumb clicking back the hammer on the Colt ready for another shot. He saw the gunman down, one hand over his chest.

Someone sat beside him and held the man's head in his lap. Angry eyes stared at Spur.

The town marshal came pushing through the crowd that had formed in a few seconds. Spur walked up and stared down at the man. He was dying. Medical doctors didn't know enough yet to save a man lung shot. Someday they might, but not now.

Spur watched the dozen men and women who circled the wounded man. They all had angry stares for him. Two of the women cried. The marshal knelt beside the wounded man, bent low to hear what he whispered and nodded.

The man on the ground let out a moan of pain, then shouted something but the words turned to a whisper as the last breath whistled out of his body.

The town marshal stood and paced deliberately toward Spur.

"Gonna have to ask for your gun, Mr. McCoy."

"What? Didn't you see it? He already had his gun out before I drew mine. He threatened to kill me. It was self defense. Anyway, I'm a federal lawman in the pursuit of my duties."

"Even so, have to have a hearing. Your six-gun please."

"Sorry, not convenient right now. I'm on an important case and my charge is missing. I have to find her or there could be serious international consequences. I told you about the situation earlier. I'm sure that you'll . . ." Spur stopped. He felt two gun muzzles pressing in his back.

"Like I said, Mr. McCoy, I'll have your weapon and you'll be the guest of Plains County until I get this cleared up." The marshal reached out and took the gun from Spur's hand.

"That was James Leslie you just gunned down. He was an important man in this town. We'll have to study all the evidence closely."

"You can't do this, Marshal. You saw what my papers said."

"I also see that you've shot down in cold blood one of the town's leading citizens. President of the First Kansas Bank, Deacon in the Wilsonville Community Church, part time teacher of English at our school. Builder of our city library, employer of over fifty people in this town. I've heard three folks say you shot first, didn't give him a chance."

"He fired first, he had his gun out all the time. If there are any honest people in this town they'll testify to that. There must have been twenty people see him draw down on me, then lower the muzzle of his weapon toward the ground."

The guns in his back prodded Spur forward and he moved across the street toward the town marshal's office. He'd seen the two small barred cells in back. Now he saw them from the other side of the locked door.

"A telegram, Marshal. Send a telegram right now to William Wood, Director of the Secret Service, 61 Pennsylvania Avenue, Washington, D.C. You'll get an immediate reply. I've got important work to do here. That girl is still missing I told you about earlier. She's a princess. Only daughter of the Prince of Mantuco on the southern coast of France. If I don't find her it could mean real trouble, international trouble."

"Yep. I can send the wire. Seems to me this is Friday. Don't know if they will get the wire until Monday."

Spur scowled. Two days, maybe three? Hard telling what could be happening to the princess in that time.

"Marshal, there's a Francine Miller registered at the hotel. Can you send someone to have her come and see me? There's still a chance I can save the princess even if I'm in here."

"Might." The marshal sat down in a chair and stared at Spur. "Jim told me just before he died that you gunned down his brother out in Wyoming three or four years ago. That true?"

"True. This Jim yelled something about it. But it wasn't until you said the name Leslie that I remembered. Tom Leslie was the leader of a vicious gang of cattle rustlers. They took over a small town in Wyoming, killed the sheriff, held the people virtual prisoners in their own town.

"He also curtailed the U.S. mail. That's when the government sent me in with five Deputy United

74

States Marshals and a twenty man unit from the Wyoming Militia and cleaned up the town. Tom and four of his men were killed. The other twelve were tried and sent to prison for from ten to twenty years. Wire the sheriff at Rocky Bend, Wyoming, if you want to check it out."

The marshal's face didn't change. "Might just do that. First I'll wire Washington. My deputy will go talk to the woman in the hotel. You rest easy."

It was almost an hour before Francine came in the front door of the marshal's office. She hurried back where she saw Spur.

"What on earth? At first I didn't believe the deputy. What's this all about?"

"No time for that. Have your found the princess?"

"No. Pierre discovered that she was in the general store and that she went away with some rancher. But we don't know who. The store man couldn't remember, or wouldn't."

"The rancher's name is Walt Urick. He's got a place about ten miles north of town on the Pawnee River. Tell Pierre that he's got to get a buggy and drive out there right now before it gets dark and bring Alexandria back here. Then I'll get this little misunderstanding here worked out and we'll get on to Dodge City."

Francine had written down the name and directions. Now she came close to the cell door.

"Stand back, Miss," the deputy said. "No contact with the prisoner."

She stepped back. "I'll go with Pierre. We'll hire a rig and hurry out there. I know it's all going to be just fine. Alexandria wanted to see what a real cattle ranch was like. I told you she acted on impulse."

75

"Yes. You warned me. Now hurry, get out there before dark."

Francine waved and rushed out the front door.

Spur sat on the thin mattress on the cell's narrow bunk. It wasn't first class accommodations. But he'd done worse.

When the town marshal came back about half an hour later, Spur was at the cell door calling to him.

"Did the telegram go through? Did confirmation of my status as a federal law officer come back?"

The marshal shook his head. "Afraid not. Telegrapher told me it's two hours later in Washington, and them offices usual close about four o'clock, which is two o'clock our time. So he said chances are the message won't get delivered until Monday morning. Best I can do."

"The telegrapher is wrong. It's only an hour later in Washington, D.C. Marshal, you can do better. You can let me out of here on my own recognizance. Let me find the princess and bring her back here where she'll be safe. Then you can do all the investigating you want to about James Leslie. You'll find it just as I told you. James Leslie drew down on me while I was forty feet away, and challenged me to a shoot out. Only he kept the advantage of having his weapon out of leather.

"Ask anyone who saw it, they'll tell you I was defending my life."

"You say. I got to go by witnesses, like you suggest. Fact is I have three written statements so far by witnesses who swear that you fired the only shot and that James Leslie never had a chance to get his weapon out of leather. They say you shot him down in cold blood."

* * *

Pierre Dupont did not like the idea of driving a buggy out across the wilds of the state of Kansas. He had insisted that Francine remain in the hotel. No use putting both the ladies in jeopardy. He had along with him a derringer with two shots, concealed in his pocket.

He had never fired it in anger and was not sure he could aim at a human being and pull the trigger. But he had bluffed with it twice. He also had the sum of over two hundred United States dollars. When all else failed, bribery usually worked wonders.

The only thing he had been able to learn from the store owner was that Walt Urick was a Baptist, that he paid his bills and that he had been a widower now for about two years.

Why in the name of heaven would the princess have run off with the man? He was almost 40 years old. Pierre had exhausted every line of logic he could propose by the time he ended his three hour drive and found the gate that proclaimed that the Urick Ranch lay a half mile to the west along a rutted trail.

As he drove up to the buildings, he saw that they were not in good repair. The house had a chimney with brick missing. One window had been boarded up. The barn was unpainted. There were only two horses in a small corral and none at all in the pasture beside the barn. He had seen no beef cattle in his drive into the place.

He stopped in the front yard and walked rather stiffly up to the front door. He knocked and heard someone come out the side door nearest to the buggy.

Pierre walked around so he could see the door

and found himself staring at a tall, slender man in dirty jeans and a ragged undershirt that was also dirty. His hair was half combed and he had a three day growth of beard.

The most disquieting aspect of the man's appearance was the double-barreled shotgun that he held aimed generally in Pierre's direction but not directly at him.

"What you selling?" Walt Urick called.

"Dear sir, I'm selling nothing," Pierre said. He moved toward the man. "You must be Mr. Walter Urick, am I right?"

The man nodded. When he smiled, Pierre could see that he had two teeth missing in the front.

"Good, good, I am Pierre Dupont, representative from the Prince of Mantuco, on the southern coast of France. I wish you a pleasant day."

"Never heard of either of you."

"Not unlikely. We are not a world power. I understand you have a house guest named Alexandria, I'd like to speak with her please."

For the first time the man grinned. "Yeah, bet to hell you'd like to talk to her. She ain't talking. She said to tell you to go home and forget her. She ain't moving until somebody called Spur comes out and rescues her. She likes to hear guns go off."

Urick shifted the shotgun and blasted a round of buckshot across the farm yard, scaring a half dozen chickens who were pecking at some seeds just out of range.

Urick laughed when Pierre took a step backward. "Got me one more round. You want me to see if I can knock down that horse of yours with the other barrel?"

Pierre backed up a step, the puny little derringer seeming like no help at all against a shotgun.

"Not at all, sir. I understand. I still would like to speak to Miss Alexandria. Perhaps I could interest you in a small cash payment for a few moments of her time. I do have a five dollar bill I could sacrifice for the pleasure. It's all the cash money I brought with me."

Urick hesitated. That was a week's wages for a working man. He scowled.

"Hell, I shouldn't. Told her she didn't have to talk to no one she didn't want to. Who is this Spur guy?"

"A man of her acquaintance from St. Louis." Pierre held up the five dollar bill.

"A fiver? Put it on the ground there and back away. Might be a counterfeit. Been some of them lately with them greenbacks. I'll look at it."

Pierre backed almost to the buggy and waited. Urick hurried forward, picked up the five dollar bill and stared at it. Then he laughed and brought the shotgun up.

"Now, like I said, you get on that buggy, Mr. Fancy Pants, and drive yourself back to town, lessen' you want a butt full of buckshot. You send that other feller out and then we can talk business."

"But sir, you took my money. Doesn't that allow me the chance to talk to Alexandria?"

The shotgun boomed again, this time near him, but only two of the whining buckshot hit Pierre in the leg. Neither one broke the skin. He winced but tried not to show any pain. He thought of running forward with his derringer, but already the man was pulling out the spent rounds and putting two fresh shotgun shells in the chambers.

Wearily, Pierre climbed into the buggy, took one more look at the ranch house. He thought maybe he'd see Alexandria looking out a window or waving. No such luck.

He pulled the buggy around in a circle and aimed it back down the lane toward town. It would be well dark before he got to the hotel. What could he do now? Francine had told him that Spur was incarcerated and they had no way of knowing for how long.

Pierre drove the rig and tried to figure out some diplomatic way to get out of this one. He definitely wouldn't wire his embassy for instructions. He would probably be in and out of more trouble than this before this trip was over.

He took careful account of the land masses he could see as he drove down the trail-like road toward town. One thing he didn't want to do was get lost and have to spend the night out here on the prairie.

Three hours later, Pierre gave a sigh of relief when he saw the lights of Wilsonville. He hadn't decided what to tell Francine. At last he decided just to tell her the truth. Spur McCoy was the only one who could get them out of this mess and he was still in jail.

Alexandria watched Pierre drive away. She giggled and twirled around in the rancher's wife's dress. It was too large for her but she had been enjoying trying on the various things in the closet.

Walt had been nice to her. He said all she had to do was cook for him and he'd let her stay. The way he looked at her she knew he meant to do more than just be nice to her, but she was not a virgin and men did not frighten her. Give them what they wanted and they became like little boys.

"Hey, woman, the old man is gone. Come down and fix me my supper."

Alexandria froze. Her eyes widened. What was she supposed to do now? She didn't know the first thing about cooking. She had never cooked a thing in her life. Not with a dozen servants to wait on her.

She put on another dress. It was too large as well, but she shrugged and walked down the bare boards stairs. The kitchen was lit by two smoking coal oil lamps and Alexandria came to a stop when she saw Walter Urick near the stove with a meat cleaver in his hand. He lifted it and chopped a freshly dressed chicken into four pieces.

"Cook it," he said.

"I'm so sorry, but I don't know how to cook."

"What? You promised." He scowled, scratched his crotch and shook his head. "If you can't cook, what can you do?"

"Nothing really. I'm a princess, I don't have to do anything."

"Sure, you're a princess and I'm the king of England." He shrugged. "Hell, I know one thing you can do. Look at the size of your tits." He walked toward her. Alexandria shivered. It wasn't supposed to be like this. He had been polite in town, courteous, pleasant.

She couldn't move. He stopped in front of her and caught her breasts with his hands.

"Oh, damn yes, big tits." He jerked the dress she wore and it tore down the front. Under that she had on her own blouse and he did the same thing to it, ripping the buttons off and showing her breasts. His hands fondled them and he bent to kiss one.

They stood near the table where he had cut up

the chicken and where a heavy iron frying pan lay. When he bent to kiss her breast, she caught the handle of the pan with both hands and slammed it down on his head.

Walt Urick groaned and sank to the floor.

Alexandria looked at him in surprise. She might be foolish but at least she wasn't stupid, she told herself. She searched for some string or rope, and found some strong cord on a shelf. She bound Walt's hands behind his back, tying his wrists together with tight knots.

Then she did the same to his ankles, wrapping the twine around them and knotting it securely.

Her mind raced ahead. What next? Next a good night's sleep. In the morning she would get one of the horses from the corral. One thing she had learned that would be helpful now was how to ride. She had ridden only jumping horses, but these flat-land ones would be easy. She could put a saddle on. Then she would simply reverse the direction they had come out here in the wagon. She'd had plenty of time to memorize the route. She had a good memory.

She washed her face, found some home made bread and cut off two large chunks. There was butter in the cupboard and a dish of strawberry jam. She ate the jam and bread, pumped some water from the inside well to drink and checked on Walter. He was still unconscious. She hoped she hadn't hit him too hard.

She took one lamp upstairs after blowing out the second one. The bedroom had been his wife's. It was a woman's room. The bed was unused and had sheets and carefully quilted spreads on it.

She undressed and slid between the sheets and soon went to sleep.

Once during the night she heard someone bellowing in rage. She knew it was Walter, but she also figured if he was screaming he was still tied up. She went back to sleep.

When morning came, she dressed quickly in the clothes she had come in, the bright blue dress, and went down stairs. Walter was still on the floor. He had a welt on his skull and had half way untied his hands. She scolded him, rolled him over and tied them again.

"Walter, you should be more polite to your guests. And that fondling me, that was not at all nice. Let this be a lesson for you."

She wasn't hungry, had only a glass of water, then saddled a horse from the barn and rode down the lane. It was simple getting back to town. She just followed the buggy tracks that Pierre had left.

It was not quite ten o'clock when she rode up to the hotel and slid off the horse. The blue dress billowed up and two men cheered but she frowned at them and they hurried on.

Upstairs there was a delightful reunion.

"Alexandria! You got away from him!" Francine squealed when she let the princess into her room. "How did you do it? Did he hurt you? Did he . . . you know . . . rape you?"

Alexandria told her all about it. Then they went and told Pierre, who was greatly relieved.

They decided the best thing would be a good breakfast. After the food, the other two told Alexandria that Spur McCoy was in jail for killing a man in a gunfight.

"I wasn't even here to see it!" she wailed. Then she brightened. "That doesn't matter. I'm working on a plan to break Spur out of jail. It won't be hard. First we find out how many deputies there are and who is on duty."

"No," Francine said. "We won't try to break him out of jail. In a day or two Washington will wire the marshal and it will all be straightened out."

"Yes, Princess, Francine is right. I simply won't hear of your doing anything that will endanger Mr. McCoy, or get us in trouble with the law. Remember, we are guests in this country and we don't want to have to use our diplomatic immunity. That would be bad publicity. I'm speaking for your father now. I forbid you to do anything to try to free Mr. McCoy."

"Yes, of course," Alexandria said.

Francine saw that gleam in the eye of the princess and she knew she had to stick with Alexandria every waking moment. The princess had something in mind and Francine had to do everything she could to stop her, or they all might wind up in jail.

Chapter 6

After breakfast the two ladies walked the streets looking in shops and buying some trinkets. Pierre had hurried away to the marshal's office to tell Spur that the princess was safe and back in town. After a half hour of shopping, the princess suggested that they go back to the hotel.

"I think I'll lie down a while. I didn't sleep too well last night."

Francine concurred. They had separate rooms next to each other and a few minutes later Francine saw the princess safely on her bed, her shoes off and her eyes drifting closed.

Francine went to her room and combed her hair. She wanted to keep it brushed and radiant so Spur McCoy would be attracted to her again. Oh, what a man! She dreamed on, remembering their time together. She could almost feel his hands on her. Marvelous.

She had no idea how long she sat there brushing and remembering the way they made love. Francine sat up suddenly. The princess! She hurried to the door and opened it. No one was in the hall. She knocked on the princess's door and waited. There was no response. She knocked again, a small frown etching her pretty face.

"Oh, no!" Francine said and tried her key in the door. It worked. The princess was not in her room.

Francine hurried down the hall to Pierre's room. He was not there. Probably at the telegraph office trying to get help for Spur McCoy. Where would the princess go? McCoy. She said she had some ideas to break him out of jail.

Francine hurried back to her room for a hat and her reticule, which had a little emergency money in it. The princess never carried any and it helped if Francine did.

She walked out of the hotel and toward the marshal's office and the jail. What on earth could Princess Alexandria be trying to do? Francine had no idea how a person could be broken out of a jail. She would talk to the lawman and tell Spur that the princess was rescued even if Pierre had already done that.

Less than a block away, Princess Alexandria smiled at the cowboy outside a saloon.

"You're a cowhand?" she asked.

"Yes'um. You bet. I work the Lazy R out a ways." The hand was young and shy now talking with such a pretty woman. He stared down at his clothes and didn't know where to put his hands.

"You have a horse and a good rope?"

"Yes'um. Cowboy always has a horse and a rope."

"You have a friend who could help us play a joke on someone? I'll pay you five dollars."

"Five. . . ." The cowboy gulped. "That's a lot of money, Miss. I shore can find a friend."

"Right now, please, I'm in a hurry."

The cowboy turned and whistled through his teeth. Two men against the wall of the hardware store ambled across the street and watched Alexandria before they looked at their friend.

"Yeah, Buster?"

"This little lady needs some help. I told her we'd be more than happy to oblige."

"Yes, Miss, sure would," one of the hands said.

"Good, get your horses and ropes and meet me down the side street right there, just by the alley. Quickly now."

The three ran for their horses a half block down. She walked sedately down the side street to where the alley opened to the street and waited. Alexandria had put on that morning a brown dress that had a small jacket and pinched in at the waist. As with all the dresses of the day, it swept the boardwalk and now the dirt of the side street.

The three horsemen came around the corner, walking their horses and not in a group so they wouldn't attract attention. They saw her move into the alley and one after another, they followed her. About half way down, she stopped.

"Right over there two buildings away is a window. The one with bars on it. I want you to attach your ropes to the bars and to your saddle horns and pull that window right out of its wall."

One of the cowboys laughed. "Miss, that's the town jail. We get in big trouble for doing that."

"If you're afraid, I bet the other two aren't. Am I right?"

"Aw, hell, we can pull it and be out of town before the old marshal knows what happened," the first man she talked to said. "Let's give it a try. Depends how solid they built that back jail wall."

They rode up to the jail quietly. There was no rear door. One man stood on his saddle and tied all three ropes to the bars of the three-foot-square window.

Then the three men tied their ropes to the saddle horns and spread apart a little. They all headed the same way and walked their horses out until the ropes were tight.

The horses, trained in cattle branding, held the pressure on the rope. The three men looked at Alexandria, who stood across the alley watching.

"Now," she said sharply.

The three men spurred their horses. The animals strained forward, hooves sliding on the dirt surface of the alley for a moment; then there came a ripping sound and one bar tore out of the top of the window frame. Right beside it another broke loose and then, as the horses dug in harder and pulled, the whole barred window jolted out of the frame and pulled half of the stud wall with it, as the horses raced down the alley.

The riders stopped, untied the ropes from their saddle horns and left them, pounding down the alley and out the near end, then scattered going around half a dozen blocks and came back to Main Street and tied their animals to a hitching rail.

Alexandria watched in fascination as the rest of the rear wall of the jail crumbled and fell outward into the alley. Two surprised men in the back cell stared at freedom for a moment, then leaped out the opening and darted past Alexandria and between buildings away from Main Street and vanished.

A pair of revolver shots hammered into the morning brightness. Then the only thing Alexandria could hear was someone swearing in the half ruined jail.

"Anybody else try to get away and he gets shot through the gullet, you hear me!" an angry voice screamed.

Alexandria picked her way back the way she had come and was on the street away from the alley before the first deputy got through the tangle of the jail cells and jumped through the opening into the alley.

"Yeah, Marshal, I see the window," the deputy called. "Looks like it's still got three ropes attached to it. No damn way to identify a cowboy by his rope."

"Bring them in anyway," another voice bellowed. "And get that damn barred window back here."

Alexandria walked toward the jail. She knew it was down this way on Main Street. She had been past it before. When she found it, she almost ran into Francine coming out.

"Oh, Alexandria!" Francine exclaimed. "I was worried about you. Where on earth have you been?"

"Out walking. I wasn't as tired as I thought. I so do like to poke around in these quaint shops by myself. Is Spur still in his dungeon? I've never been in a Western jail. Would the marshal mind, do you think?"

Francine frowned. This princess was playing it too innocent. She just might have had something to do with the wrecked jail. She shrugged. "He didn't seem to be in a good mood at all, but we can ask him. From what he says visiting privileges aren't guaranteed out here in the West."

There was a slight smell of powdered plaster in the air as the two women entered the town marshal's office. A counter across the width of the room separated the civilians from the lawmen. A deputy looked up from his desk.

"Something more, Miss Francine?"

"This is my friend, Alexandria. She knows Mr. McCoy as well and wondered if she could visit him. She's from France and has never seen a Western jail before."

"Why of course. I don't see any reason not . . ."

The marshal stormed into the room from the back at that moment.

"No visitors!" he barked. "No more damn visitors until we get the jail secure. Deputy, get these women out of here and lock the front door until I tell you to open it. We already lost two prisoners who were to go to trial tomorrow." The deputy looked at the marshal with his mouth open.

"Now! Deputy. Get those women out of here. . . . NOW!"

Alexandria stood transfixed. "Beautiful!" she said. "Now that is the way a rough tough lawman should act out here in the West. I love it!"

The marshal turned and looked at Alexandria for the first time. "Miss, I'm going to have to ask you to leave now. We have a problem in the back. Kindly step out to the boardwalk."

Alexandria smiled her best and nodded. "Yes, of course, Marshal, but could I kiss your cheek first? Just so I'll have something to remember you by."

The deputy chuckled softly.

The marshal sent a withering look at him and nodded. "Well, Miss, I guess that might be all right."

He moved over and pushed his face down beside hers and she pecked his cheek, then turned on her small booted heel and walked out to the boards in front of the office.

Francine giggled. She caught Alexandria's arm and they marched down the boardwalk.

"You are so naughty, Alex. Just plain wicked. I never would have had the courage to do that. You turned that raging, furious man into a little puppy dog."

Alexandria laughed softly. "But not as good as you did to Spur McCoy in that vacant train compartment a couple of nights ago."

"Yeah!" Francine said and both young women laughed as they continued along the boardwalk toward the hotel. They stopped at a women's wear store and before they came out, each had bought a perfectly ugly hat. They wore them proudly to the hotel.

Pierre waited for them in the lobby. He stood quickly when the princess came in. The two women saw him and waited for him to come to them.

"Looks like we won't have to break McCoy out of jail after all. I wired the embassy. The ambassador had an emergency conference with the Secretary of State, and that office talked with the Justice Department all within an hour. By now a telegram will be on its way to the local marshal. Spur should be a free man before supper . . . that is, dinner time. I do get caught up with the Western way of thinking."

Pierre frowned. He stared over the heads of the women at someone near the door. Alexandria turned and looked the same way.

"Oh, dear, I forgot," Alexandria said. "I hired that cowboy as a guide and never paid him. Francine, bring your purse and help me."

The two went to the front door and out to the steps of the hotel. Two more cowboys in range clothes and wide hats came up and stood beside the first one. Francine dug in her reticule and came up with three five dollar bills. She gave them to Alexandria.

The princess gave one of the bills to each of the three cowboys. "I want to thank you for your help. It was the best joke I've played on anyone all day."

"Shore enough, Miss. Anytime you need any help, you just call on old Buster here." He touched the brim of his hat and turned and the three young men ran toward the closest bar.

Francine lifted her brows. "Three guides? You needed three guides for a half hour walk around town?"

"Tell you tonight," Alexandria said. "Maybe it's time I really have a nap."

Francine grinned. "Me, too. If we're going to be taking the train soon I better rest up. Sometimes I don't get much sleep on trains."

Alexandria punched her playfully in the ribs and the two laughed out loud as they went into the hotel and up to the second floor to their rooms.

Pierre never did figure out what they were laughing about.

It was almost six that evening when the marshal unlocked Spur's cell and waved him out. "Got some talking to do," the man said. In the marshal's small office he motioned to a chair.

"Your princess is safe, you're free to go. I had a wire from Washington, D.C., your boss. He thinks rather highly of you. Also had two women come in and tell me that Leslie did draw first and that he fired first but missed. Your story holds up.

"Also wired that sheriff up in Wyoming. Amazing what you can find out in a short time. That Rocky Bend, Wyoming, sheriff said that indeed you were in on the Tom Leslie fracas up that way. He praised you highly. Also said that Tom's brother was in on the deal and evidently left the gang a few days before the final shoot out. He had the gang's stolen money and was supposed to put it in a safe bank somewhere.

"My guess is that if we dig into James Leslie here in town, we'll find some shady and downright crooked dealings as well."

The marshal held out his hand. "Sorry for the minor inconvenience."

"No hard feelings, Marshal. It's happened before. Now, I feel like a good long bath and a big supper. Where's the best place in town to eat?"

The next morning, Spur and his party of four caught the 10:10 westbound heading for Dodge City.

A day's journey behind Spur, Darlene Benoit rode in the second class coach on the spur line down toward Dodge City. It had taken her two days to track down the tall man in the black hat and his party of four. At last a twenty dollar bill had loosened the tongue of the railroad ticket agent. He had sold the man tickets to Dodge City. He also sent some telegrams for him and knew that his name was Spur McCoy.

Now Darlene settled in the lumpy seat. Her two men were in the seats just across the aisle so they could all see each other. She felt with her feet to be sure her small carpet bag was still in place between her legs. In it were four five pound sacks of black powder and ten feet of burning fuse. The next time she would make sure.

She had no idea how far behind the princess she was. Two days, three days, one day? Dodge City, a cow town. What would they do there? They might move on quickly. Damn! Why did the fates step in and send her carriage down that side street where Eduard was their only attacker? It should have been over right there.

Darlene would have gladly run up and fired point blank at the princess and ripped the heart out of the Prince. Darlene knew she would have been killed, but it would have been worth it. A life for a life, the Biblical instructions. Gladly.

It grew dark quickly and Jacques came and sat in the empty seat beside her. She was next to the window. Jacques had been more and more insistent lately. She had promised him but never taken care of his needs. She had to soon. Maybe with a blanket.

"We will find her," Jacques whispered. He turned sideways in the seat to shield them partly from the aisle and his hand crept to her thigh. She did not remove it.

Encouraged, he pressed closer. "We will find her and throw bombs in her room and blow her to hell," Jacques said softly so only Darlene could hear. His hand crept over her thigh and slid with the skirt deep between her legs and inched upward.

"If the bombs don't kill her, we will wait for her to come from her room and shoot her body full of holes."

"Oh, yes!" Darlene whispered.

His hand came to her crotch and he massaged her through the cloth. He caught her hand and moved it toward him and placed it over the swelling behind his fly. Deftly she unbuttoned the fly and worked inside.

The lights, now turned low, were soft, and glowed at the center and ends of each car. No one could see them. She let him rub her but it did not arouse her in the least. She let them use her, so she could use them in her plans.

She freed his hardness and worked it back and forth slowly.

"Yes, oh yes!" Jacques whispered, his hips moving gently against the thrust of her hand. "We will kill her many times. Yes, that is good!"

She bent and kissed his lips, then pulled his face to her breasts. He moaned softly and his hips humped in a series of spasms and his whispered words to her made no sense in French or in English. His body tightened and he moaned softly again and then relaxed.

She moved her hand, then patted his cheek. A moment later he was sleeping, his hand still at her crotch. She moved his hand and straightened in the seat, setting it as far back as it would go. Sleep would be strange and difficult, but it would come.

She thought about Dodge City. Surely they would catch them in Dodge. All night the train would grind across the flat country. Then late tomorrow afternoon they should get to Dodge City.

Jacques mumbled something and reached for her. She put his hand on one of her breasts. He fondled it gently in his sleep, then sank back into a deeper slumber. She moved his hand back beside his legs and tried again to sleep.

At last she did sleep. Almost at once it seemed that the reoccurring dream came. She was in prison in the Principality of Mantuco. It was evil-smelling and cold and wet. The stones were huge and the door small and no windows. Guards came past and looked in through a small hole.

But she wasn't the one they looked at. They checked on Didier, her brother. They shouted at him, called him terrible names. No one could see her, not even Didier. She tired to talk to him, but he lay on the lice-filled straw for a bed and moaned and cried out in his pain and his agony.

Then the guards came and beat him again. Tied him to chains on the high wall and flailed his naked body with whips and quirts and small chains until his back was a mass of blood and only then did they take him down and throw him back in the cell.

He screamed now, screamed as if he wanted to die because he hurt so bad. When he screamed, she did too and now he could hear her and he looked up, pleading with her to help him. His voice came softly from a great distance, begging her to save him, to stop the guards from beating him.

But then his screams brought the guards and they took him to the wall again and beat and whipped him and the cycle repeated over and over and over again until she couldn't stand it and she sat up and cried out in pain.

The click, click, then click, click of the rails below the train tracks told her she was awake and she was on the train. Jacques came awake beside her. He held her face and watched her in the dim light.

"The dream again?"

She nodded. "It won't go away. I have to kill her before the dreams will end. Only then will my brother be satisfied and avenged. Only then will I ever get a good night's sleep again."

Jacques pulled her toward him and put his arms around her and sang softly to her a French lullaby. She fought it a moment, then remembered her mother, who used to sing the same song. She relaxed and tried to let her mind be at rest for a few moments, and then she was sleeping.

A moment later the dream came and she was in a prison, deep in the ground, and the walls were of huge stones, only they were cold and damp, and far below in his cell she saw her brother. Didier was screaming again . . .

Chapter 7

Dodge City was a disappointment for Princess Alexandria.

"It's just a little place with one street and lots of cows waiting to get on the train to go to the slaughterhouse," the royal one from the Principality of Mantuco said. A growing pout was evident.

She stared out the window of the Dodge City Hotel, the best one in town. They were on the second floor, where they always stayed.

"It's not even exciting. No cowboys shooting at each other, nobody riding his horse into a saloon. I know, I know what I want to do!"

Princess Alexandria turned to Francine and the English girl knew exactly what this woman had been like when she was a youngster. She had a sweetness smile and held her hands together like she was ten.

The two women were alone in the room. Alexandria did a little hop and laughed.

"Francine, dear, wonderful, marvelous Francine! I want you to arrange it so I can go to a brothel! I want to see a genuine, Wild West whore house!"

Francine leaned back in surprise. "Why Alexandria Elizabeth! I'm shocked. What in the world ever made you say such a thing? That's totally impossible. It just can't happen. No, I won't even repeat what you said. And I don't want you sneaking off and walking into one, you hear? Your father would be so upset he might disinherit you."

"He can't, I'm his only heir to the throne." She reached out and touched Francine. They had been best friends for five years now, no, six.

"Darling, Francine. If you don't think I should, then we'll just forget all about it. Let's find Pierre and do a tour of the town. Two ladies alone might stir up the local he-men too much. With the Colonel along, we'll be safe as babes in a nursery."

They toured Dodge. Spur McCoy was off somewhere making arrangements for the four of them to be guests at a real working cattle ranch about two hours ride out of Dodge. There would be horses and cattle and even some branding demonstrations. It wouldn't start until the next day.

The three walked both sides of the three block street, and poked into a leather goods shop. Alexandria was entranced by the pungent smell of the tanned leather.

"That is such a good scent," she said to the proprietor, who worked on some finishing touches on a saddle he had crafted.

"Yes, ma'am. Does smell good. Part of the reason I went into the trade."

"How long does it take you to make a fine saddle like that?" Pierre asked.

The saddlemaker grinned and tied off a length of lacing. "Now if I could work at it full time, I could do a fine riding saddle in about ten to twelve days. Course I never get to work full time. Somebody's always got a pair of shoes to be fixed, or a pair of saddle bags to get mended. Then I make a fine leather traveling case or two as well."

Alexandria bought one of the small cases and pointed at Pierre, who promptly wrote a bank draft for the amount.

"Don't know this bank," the merchant said. "Out here we don't much hold with bank drafts from back east. I'd prefer gold coin, you have any."

Pierre tore up the check, reached into his purse and took out fourteen dollars in gold coin. The traveling case had a price of six dollars. Alexandria held up her hand and bought another one and gave it to Francine.

They all had supper together in a cafe across the street that guaranteed all you could eat for 75 cents or your money back.

The restaurant was fancied up for the easterners who came out to Dodge these days to sightsee. The tables all had cloths on them that had been cross stitched with half a dozen cattle brands each. On the walls were a dozen or more longhorn steer horn sets, mounted and usually used for holding hats on the sharply tipped ends.

The walls were of vertical boards, painted a dull brown and dotted with full pages of the local newspaper set in frames and behind glass. Each was the account of some deadly shootout on the streets of Dodge.

The food was better than advertised. McCoy put away two big steaks an inch thick and plate wide, along with coffee, half a dozen big slices of fresh baked white bread and side dishes of creamed potatoes and new peas, boiled carrots, fried parsnips, and a choice of four desserts.

The princess stared in wonder at the food. She ate sparingly but seemed to want more. She held up her hands when the waitress offered her another steak.

It was almost nine o'clock when they got back to the hotel. The princess had been nodding off near the end of the meal, and Francine saw that she was really tired. Back in the hotel lobby, McCoy gave them the time table for the next morning. A two seater carriage would be on hand at 8 a.m. to take them the two hour drive out to the Circle K ranch for their Wild West cattle day.

They would be there all day, and have an old-fashioned cowboy hoe-down in the evening around a trail-like bonfire. The following morning they all would be outfitted in riding clothes and go for a one hour trail ride to see how the cattle were worked on the average ranch. Then it would be back to Dodge and a long hot bath to relax sore muscles.

Princess Alexandria heard some of it but dozed off again as they stood there. Francine grinned and helped her up the steps to their room on the second floor.

Francine had to decide if she should undress the princess or let her sleep in her pink dress. At last she decided she better get her out of some of the clothes. She took off the pink dress with no cooperation from the sleeping princess. Two petticoats later, Francine gave up and pulled a light sheet over the snoring royalty. She put away the clothes, then hurried out of the door and locked it from the outside with her key.

She slipped into her room and fumbled for a match to light the lamp. When she got it lit, she put the glass chimney back in place and turned down the wick.

"That should do it," a voice said from the other side of the room. Francine whirled, almost dropping the lamp before she recognized McCoy's deep tones.

"You frightened me!" she said. Francine put the lamp down on the dresser and walked over to where Spur sat on the bed. "You come in for a good night kiss and to tuck me in for the night, or are you ready to be nice and stay all night?"

"Little of both. How is the princess?"

"Dead to the world. I've never seen her so tired. I had to undress her." Francine glanced up with a wicked gleam in her eye. "I know, you would have been glad to help me. You undress women extremely well."

"Are you sure she was sleeping?"

"Spur, I slept in the same room with her for four years in school. I know how and when she snores and when she doesn't. She was out like a coal oil lamp in a tornado."

Spur frowned at her. "It seemed to happen so quickly. Usually she listens to every word when I'm talking about taking her on a new adventure. Seemed strange."

"Hey, you unbeliever. I have the key to her room. We can check every two or three hours just to make sure." Francine unbuttoned the top of her dress. This one had buttons from top to bottom, but only a third of them needed to be opened to remove it.

"Would you be a darling and help me with these buttons?"

"More than happy."

103

In the next room, Princess Alexandria stood next to the door and listened. She hadn't heard a thing since Francine went into her room and locked the door. Now she heard voices through the thin wall and figured Spur McCoy would be in Francine's room. That would keep Francine busy for two or three hours at least.

Alexandria had dressed in the only garment she had that was open at the throat. She undid one more button so she could almost see a line of cleavage, then she grinned. This was going to be the best adventure of any of them!

She turned the key in her door gently without a sound, opened it and edged into the hall, then closed the door silently and locked it.

Five minutes later she walked the main street of Dodge and came to the spot she wanted. It was half a block down from Main on a street called Rustler's Row. She grinned with a surge of emotion and walked up the green steps and toward the green door.

A man came out, stared at her a moment, smiled and nodded and went on down the steps.

She pulled open the heavy door and saw at once that it was all she had dreamed it would be. The entryway room was twenty feet square and blazed with color. A thick carpet on the floor had to be two inches deep. Vivid purple drapes covered one wall. The other wall had curtains around the front windows of some kind of shimmering silk material in light blues that faded to white and back to blue.

On the far side of the room an upright piano sat with the top open and a small colored man tapped one foot as he pounded out a soft, sentimental tune.

On the other side, a dining room table labored to hold up dozens of silver trays of cold cuts and slices of melon, cut fruit, dried fruit, figs, peaches, delicate crackers and small squares of cheeses of a half dozen types.

Below the purple drapes, a long couch rested, decorated with a fabric that looked like leopard skin. Two girls sat on the couch. Both wore flattering dresses that had been cut low to show a swell of bosom and deep cleavage. The skirts were so short that they barely covered the women's knees. They stared at Alexandria with surprise, then one of them nodded.

"Your name Peaches?"

Alexandria hesitated, then bobbed her head.

"Belle wants to see you right away. We're short two girls and she's working our little asses off. Through the door and up the stairs. First door on the left. Knock before you go in and wait for her to come to the door or she'll slap you silly. Move, get dressed before the rush starts."

Alexandria took a deep breath and went through the door. She wanted to giggle as she climbed the stairs. They thought she was one of the courtesans! Thought she was a whore! How perfectly delicious! She would have a wild story to tell Francine tomorrow.

She found the door and knocked. A moment later the door swung open and Alexandria walked in. It was a bare room, with no rug on the floor, a desk to one side, a single bed to the other side, not a picture or decoration on any of the walls. The window looked down on the alley.

A woman hurried ahead and sat down behind the desk. A single lamp burned there. The woman had henna red hair that stood out like a freight

105

train had just missed her. The woman lit a long brown cigar and blew the smoke at the ceiling. She appraised Alexandria for a moment.

"A little skinny but I guess you'll do. Peaches isn't it?"

"Yes."

"Good, I don't like talkative ones. Do what you're told, be nice to the customers and never fault one. I don't stand for that. They pay their money they get their money's worth. Understand?"

"Yes, ma'am."

"Good. My name's Belle. Don't call me unless you're really in trouble. I don't stand for no cutting or hitting my girls. Other than that, if it don't hurt, do it. You'll be in room twelve at the end of the hall. You got any other clothes, a robe? Yeah, a robe for the first night."

Belle stood and frowned. "Get on the robe and nothing else and come back. Hear you worked in Denver for a year. You look older than eighteen."

Belle snorted and went back to the desk. "You get fifty cents for every two dollar poke. More than most pay you. I'm easy. No holding back. I keep a tally. You pay up prompt every night before you go to sleep. We stay open as long as there are any customers. Any questions?"

"No."

"Good, go get undressed, I want a better look at you. I like my whores to have a little more meat on the bones, but some men like them skinny. Get out of here."

Alexandria hurried to the door and went out. She hesitated at the stairs. She was supposed to go to room 12 and get into a robe. She didn't have a robe. Maybe there was one there.

She grinned and hurried down the hallway to

room 12. No one was inside. She heard moans and screams coming from one of the rooms.

In number twelve she saw it was not much wider than a single bed along one wall. There was space to turn around and get undressed but not much more. A chair was the only other furniture. No fancy drapes here, no pictures on the wall. Nothing else. A tattered robe with a streak of blood on it hung on a hook. She looked at it and then at the crib and shook her head.

Alexandria backed out of the room and turned toward the stairs. She saw Belle coming up the steps with a dozen men right behind her. The men were holding whiskey and beer bottles and singing and laughing.

Belle parcelled them out into rooms along the hall. Alexandria had backed up quickly when she saw Belle coming. There was no way to get around her. Belle looked up and saw Alexandria standing in front of room 12.

"No, no, Peaches. We don't have time for pick and choose. These sidewinders take who I give them or I throw them out. Now get back in your room and strip, I've got a real hungry man for you."

Alexandria hesitated. Belle scowled at her. "Look, little twat, when I yell, you jump. That's the way it is around this whore house. Got to be."

She was at room 12 then and pushed a big blond-haired cowboy toward the door.

"Inside, cowhand. You got only a half hour so make it worth your while. We're busier than a convention of cattle rustlers. A half hour and no more." She pushed the six-foot cow hand into the room and pulled the door shut.

Alexandria stood by the bed at the far side.

The cowboy stopped just inside the door. He looked big enough to reach the walls by stretching out his arms. The smile on his face softened.

"Hey, you're new here, right? You're Peaches? Fine name. Never knew anyone called Peaches."

He motioned to the bed. "Best you sit down."

Alexandria shook her head.

The cowhand chuckled. "Hell, this your first time or something? Never seen me a whore nothing like you. Is this your first time?"

Alexandria nodded.

"Well, whyn't you say so? I can be right down tender and easy. Come here, little darling. Jed can do things right. You have been with a man before, haven't you?"

Alexandria nodded again.

"Oh, damn, that's good. I hate to get a virgin. More screaming and crying and bellowing and howling I never did hear. Never again a virgin for me, no sireee." He sat down on the bed and pulled off his boots.

"You going to . . . to undress?" Alexandria asked.

Jed grinned. "Hell, Peaches, best way is skin to skin, I can tell you that. Ain't the same with clothes on. I know. I tried it both ways. Clothes on is when somebody might come and catch you. Kids do that a lot. Hell, we ain't kids and we got a whole half hour."

"Couldn't we . . . couldn't we just talk?"

Jed laughed. "Not a chance in a cornfield, little heifer. I came to get me a poking and I paid my two dollars and I intend to get my lily all drained."

"I . . . I . . . I can't. I'll give you your money back. I'll give you five dollars if you help me get out of here."

He frowned. "Five dollars. Well, maybe." She

moved toward him and he caught her wrist, pulled her on the bed on her back and lowered himself carefully on top of her, crushing her into the hard mattress.

"No!"

Jed lost his patience. "Little whore, Peaches. I paid my money and I'm getting my poking, you like it or not no nevermind to me. Now hold still or I'm gonna have to hurt you."

Less than two blocks away in the Dodge City Hotel, Francine lifted away from Spur McCoy. He lay on his back, one hand thrown across his eyes and he was still panting.

"I better check on Her Majesty," Francine said. She pulled on a robe, tied it in front and slipped out the door. Twenty seconds later she was back shaking Spur.

"She's gone! The prettiest dress of the wardrobe is gone, too!"

As Spur dressed he questioned Francine, who was frantically pulling on her own clothes.

"What did she say tonight? Did she have any wild schemes. Think girl, think."

"Tonight she was really tired, or I thought she was. She hardly said a thing. This afternoon we talked. Crazy things. One time she said she wanted me to take her to a real Wild West whore house."

Spur stopped pulling on his boots and looked up at Francine.

"She wouldn't, would she? On her own, at night, alone?" He finished dressing. "Go get Pierre. Tell him what's happened. And that we have to check out every whore house in town. Not the saloon whores, just the houses. Have him take this side of the street and the cross streets. I'll be on the other side."

Spur paused at the door. "Tell Pierre to ask the girls or the madam if they have had any new girl who started tonight. If they did, it could be Alexandria. Now hurry!"

Spur took the steps three at a time. The clock in the lobby struck eleven o'clock. It would be busy time at the houses of ill repute. He checked the first cross street and saw one house that might qualify, but it wasn't right. He crossed the street and caught the faint piano music coming from the open front door.

The madam had been polite but firm. She hadn't taken on a new girl for three months.

It was a half hour later that he found the fourth whore house on his side of Main Street. It was half a block down and he was struck by the dazzle of color as he stepped into the parlor. The piano man turned and grinned. He was a small black man Spur had known in Denver where he plied the same trade.

"Sam," Spur said.

"Evening, Mr. McCoy. You do travel about a bit."

"As you do too, Sam. You have any new girl in here tonight, one just starting?"

"You heard. Yeah, brand new to the business I'd say. She calls herself Peaches."

"Girl about five-three, long brown hair, big tetas."

"Sounds like her. Room 12 upstairs in case you're in need."

Spur took the steps three at a time and brushed past one nude-to-the-waist girl on his way. He got half way down the hall when a bellowed command behind stopped him.

"Where the hell you going, Jasper?"

Spur turned and looked at the woman who filled the hall. She was tall and square and had a pound of dance hall makeup on her face and her henna red hair looked like it had been combed by a cactus branch.

"Peaches. She down here?"

"Who wants to know?"

Spur drew the .44 so quickly the woman couldn't move before he blasted one round into the ceiling. The roar of the six-gun in the confined space boiled through the building for 30 seconds. Spur couldn't hear anything the woman said except a long shriek.

The sound died down. Three doors down the hall opened and heads poked out, then vanished suddenly back inside.

All was quiet for a moment, then Spur heard a scream. It was one that couldn't be missed. He knew at once it had to be Alexandria. Spur McCoy turned and charged for room 12, the big .44 high in his right hand, his left foot lifted to smash into the door right beside the latch.

Chapter 8

The door to the crib at the Green Door brothel crashed open behind Spur's heavy boot kick and swung wide hitting the wall. The tall cowboy had Alexandria's hands held above her head with one fist and his other hand probed between her legs.

Spur saw the top of her dress torn down showing one pink-tipped breast.

The cowboy had only time to grunt in surprise and turn his head before Spur's solid fist smashed into his jaw. The blow slammed the cowboy to the side. He rolled off the edge of the bed and came to his feet ready to fight.

Spur slashed the barrel of his .44 down across the man's head. The front sight drew a line of blood across his scalp and drove him to his knees. Spur grabbed the man's jaw in his hand and tilted his face upward.

"The next time a lady tells you no, cowboy, you're

gonna remember that she means no."

Spur's right knee hammered upward, catching the cowboy's jaw and ramming him upward and back. He landed on the bed, unconscious.

Alexandria had pulled the torn dress together to cover her breasts and held it with her hands.

Spur looked at her. "Are you all right?"

She tried to speak, but couldn't. Alexandria nodded instead, her lower lip quivering. Spur looked out the doorway. Six heads showed along the hall. He waved the .44 at them and they vanished and doors slammed shut.

"Let's go, Alexandria," he said softly. She nodded and moved to the hall. She hung back just a moment, then lifted her chin and marched down the hall. Spur was right behind her with his Colt in his steady right hand.

Nobody bothered them going along the hall or down the steps. One door closed softly, but Spur saw no one. In the fancy parlor, only Sam sat at the piano playing softly.

"Good-bye, Mr. McCoy. I see you found what you come for."

"Good night, Sam."

Outside, Alexandria sagged against Spur and he put his arm around her for support. They walked the two blocks that way back to the hotel. The few people on the street paid no attention to the couple.

At the hotel door, Alexandria straightened and marched into the room, her head high, her eyes straight ahead. She went up the stairs and then stumbled on the second floor and Spur was there to steady her. She leaned against him again until she was in her room.

Francine hurried in behind them. Alexandria sat

on the edge of the bed. She dropped her hands and
her dress came open again, but she didn't notice.

"Oh, god but I'm tired," the princess said. She
slumped backwards on the bed and let out a long
sigh.

Francine shooed Spur out of the room and locked
the door behind him. She went to the princess and
lifted her feet and legs onto the bed, then slipped
off her shoes. Alexandria had one arm over her
eyes. When she moved it, there were tears streaming
down her face.

"I've never been so terrified in my life!"

"You had reason. You also brought the trouble
on yourself, remember that."

Alexandria nodded. "I know. But it was exciting.
They actually thought that I was one of them, a
common whore! That was the thrilling part."

"We'll talk about it tomorrow. Sleep, you need
some rest. Help me get you undressed."

When Francine came out of the room twenty
minutes later, Spur waited in the hall. Pierre had
come back after a hilarious trip through half the
brothels in Dodge City. He was still laughing, and
thankful that Spur had found the princess.

Spur looked at Francine.

"She's fine, just a bit scared. She got pawed a
little and petted but that's all. You got there just
in time."

"I'm glad. Maybe this will calm her down a little.
She could have been beaten up and then raped in
that place. The customers don't expect amateurs."

"We don't have to worry about her going into
whore houses any more." Francine pointed to her
room and then to Spur. He shook his head.

"We both better get some sleep. Tough day
tomorrow."

Bright and early the next morning, Spur had the carriage by the front door slightly before eight. The three visitors were still having breakfast at the hotel dining room. He went in and rounded them up. Even so, they were a half hour late getting started.

Spur drove the pair of flashy blacks the livery had hitched to the rig. It was a warm morning and by the time they had taken the trail north for a half hour, the sun came out seriously.

Alexandria seemed to have recovered from her scare the night before and chatted with Francine and with Pierre. It was turning out to be a good tour after all, she said.

Spur followed the directions and brought the carriage into the home ranch buildings at the Circle K a little after ten-thirty. He met the owner, Cadell Scott. The old-time ranch owner had on his range clothes, jeans, chaps, brown shirt and leather vest. He doffed his high-crowned white hat and grinned.

"Morning, folks. Welcome to the Circle K. We'll try to show you what happens at a cattle ranch. Not a lot. Mostly we just sit around and let the cattle grow."

They all laughed and he took them out to the corral. It was made of poles and posts set firmly into the ground. Inside a cowboy was in the process of breaking a horse to ride. Both women had worn dresses and now had to lift the skirts to keep them out of the thick dust around the corral.

Princess Alexandria watched the rider with fascination.

"Why doesn't the horse let him ride?" she asked Scott.

The rancher chuckled. "That horse has been running wild for most two years now. He don't know nothing about a saddle. Never had one on his back until this morning. He'd been one of a bunch of wild horses that roam around. We caught six last week and now we got to break them to ride.

"Don't hurt them none, Miss, and after he calms down and gentles, he'll get more to eat than he ever found on the range. Make a good cattle pony after a year or two of learning."

"He looks so frightened."

"Deed he is, Miss, but that's part of what he'll get over."

The cowboy got bucked off the horse and caught him and with the help of two horses and riders got back on the saddle and the learning process went on.

Scott took them to the ranch house where there were refreshments set out. They sat in the kitchen around a big plank table that had been varnished to a high gloss. The cook had fixed lemonade for them and coffee and had baked a fresh batch of cinnamon rolls. They were heavy with cinnamon sugar and small and delicious.

The princess had two of them and two glasses of lemonade. She brightened. "Where are the rustlers, Mr. Scott? Have you ever hung a rustler?"

Scott laughed and had a drink from his coffee cup. He put the brew down and nodded.

"Mostly we don't get many rustlers around here, Miss. Ain't too healthy. When some bunch tries to steal some of our cattle we look on it with kind of a sour face. Far as hanging them, most of us leave that up to the sheriff now. Don't believe all them stories you read in the newspapers about the Wild, Wild West. It ain't all that wild no more. Don't think there's been a rustler hung without the benefit of

117

law around here in four or five years now."

He took them into his office and den. On one wall was a big map drawn to a large scale that showed the town of Dodge City, and the outline of his ranch. There was one small stream that centered the big plot.

"How on earth could you buy all of this land?" Francine asked.

Cadell Scott shrugged. "Well, Miss, fact is I didn't. Way you start a ranch is to get a homestead, usual a hundred and eighty acres of land. Now the law don't say how it has to be laid out, so most of us stretch it out a quarter of a mile wide and as long as it takes to make up that 160 acres. We stretch the claim several miles along a stream and any lakes we can find.

"Water is the secret to raising cattle. No reliable stream and you got no ranch. Once we got the claim along the water, we claim what we call range rights for ten miles or so on each side of the stream. Makes for a nice-sized ranch that way."

"But that must be hundreds of thousands of acres," Francine said.

Scott nodded. "True, miss. But when it takes 25 to 30 acres of land to feed one steer, a rancher needs a lot of land."

"That much?" Pierre asked.

"Sometimes less, but on average. Depending on the summer rains and the winter snow pack. Well, enough in here, let's take a short ride in the carriage and I'll show you part of the herd."

The ride was less than half a mile on north along the edge of the good-sized stream. They came around a small bend and a sea of brown and white and tan and black-backed animals spread out for what looked like half a mile.

"Oh my!" the princess said. "So many cows."

"These are steers, Miss. They've been neutered so they'll grow bigger. This bunch is about ready to go to market. Takes usual about four years for a calf to get to this point where he's ready for the dinner table."

"Four years!" Pierre gasped. "I say I'd rather raise chickens, I think. Three months tops and you have a good frying chicken."

"But not one that weighs a thousand pounds," Scott said and they all laughed.

They heard a ringing sound in the distance. Scott motioned for Spur to turn the rig around.

"Time for dinner," he said. "That's the dinner bell. Oh, we eat breakfast, dinner and supper here in the West. We don't hold with that fancy French word of 'lunch'. We work hard and need three big meals a day."

Back at the ranch they went into the kitchen again and the cook had spread a meal on the table. There were small dinner steaks, side dishes of baked beans and cabbage and carrots and heaps of mashed potatoes and brown gravy.

"Oh, my, I shouldn't eat so much," the princess said. Francine grinned at her.

"Your only chance for a real Western ranch dinner, Alexandria."

"Well, then I better eat."

Spur grinned at the way she put away the food. She ate like a man just off a trail drive.

After dinner they had an hour to rest. The women were put in a big bedroom on the second floor of the ranch house.

"This was my wife's bedroom," the rancher explained. "She died of the fever three years ago. I ain't changed it much. I don't figure it's time yet.

119

The room will be glad to have a woman's touch again."

Two hours later the group assembled in the big living room with its large fireplace.

Scott took off his hat and smoothed down his thinning gray hair. "Now, wanted to take you down to the south pasture and show you something special. We can go in the carriage. Tomorrow we may have you all riding horses, so get ready for that."

The carriage went through a gate and down along the river again toward a small herd of animals they could see in the distance. Ten minutes later they were among the animals.

"Oh, look, a baby!" Princess Alexandria crooned.

"Call this the nursery," Scott said. "We find a cow having trouble birthing or a calf that can't quite make a long trail drive, we bring the cow and calf down here and keep watch on them. Usually we have forty or fifty down here in the spring. Found we can save most of the new calves that way. So it's worthwhile."

"How many animals do you have on the ranch," Pierre asked.

Scott scratched his head and twisted his mouth figuring. "Not just sure. We have about three thousand steers ready for market in that other herd. They'll be going out in a day or two, soon as the stock pens at Dodge empty out. Getting so you have to put in a reservation to get a cattle car these days.

"Beside that we have about four thousand brood cows, and the breeding animals to service them. Then maybe six thousand steers from one to three years getting grown up."

"That long?" Alexandria asked.

"Yes, Miss, takes a while. Up ahead here is old Annabelle. She always has trouble with her calves. Got to be sort of a pet around here. Would you like to pet her calf?"

The little white face had bright eyes and his ears came forward when he saw the carriage. He moved toward it and stopped to watch. The rig paused and they all got down. Princess Alexandria walked slowly up to the calf that was only two weeks old, Scott told them. He stood his ground. Annabelle was thirty feet away but watching closely. She bawled softly once, then relaxed and grazed.

Alexandria knelt in front of the small calf. He watched her. She reached out a hand and let him smell it the way she had been taught to with a dog. He was not troubled.

She raised it and scratched his ears, then the space between his eyes and then his chin. He took a step forward and his tongue came out and sand-papered her hand.

"Oh, my! What a rough little tongue you have!" She smoothed his straight back and his sleek flanks, then stood and moved away six feet. He followed her. She crooned to him and scratched his ears again.

"I want to take him back home with me," she said.

Scott grinned. "You'll have to talk to Annabelle about that. Don't think she would approve." The cow made some soft noises and the calf turned and ran to her and nuzzled at her teats until he caught one and began nursing.

Alexandria watched a moment and smiled. "I guess he better stay with his mother," she said.

They moved through more mothers and calves, many about the same age, a few older. Under a

121

small tree by the stream, they found a mare and her foal. The small horse was less than a month old, Scott told them.

"Normal we don't let our mares foal. This one kind of sneaked up on us. Quicker and cheaper to buy good cow horses than to raise them. But kind of nice to have a foal around now and then."

The foal saw the rig coming and pranced up toward it, curious. He stopped a short distance away. His mother came up and stood between him and the carriage. He moved so he could see the strange rig under her neck. Then he pushed forward closer to the rig. Scott said something to the mare and she stayed where she was.

"Better not get out this time," Scott said. "This mare is still a bit protective of her foal. I haven't even touched the critter yet. A little colt, I think."

Soon they drove on up the river to a four foot falls and stopped. There was a blanket spread and cold lemonade ready for them. Small sandwiches covered a plate and they sat and had the snack and enjoyed the shade under the trees and the chattering of the river.

"This is the Wild West I'll remember," Princess Alexandria said. "So peaceful, so quiet, so beautiful."

A half hour later they had to start back.

"Have a little barbecue planned for you tonight," Scott said. "Couple of the boys saw a mean fiddle so we'll have a small hoe-down as well." He stopped and grinned. "Now ladies, these lads gonna want to show you some dances. They ain't exactly the best smelling gents. They been working all day in the hot sun and don't get a chance to take a bath too often. Hope you'll understand if the perfume ain't exactly roses."

"It won't matter at all if they show us some of the local dances," Alexandria said.

The barbecue was done over a fire pit four feet long filled with hot burning coals and a quarter of a beef on a long iron spit a foot over the fire. On the far end, a man sat in a chair and turned the beef around and around in a slow rotation so it would cook through and not burn. It had been on the spit for an hour already and would be ready in another hour.

The four relaxed and washed up and rested. Spur took the chance to talk with the hands. Most were pleased with their work for Scott. He was a good boss, but still the boss. The work was the same as when Spur had done it: tough, dirty, wet when it rained and mean when the animals got ornery. Spur remembered his six months on a trail drive and wished them luck.

The barbecue supper was a smashing success and they all ate more than they should. Then before they had digested the feast, two fiddlers and a man with a guitar came out of the darkness and sat on the steps of the big covered porch.

They began playing and stomping and a cowboy came up and bowed to Francine and she smiled and stood. He showed her the simple steps and she proved to be a quick learner, picking up the moves quickly and following him with the smallest hint of his change in direction.

A few minutes later another cowboy asked Alexandria to dance. She stood and he swept her away. She had taken many dancing lessons in France and adapted to the steps quickly.

A half hour later six different cowboys, all previously selected and approved by Scott, had danced with the ladies.

Then it was over. The fiddlers and the picker returned to the bunkhouse and the rest of them went into the big living room where a small fire burned in the six foot wide fireplace box.

"So far you've seen a big part of the life of a rancher here in Kansas in the 1870's," Scott said. "Any questions?"

"Do you have any children?" Francine asked.

Scott hesitated a moment. Then lifted his brows and nodded. "Martha and I had two. Our small daughter died shortly after she was birthed, and our son, Joseph, who was twenty, was killed in a stampede about three years ago."

"Oh, I'm sorry," Francine said.

"That's all right, Miss. Just part of life here on the ranch. You folks enjoy. You have your bedrooms. Breakfast will be whenever you want it in the morning. About ten o'clock we'll head out in the carriage and go back toward town, then turn off and I'll show you a branding and cutting demonstration. That's the last part of a real ranch you haven't seen."

The next morning, Spur was up at 6:30 as usual. He had breakfast with the hands and trailed them out to work. They teased him into taking a turn on the bronc they were breaking.

"She's almost tamed," the foreman said. "You told us you did some cowboy work. Show us how to tame this one."

Spur borrowed a pair of chaps and eyed the maverick with a critical stare. The mare seemed about ready to take to the saddle. They dropped the leather on her and cinched it up while they had her nose tied close to the poles with somebody holding her tail wrapped around another rail.

"All set," the foreman said.

Spur climbed the fence and eased into the leather, found the stirrups and close-hauled the reins around her neck.

Then the hands let loose of the rope holding the mare. She bolted straight across the corral, skidded to a stop inches from the far rails and tried to scrape him off. Then she went straight into the air and came down stiff-legged on all four feet and almost jarred Spur from leather. She bucked, kicking her hind feet high into the air.

Spur held on to the reins with one hand. It was cheating to hold onto the saddle horn. He knew he should be spurring the horse along the front flanks but he couldn't manage it.

She took another run across the corral, stopped and fishtailed and almost unseated him. As soon as she came down she bucked six times in a row and each time he lost a little security from the saddle and in the stirrups. On the final bounce, Spur sailed off the leather and came down on all fours before he rolled in the dust of the corral.

He heard wild cheering from the sides of the corral and looked over to see the two girls and Pierre applauding him.

Spur picked himself up and slapped the dust off his pants and climbed the rails to get out of there.

It took him another five minutes to get the dust out of his shirt and pants. The hands chuckled. The foreman said he lasted a lot longer than any of them figured he would.

"Truth to tell, Mr. McCoy. Nobody has ever ridden that mare to a standstill. She just won't gentle down. We played a little trick on you."

Spur laughed. "I had it coming. That's a tough way to make a living."

"Always has been, always will be," the foreman said. "But, long as folks eat beefsteak, there'll have to be cowboys."

The women watched Spur. "You get hurt?" Francine asked.

"Just my pride. You ladies get a good sleep?"

"Oh, my, yes," Alexandria said. "Now we're excited about the branding. Does it hurt them?"

"A little, but mostly the animal is upset by being held down. You'll see."

It was a little after 10:30 that morning when they came to the branding.

"These are a late gather we brought in last week. Most of the critters were rounded up earlier. We brand the new yearlings and cut the bulls."

The carriage came to a stop near a group of cowboys who seemed to be waiting. Scott waved at them and they began.

A fire burned hotly nearby and the long branding irons that projected from the fire had their brand ends glowing red hot.

Two mounted men rode into a herd of cattle and one man cut out a yearling without a brand. The horse did most of the work, anticipating each time the animal turned one way or the other. Slowly the rider worked the animal out of the herd. Another rider came up and roped the yearling around the head.

The first rider behind the animal threw a loop under its two rear feet and pulled the rope tight around his saddle horn. The rear horseman stopped holding the steer's rear feet together by his rope. The lead cowboy walked his horse ahead slowly until the animal fell on its side.

"Iron's hot!" the man at the fire called.

Another cowboy ran up with leather gloves on

and grabbed the hot iron by the long cooler handle and ran it to the downed steer. The hand put his knee on the animal's rear leg, lowered the branding iron to the steer's hip, held it for precisely the right time and pulled it away.

There was a hissing as the iron burned through the hair and halfway into the tough cowhide. The steer bellowed in anger and some pain, then before he knew it the ropes came off and he was herded to one side with the other just-branded animals.

"That is the way we brand the young steers so we can prove they belong to us," Scott said.

They watched the branding for another half hour, then the small gather was done and the cowboys headed for the ranch.

"That's about it, folks," Scott said. "Hope you have a good trip the rest of your time in the country. So long." Scott touched the brim of his high-crown white hat and turned and rode after the other cowboys.

Two hours later they were back in Dodge City in their hotel. Spur settled into a long hot bath and didn't emerge until the water cooled. At last he had the dust of the corral washed out of his hair and ears. He grinned. It had been a little more of a cattleman's demonstration than he had planned for the princess, but at least she didn't get into any trouble this time.

Control was the clue. He had to keep her so busy that she couldn't get into any mischief. Then he wouldn't have to risk limb, life and diplomatic immunity to rescue her.

It was to be hoped, but somehow Spur felt he might not be so lucky in the days to come as he was today.

Chapter 9

Darlene Benoit sat in the small cafe across from the Dodge City Hotel and watched the front door. She had been there most of the day. Twice she had been out for walks, but only long enough so she could keep her watch on the door.

She knew they were still in Dodge. The ticket agent said no one with Spur McCoy's appearance had bought tickets for four persons to anywhere in the past two days.

A five dollar bill for the room clerk had bought the information that the four were still in the hotel, and all on the second floor. Another dollar had provided her with the exact room that the princess was staying in.

They were not in the hotel right now, hadn't been all day. She had knocked on one door then the next until she had touched all four and no one had answered. They had to be out of town somewhere, but they had not checked out. They would be back.

She would wait. Didier was in no hurry, so she would not be either. It mattered not a whit whether the whore princess was killed today or tomorrow—just so she was killed.

Darlene went out the front door of the cafe, and down the block. She found a chair in front of the hardware store and sat there as if waiting for a friend. Two hours later she walked the other way past the hotel to another cafe and ordered coffee. She broke down and got a donut. Had to keep her strength up.

Darlene knew she looked unkempt. She had been traveling and working, trying to do one last duty. It had left her no time to take care of herself. Now she decided that no matter what happened here, she had to have a bath and wash her hair and get it fixed somehow so she would be presentable enough to pass in a crowd.

Jacques and Bernard were in a boarding house a block down the street and a block north. It was less expensive to stay there. She had a room at the only other hotel in town, which cost her fifty cents a night. Too quickly she was running out of money.

At least the dream had not come last night. She prayed that it would only come when she needed to fire her determination. Poor Didier!

He'd had everything to live for and those people had ended his life. She would kill them all if she could! But she knew better, and now waited for the flower of her father's heart, the princess who also had much to live for. It would be a good trade.

She looked up in time to see a carriage stop at the hotel. A tall man with slightly reddish brown hair under his wide-brimmed hat stepped down and helped out two women and a man. It was them!

She left the cafe at once and walked across the street, but by the time she got to the hotel, the quartet had vanished inside. There would be no chance for escape if she shot the princess in the hotel lobby. Damn!

Darlene went inside the hotel and saw that the four had already vanished up the steps. Their rooms were on the second floor. A moment later she saw a young lad from the hotel carry two buckets of water up the stairs to the second floor. She followed him.

Yes! The fragile princess would need a bath after a two day outing! Perhaps Darlene could take the little lady some extra towels for her bath, with the revolver hidden under one of them. Yes.

She waited for the boy to come back from the second floor bath room. She stopped him by holding out a fifty cent piece.

"I'm in room 21 down the hall. I need one of those big fluffy white towels. Could you bring me one?"

"Right away, Miss," the lad said. He looked to be no more than fifteen and would be delighted to make an extra fifty cents.

She waited down the hall until the boy appeared with two more buckets of water. He had the towel on his shoulder. She took it and gave him the fifty cents and walked down the hall.

When he went into the bathroom, she stepped up the steps to the third floor to be out of sight. She watched as he came out of the bath and knocked on room 22. The door opened a crack, and he said, something, then went back down the hall.

The bath was ready. The Princess would be coming out soon. A moment later the door opened; only it was the other woman, the one with long blonde hair, who came out. The princess might not have a bath for hours, or maybe not at all. Darlene tossed the towel on the steps and went down to the lobby and out the door.

They would try Jacques' idea. He said it would succeed. By now she just wanted to get the job done and be on her way home. Strange places did not agree with her.

At the boarding house, the owner called Jacques down and he and Darlene went for a walk.

"Your way, tonight. Be sure to use your knife. That way we can be on the midnight train heading for New York. Agreed?"

"Of course. It makes me happy to be able to work with you and for the glory of France. I will be ready. I need to buy a few things at the store."

They walked to the store and Darlene went on by and to her hotel. She would be with Jacques tonight as far as she could go. Perhaps the street in front of the hotel would be the best spot to make sure it all went perfectly.

Again she waited across the street. None of the four came out of the hotel until nearly six o'clock. Then McCoy left the hotel and went to the train depot. There he bought tickets, talked to the station master and left in good spirits.

She went in a short time later and asked if her friend had been in to buy the four tickets. He was to meet her there.

"He bought them and left a few minutes ago." The ticket seller shook his head. "I envy you the cool weather you'll find in Denver and the Rockies. Beautiful there this time of year."

"I'm sure it is. What's the exact time the train leaves?"

"Tomorrow, Ma'am, promptly at 12:06."

"Thank you." She turned and left before he could continue the conversation. She knew where they were heading next. But in her heart she knew that she wouldn't need it. If Jacques worked his plan the way he had outlined it, she saw little chance that it could fail.

It would be a hot night. The windows would be open. It was perfect. Yes, it would all be over in a few hours and they could get away on the midnight train to the east. She could buy a ticket at the last minute or pay for the ticket on board. There was still a little money left, but not much.

She went to her small hotel and lay down. It had been an exhausting day, watching and watching. Darlene slept for three hours and came awake promptly at nine-thirty. She checked her clothing, brushed her short hair and hurried out the door.

She met Jacques in the alley behind the big hotel. He nodded.

"She's there. I saw them eat in the hotel restaurant and then all go back upstairs. The light is on in her room. Should be easy." He pointed to the wooden ladder nailed to the outside of the hotel in back. "They even provided me with a ladder. You can watch the show out front."

Jacques looked up and down the deserted alley, then looped the coil of half inch rope over his shoulder and climbed up the ladder. When he made it to the top, Darlene turned and walked around to the front of the building and across the street. She slouched in the door of the hardware store and watched.

Nothing happened at first. A drunk came by, mumbling to himself, sipping from a small whiskey bottle. He never saw her.

Two men walked past talking in hushed tones. They failed to notice her as well. Then all was quiet on the street. On the second floor she saw that there were lights on in all four of the center rooms. Then the ones in the middle went off. A short time later the third one was snuffed out, but the fourth light, which she figured was either Spur McCoy or the diplomat, remained on.

She gasped when she saw a figure at the top of the third floor of the hotel. Slowly the figure edged over the false front of the building and stepped into space. She couldn't see it, but she knew he was held by the strong rope. Jacques worked down the side of the building slowly, stepping on the face of the building, and leaning out as he played out the rope a little at a time.

He went past a dark window on the third floor, then down to the second level. For a moment he headed for the lighted window, then he stepped past it to the second one over. Darlene could see white window curtains blowing out of the window. It was open!

Darlene held her breath as the figure dressed in black edged around the window and then silently slid through the opening. It would be over quickly.

In the room above, the woman had tossed one way and then the other, not able to go to sleep. She watched the moon through the window a moment, then turned on her side away from the light. A moment later she turned back. She could just see the edge of the moon. If she watched it long enough it would travel across the window and be out of sight. The moon seemed to move quickly, but she knew it was really the earth rotating as the moon orbited the planet that made the moon appear to move.

For a moment she thought she heard something, then it quieted. Again a sound came from outside near her window. She sat up in the bed and stared at the window. Slowly a shadowy figure moved around the second floor window and eased through it to the room on the floor not ten feet from her!

She grabbed the derringer from under her pillow and held it with both hands in front of her. The man crouched for a moment, then he came forward. She saw the knife at the last moment and when he was three feet from her, she fired the rugged little gun with the .45 caliber slug.

The explosion of the powder in the box-like room blotted out her scream. She saw the bullet strike the man. He staggered, then lunged forward. She pulled the trigger again and the second barrel fired, the bullet hitting him higher, this time in the neck, she thought, as she rolled to the left and well away from the falling form. . . .

A moment later Francine dropped the derringer and rushed for the door. She fumbled trying to unlock it. Another key from the outside unlocked the door and McCoy rushed into the room.

"Francine, are you all right?" McCoy struck a match and found the lamp. He lit the wick and slipped the tall chimney in place. Then he saw the man face down on the bed.

"Your shots?" he asked.

"Yes," Francine said so softly he barely heard her.

Spur had his Colt in his hand as he turned over the man lying partly on the bed. Half the side of his neck had been blown away and blood drenched the quilts. Spur turned him face down again.

Pierre was there a moment later. He pulled the other two out of the room and locked the door.

"Damn good thing you made the girls switch rooms tonight," Pierre said. "Old trick you learned years ago, you said. Damn glad you did. Now, let's check on the princess."

They opened the door slowly. Alexandria sat up in her bed.

"Francine? Is that you?"

"Yes, yes, I'm here, Alex. Everything is fine. Go back to sleep."

Spur motioned Francine toward the bed. She shook her head. They closed the door gently and locked it. He led Francine down to his room.

"You stay here tonight. I'll be in the hallway outside the princess' room. Now, are you really all right?"

She fell against him and put her arms around him. "He tried . . . he would have killed me. He came down from the roof, must have used a rope. I heard him."

"You always carry a derringer?"

"Always. I owe my life to having one under my pillow tonight." She shuddered and he held her tighter. She looked up. "It's strange. You're holding me close. I'm almost undressed and yet I don't have the slightest urge to make love."

"Almost getting killed will do that to a girl." He let go of her and led her to the bed. She slipped into the sheets and let him cover her.

"You stay here. I'll be in front of Alexandria's door the rest of the night. So far, that's two points for us and none for the bad guys. Any idea who they are?"

She shook her head. "A kiss goodnight?" He kissed her cheek and she frowned, but before she could speak, he hurried to the door and into the hall.

Spur checked the rounds in his revolver. Twice someone had tried. He'd bet they would find those three small triangles tattooed on the latest victim. Who were they?

He sat down with his back against the Princess Alexandria's door and waited. He heard nothing from inside her room. Some late night hotel guests returned, but found their rooms before they came to Spur.

Pierre came into the hall once, saw McCoy there and nodded. "Want me to relieve you in three or four hours?"

"No. I'll be fine. I can rest a little here. If anyone comes down the hall, I'll know it before they get two steps forward. Go to sleep. They tried once tonight, I doubt if they'll have another go at it. We'll just have to wait and see."

On the street below the hotel, Darlene had heard the shots above. She pushed back against the hardware store. No one looked out the window. Neither did Jacques come out the window and go up the rope. She had told Jacques not to take a gun with him, but he might have.

Darlene knew that she had to go up there. She looked at her reticule. It was a large one and heavy. Inside was five pounds of black powder, two feet of the burning fuse and the sawed off shotgun. She had matches that would light easily. Jacques was captured or dead. If they captured him alive one of them would take him to the sheriff's office. But wouldn't they be coming already?

No, no one was coming. So Jacques must be dead or badly wounded. She had to go up there with the bomb.

Darlene shivered, then straightened her shoulders and walked across the street toward the hotel. Once inside she saw more activity than she expected. Two men she figured might be the owners or managers were shouting at each other.

She walked past them and up to the second floor. She looked down the hallway, and without pausing continued up to the third floor. That man, that Spur Morgan, was sitting in the hallway below in front of a door. So that's where the princess was now. Darlene knew she had to do something quick.

The shotgun. With him on guard, there was no way she could use the bomb. She went to the end of the third floor hallway where a window looked down on the street. Quickly she opened the large reticule and took out the shotgun. It had been sawed off twice and now the barrels were only six inches long. The stock had been cut down as well, so the whole weapon was only 18 inches long. She checked the barrels. Both were loaded with double aught buck, 13 .32 caliber balls that would tear up anything they hit.

She snapped the breech closed and held the deadly weapon alongside her leg as she walked back to the stairway. One round for McCoy, and then she would kick the door open and loose the second barrel of deadly shot into the princess. The sound in the hall would awaken her and she'd be sitting up in bed or standing. Perfect.

Darlene came to the steps and looked down. It had to be now, she would never have another chance. Easy. She would walk down the hallway toward the man on the floor, shoot him from twenty feet away, run up and do the door.

She descended to the second story level; automatically she turned into the hallway and walked forward. Her right hand held the shotgun at her side behind her long skirt. McCoy couldn't see it, she was sure.

Darlene Benoit was 30 feet from the man when he looked up, came to his knees and began to draw his six-gun. She whipped up the sawed off weapon and when it aimed down the hall, she pulled the trigger.

Too far away! She knew it the moment she fired, but there was no other course. The six inch barrel would scatter the shot into the side walls, not force it down the hallway. She saw some of the shots hit the wall fifteen feet from the target. The ugly Colt revolver in the man's hand barked once, then he dove away and down the hall.

She turned and ran. He had missed her. He'd had no time to aim, not even point-and-shoot aim. Before she was to the end of the hall, she heard sounds behind her. Just as she turned around the corner and down the first few steps, the revolver fired again, but he was too late. She dropped the shotgun on the stairs, walked the last few steps to the lobby and then to the side door.

The room clerk looked up at her, nodded and went back to the book he had been reading.

A moment later Spur McCoy ran down the stairs. He had a scrape on one cheek and blood showed on his left arm, shoulder high. He was hatless and anger boiled out of his face.

"A woman just come down here?" he bellowed at the clerk.

139

"Yes, went out the side door."

McCoy ran that way. He still might find her. The side street was as dark as a coal mine. He looked up and down the dirt lane but saw no one. He darted into the street and ran half a block away from Main. No one was there. He saw nothing move in the darkness along the street that had no houses and no lights.

Back at the hotel, Spur McCoy pounded his palm against the wall and went in the side door. By then the hotel manager had sent the night clerk for the sheriff.

"Shotguns going off in the hall, an intruder crashing into a room on the second floor and a dead body in room 22. I don't know what I'm going to find next. You're McCoy, the one who is ushering this special party?"

Spur nodded.

"This is your notice, Mr. McCoy. I want you and your party out of here by noon tomorrow. Not another night. You folks have been trouble for me since you arrived. I want you out; whether on the train or in jail will be up to the sheriff. He's on his way over here now to talk to you about that man up there shot to death."

Chapter 10

The sheriff arrived ten minutes after Spur McCoy got back to his room. Francine was still sleeping. He waited in the hall. Sheriff Potts was a small, slender man with a goatee and handlebar moustache. At nearly midnight he was angry because he had been called out.

"You Spur McCoy?" the lawman asked.

"Right. You the sheriff?"

"I am. The body in there?" He pointed to the open door.

Spur nodded and they went in together. Spur lit the lamp and gave it to the sheriff. He rolled the body over on the bed and grunted.

"Somebody did him in for good. Who is he?"

"We don't know, Sheriff. He came down from the roof on a rope, swung in the window with a knife to kill the young woman sleeping here.

She heard him, used her derringer and there's the result."

"Where's the knife?"

They found it on the floor beside the bed. The sheriff looked at the end of the rope still trailing in the window. He leaned out the window and pulled on the rope. It was fast above.

He sat down on the room's one chair and rubbed his left knee.

"Seems to check out. Where's the young woman who did the shooting?"

"Sleeping next door in my room. She's part of a group of three foreign diplomatic visitors from a principality on the southern coast of France called Mantuco."

"Never heard of it."

"Neither had I until I took this job. I'm supposed to be guide and bodyguard to the Princess of Mantuco. She's sleeping in the room on the other side. I work for the federal government."

Spur handed the sheriff his new identification card with a small tin type picture on it. The sheriff studied it in the lamp light.

"That really the president's signature?"

"I didn't see him sign it, but my boss says it is. Do you have some statement or release form we can sign and get this taken care of?"

"Not without a lot more questions."

"The dead man is a member of a group from France trying to kill the princess. They tried in St. Louis and wounded another member of our party. You can send a telegram to Washington, D.C., right now and get an answer in the morning."

"Come down to my office and write out a statement. I'll check with the federal folks in the morning."

"I can't leave just yet. They tried twice for the princess. I've got a .32 caliber double aught buck slug that sliced through a half inch of shoulder. Shotgun must have been sawed off, otherwise I'd be a dead man.

"I can't leave the hallway until it gets daylight. Then I'll come in with Francine and we'll sign what we need to. We have tickets on the northbound 12:06 for Denver."

"Should be enough time. I'll get me some more sleep then, if you don't mind."

Spur watched the sheriff walk down the hall, looking at the bullet marks on the walls. He pointed to one in the dimly lit hall.

"This from the shotgun?"

"Right. She let loose about thirty or thirty five feet down there."

"No wonder you got out of it alive." The lawman waved and went on down the stairs.

Spur looked at the princess's door. It was closed and locked. He slipped into his room and found the chair in the darkness, then set it near the door so he could see down the hall toward the stairs and sat down. He closed his door almost shut and settled down to wait.

He'd been lucky in the hall when that scatter gun with the chopped off barrel spread out those double aught buck rounds. Now he had a more secure guard spot and one just as effective. He still had a lot of the night to go.

Tomorrow with any luck, they would be on that noon train heading north. They'd take a branch line to the Kansas-Pacific railroad and be off to the west for Denver.

The next morning, the sheriff was more cooperative. He had Spur write out a statement about how the death happened. There was no identification on the body and it would be buried in boot hill by the county. Francine did not have to appear.

Spur worried about boarding the train with the assassin still out there. If there were two of them, there must be more. He used a buggy and took the princess around to the far side of the depot and came up on the off side of the train. The conductor arranged to let her board there and go directly to the compartment car.

Francine and Pierre boarded the usual way and five minutes before time for the train to pull out, all four were in the first compartment.

"We made it," Spur said. He nodded at Pierre. "Take care of reloading Francine's derringer, would you? I want to watch the platform to see if I can spot anyone who might be in the group that's following us."

He paced the platform until the conductor called his all aboard chant and then Spur stepped on the last car as it moved slowly out of the station. He hadn't seen anyone who even faintly looked suspicious.

Back on the train, he wandered up through the two passenger cars casually observing everyone riding north. He saw no one he recognized, but he imprinted the face and form of the thirty-odd people into his memory. If he saw any of them again, he would know them. He went into the compartment car and settled down where Pierre was reading some French magazine.

"You're worried, Pierre."

"How did you know?"

"You always read that same magazine when you're worried about the princess."

"I asked her if she'd had enough of the Wild West and if we could go back now. She said the tour was just starting. She said with you to protect her, nothing bad could happen to her. I even wired the embassy in Washington. They said whatever the princess wanted to do, I must do."

"Quickest way to end an argument is with a royal decree."

"I should be used to it by now, but I'm not. McCoy, you've got to figure out all the precautions that you can to keep that little lady safe."

"I'm trying, Pierre. I wish I knew who these assassins are. Any help there from your embassy?"

"They don't have a thing. There hasn't been any group espousing the overthrow of the Prince. From time to time some group in France spouts off about regaining Mantuco as a French colony, but they aren't active right now."

"Which gives us absolutely no help."

"How long until we get to this place, Hays, Kansas?"

"Conductor said about three hours, if we don't have any holdups along the way. A big rainstorm up in here last night that might have washed out some track. They'll be watching for it."

Spur couldn't sit still. He took another stroll through the passenger cars, but found nothing out of place. He sat down in a window seat at the end of one car and tried to decide if any of the passengers had been unusually interested in him. He could have been spotted with the princess by now and been the one to follow.

If one of the assassin group was in the car, he didn't give himself away. Spur went back to the compartment and found Pierre engrossed in a game of cards with the two women. He begged off from joining them.

They had been underway for about an hour when the train suddenly lurched as the brakes were applied hard. Spur came off the seat and out the compartment door.

"Stay here and lock the door behind me," he shouted, then ran down the swaying train to the nearest entry way. He stepped down on the platform and looked toward the engine. The engineer hung out his window looking backward. The train skidded now with the wheels on the engine locked and throwing out sparks from the steel on steel slide.

As soon as the train stopped, Spur dropped to the right of way. He saw the conductor come off the train the car in back of him. They both ran for the engine.

The engineer shook his head. "Not my doing. Must have been the emergency cord. Did somebody pull it?"

The conductor shook his head. "Not where I saw."

"Oh damn!" Spur said softly and raced back along the cars toward the compartments. He got on at the front of the car and opened the inside door quietly. He saw no one in the narrow aisle along the windows. A moment later someone came out of the compartment next to his and Pierre's.

A woman. His mind flashed through the people he had seen in the second class cars. Yes! She was one of them. A young woman, maybe 30, slender, on the short side, with dark hair rather rumpled.

He hurried toward her but already she was out the other door and into the passenger cars. He stopped at the compartment door and tried the handle. Locked.

He rushed to Pierre's door and opened it. They all were there. "Out!" he said sharply. He caught Francine and pulled her toward the door and pointed down the hallway toward the front. Away from the locked compartment.

"Go, go!" he urged. Alexandria rushed past him and Pierre struggled to get around the small table that they had set up. Spur pulled him the last half dozen feet and they rushed down the narrow aisle of the compartment aisle.

They were just to the end when Spur felt a giant fist smash into his back. It drove him forward and he and Pierre went down in a flailing confusion of arms and legs and sudden pain.

Then the sound billowed out, storming after the shock wave of the explosion. It crashed around them and Francine covered her ears. They heard glass breaking in the windows and the sound and the air rush seemed to reverse and charge past them again and out through the windows and out of the closed box.

Spur rolled over and sat up. Pierre leaned against the wall. He held his left arm tenderly. "Bruised but not broken," he said. Francine blinked back tears. Alexandria knelt beside Pierre. She opened buttons on his shirt and pushed his hand inside to form a sling. Then she took off a scarf she wore and tied it around the arm and around his neck for more support.

Spur jumped up, checked to see that his .44 was still in place and walked down the hall. The smell of the black powder explosion was pungent in the hallway. Most of the smoke and fumes had been sucked out the broken windows, but there was still enough to make Spur's eyes smart and bring a small cough.

He saw the conductor from the other end of the car coming toward him.

"This compartment," Spur said. "I saw a woman coming out of it, but when I tried the handle it was locked."

They stared inside through the smoke. The interior of the compartment was a trash heap. Part of the bedding smoldered. The conductor threw part of the bucket of water he had brought with him on the fire producing more smoke and steam.

Spur estimated the situation. "Looks like the bomb was placed on the wall next to my compartment. Which means I know who it was and why it was done. Let's find her before she gets off the train."

They looked in his and Pierre's compartment. The wall had been blown out and the inside of the small room was a shambles. Nothing burned, but everything was dumped on the floor or smashed against the windows.

They hurried toward the passenger cars. Spur had the woman's appearance in his mind. About five-two, brown short hair, unkempt. A brown dress with puff sleeves. Nervous hands.

They went through the first car but the woman was not there. In the second car they slowed, checking each woman, but by the time they got to the end of the car, Spur realized that either they had missed the bomber or she had left the train.

He looked outside. They were in the middle of the plains, and the horizon stretched a hundred miles each side of the train. Far off, maybe ten miles, he saw the smokes of a small town. But between here and there he saw no form, no sign of movement.

The conductor went back and checked the compartment car. It was not damaged in the rolling sections. They would continue on to Hays.

The four travelers went back inside the women's compartment. Spur checked the damaged one and found their luggage and everything they had taken out and repacked it. He pushed the carpet bags into the women's compartment. "I'll be outside," he told them and left.

At the near end of the car door, he found the conductor. He would be a guard there until they came to Hays. No one would get into the car unless he or she could show a compartment ticket.

Spur wandered through the two passenger cars again. No one seemed nervous. No one watched him with more than casual interest. Somehow he knew the bomber still had to be on the train. How could he miss her? Was she pretending to be sleeping and her face covered? He saw no one like that.

He heard the conductor call for the next stop at Hays, Kansas, when he thought of it. A wig! The woman could have put on a long-haired wig to cover her own hair and a light jacket to cover up her puff-sleeves dress. Why didn't he think of it before.

But he couldn't pull on every woman's hair and see if she had on a wig.

He rushed back to the compartment and got the women and Pierre ready to leave.

"Wait for the last moment before you get off, then go directly into the depot and find as many people as you can and wait near them."

He rushed back to the second passenger car, and was first in line to get off when the train stopped.

He watched every woman, especially those short enough to be the bomber. He could watch only one car. He was sure the bomber even with a wig had not been on the first car. He ran toward the second but already most of the passengers had left. He saw a small woman just passing the side of the depot. She turned and looked at him and for a moment he saw such hatred, that he knew she had to be the bomber. She had long dark hair and a light jacket.

Spur charged around passengers and to the edge of the depot building. Ahead was an empty street, a half dozen buggies, and three men walking away. Nowhere could he find the small woman.

He checked in the buggies and a wagon, but she was not in any of them either.

Spur went back to the depot, made sure their tickets were good on to Denver and waited with the others for the new train to arrive from down the tracks to the east.

It was a half hour late. That much more time to make sure the princess stayed safe. So the gang had a woman in it. Or was it headed by a woman? Either way he would know her now wherever he saw her, with her wig on or without it.

He talked to the stationmaster and he found a room where the princess could wait out of the main part of the depot. It was safer there.

Denver. What would he let the princess do there? There were high stakes poker games, mines near by to explore, the wonderful scenery. A pleasure tour of the Rocky Mountains, then a short train ride up to Cheyenne, Wyoming, and back on the train to St. Louis. That should be enough of a tour to satisfy the princess.

An hour later, the train came in and the new passengers were ushered on board. Spur stood at the gate and watched each person who went through it heading for the train. He checked each one carefully, looking for any woman about the right size no matter what she was wearing.

When the train pulled out ten minutes later, Spur was sure that the assassin was not on board. He made one last walk through the three passenger cars and then went to the compartment car and relaxed for a moment.

A man and his 12-year old son watched the tall man with the black cowboy hat walk through the train. The boy made a funny face at Spur, who grinned and went on by. When Spur had walked on through the car, the young boy turned to the man.

"That was Spur McCoy. He's the one who will give you trouble. Kill either him or the diplomat if you can't get to the Princess. With either of them out of the way, It'll be easier."

The "boy" scowled. The person with the boy's cloth cap and the town pants and new shirt was really Darlene Benoit. She'd had plenty of time in Hays to buy the new clothes and change into them before the train came. McCoy had stared at her several times and didn't know who she was. If they could get lucky once more, the princess would be dead.

Bernard had volunteered for the next try at the princess. They were out of the black powder bombs. Two had been lost in their luggage when it didn't get transferred. She had dropped the shotgun so she could walk out of the hotel. They were down to her derringer and the six-gun that Bernard carried in side leather.

"Be careful. We'll go back to the compartments just as they call a stop. Then we can shoot her and get off the train and vanish into the little town. The sooner the better."

The conductor came through the car five minutes later announcing the next stop as Pleasantville. The "young boy" and his father left their seats in the first car and worked toward the fourth one, the compartment car.

"We'll take the first one that Spur McCoy comes out of," Darlene said. They stood on the end platform of the car watching the country. Shortly the train slowed and they saw a house or two. Then the train shuddered as the brake hit and they slowed rapidly.

One of the compartment doors opened ahead, the fourth one.

"Now!" Darlene whispered. They pushed into the compartment car and hurried ahead. The door finished opening and Spur McCoy looked down the narrow aisle.

Bernard had his six-gun out but it was behind his leg. McCoy looked at them and started to move so they could get past. Bernard swung the six-gun down on McCoy's head and he slumped. Bernard looked around the door, saw only the other man in the compartment. Pierre swung up a pistol and Bernard fired twice. Both slugs caught the older man and he slumped into the day seat.

Bernard rushed ahead to the next compartment and tried the door. Locked. He fired into the lock twice but the door wouldn't open. McCoy sat up groggy and reached for his six-gun. Darlene stepped around the compartment door and kicked the weapon out of his hand and down the aisle. She rushed past him, saw Bernard fire once more into the door handle area. The compartment door still wouldn't open.

152

She pushed Bernard forward down the aisle and out the door of the train just as it stopped. They sprinted across the tracks, through the rail yard, and were soon lost in the cars and engines and tracks and buildings beyond.

Spur McCoy stood and shook his head, then hurried down to where his Colt .44 lay, grabbed it and rushed to look outside. The pair was gone.

He headed back to the compartment, went past his own and knocked on the compartment in back of his, the one the gunman didn't try to open. He knocked again on the women's door. "Alexandria, Francine? Are you all right?"

Chapter 11

A moment after Spur knocked on the women's compartment door, it opened and Francine looked out.

"Didn't I hear some shooting?"

"You did, are both of you all right?"

"Yes, we were having a nap."

"Lock it and stay inside."

Spur hurried back to his and Pierre's compartment. The door was still open. Pierre was trying to sit up on the bed. Blood washed down the side of his face. His left arm was bloody as well.

Spur jumped to his side, checked the head wound. It was minor a bullet crease, but bled like a stuck buffalo. The arm was hit high and Pierre couldn't move it.

"Broke the damn bone, I think." Pierre said. Spur ran outside and called to the conductor. A minute later the conductor held the train while Spur helped Pierre off.

"I can get to a doctor on my own. You stay with the ladies. Keep going. The assassins are somewhere in town. I don't want Alexandria here." He winced and leaned against the side of the building.

The conductor had sent a boy running for a doctor. Spur saw a man with a black bag walking rapidly toward them. The conductor called out his all aboard, and Spur hesitated.

"You sure you'll be all right? I'd suggest you get back to Washington and let your doctor there look at it after you're patched up here. You have funds enough to get back?"

Pierre nodded. "One thing I have is funds. I sure as hell don't have a fast draw."

Spur ran for the train just as it began to move. The conductor grinned, swung aboard and left room for Spur.

"Figured if we moved, you'd run and catch us."

Back in the compartment, Spur cleaned up in the space he and Pierre had used. Francine knocked on the connecting wall and he went out to her door.

"All clear?"

"Yes. Pierre got shot in the arm. I told him to go back to Washington."

"That just leaves the three of us," Francine said. She reached up and kissed his lips.

The conductor knocked on the partly opened door.

"Mr. McCoy, I'll need you to help me fill out a report I got to make on the shooting. Not so worried about your friend, but that next compartment has three bullet holes in the door. Company will want to know what caused them and why."

"Come on in, and I'll tell you all about it."

The conductor listened as he was told about the Princess and Mantuco and the gang of assassins after them.

"The bad thing here is that both of them got away. At least we know there are two more of them. They did get on the train right under my nose. The woman dressed up like a young boy. Fooled me completely."

The conductor finished taking his notes and nodded. "Anything I can do for you just ask."

"How long before we get to Denver?" Francine asked.

"Scheduled to get in there about ten tomorrow morning. Be on the rails all night. Good sleeping in these compartments. It's about three P.M. now. Unless we hit a washout or a prairie fire we should show up in Denver's station along a couple hours before noon. We did put on a dining car last stop. It's just to the rear of this one."

"Thanks. There isn't anyway those two who got off the train back there can get ahead of us, is there?"

"Lord no. Not unless they climb on a big bald eagle and fly faster than we do. Your lady should be safe for a couple of days now, at least. There's another train through here tomorrow morning that they could catch."

Spur thanked the trainman again and he went into the hall, mumbled as he looked at the holes in the compartment door and then moved on down the aisle.

Francine reached over and closed the compartment door and pushed the lock, then stood so close to Spur that her breasts touched his chest.

"See anything interesting, Mr. McCoy?"

"I see a whole lot of interesting lady, but right now isn't the right time. Let's talk to the princess."

"Oh, damn. I was all worked up." She reached up and kissed him and pushed her breasts against him, then reluctantly came away from him and led the way out and to the next compartment.

Francine eased the door open. Alexandria sat up on the opened seat combing her hair.

He told her what happened to Pierre.

"Now, don't worry. He isn't critical or in any danger.. That arm will bother him for some months, but the head wound was just a crease with a lot of blood."

"Thank God! He'll be catching up with us?"

"I've suggested that he go back to Washington. They have better doctors there. Last we talked, he planned to do that."

"So you have one less foreigner to play nursemaid to." Alexandria laughed. "I know what you said to your chief. He told us. Said we should be careful not to make you hate us."

"No chance of that happening, Princess Alexandria."

"You don't need to. . . ."

He held up his hand. "Right then, I wanted to. Now, a report on our schedule. We get into Denver tomorrow morning about ten o'clock. Around that time. These train don't get in on time very often due to breakdowns, Indian raids, buffalo on the tracks and washouts of the tracks by a cloudburst."

"I want to see buffalo on the tracks," Alexandria said. "I haven't seen a single buffalo yet. You promised."

158

"Watching out the window may be our best chance," Spur said.

"I have been watching. Let's play cards. Poker anyone?"

They used chips that Francine took out of her carpet bag. It was a wild, no holds barred game and Francine beat everyone.

"I know nothing about the game," she said. "With me it's just plain luck. You think I'm bluffing when I'm not. You think I have a good hand when I don't."

Alexandria beamed. "I'm taking her with me to those high stakes poker games in Denver." She stopped and frowned. "Oh, our money man left us."

Spur shuffled the cards. "I can take care of cash for a while."

"How long?" Francine asked.

"Long enough to finish the tour. We're going to Denver, then up to Cheyenne, Wyoming, and then heading back to Washington on the good old Central Pacific railroad."

"You're cutting my 30 day tour short," Alexandria said.

"Not cutting it, just compressing a few of the points of interest. Two of those people are still at large and aiming revolvers, rifles and black powder bombs at you to say nothing of knives."

"I'm sorry if anyone was hurt because of me," Alexandria said. She stood and stared out the window. "But this will be my only chance to see America, and I want to see all of it. In two years I'll be married to some prince or duke or earl and I'll have to do exactly what he tells me to do."

"You'll have enough of the West before we get through, Alexandria, I promise. If not we'll buy some horses and ride for thirty or forty miles. After that I'm sure you'll agree that the train is much better."

Francine stood and looked out the windows. "I don't know about you two, but I could use a short nap before dinner. We have a dining car on this train, Alex."

"Good. Yes, a nap." She glanced at Francine. "Will you be napping here, or with Spur?"

The women both giggled at Spur's expression. Francine grabbed his arm and kissed his cheek. "Don't worry, Alex knows all about our little late night meetings. We tell each other everything."

"Everything?" Spur asked.

Francine nodded. "At least I do. We'll see you for dinner about six."

Spur went out the door, waved and listened to be sure that Francine locked the door as he left. In his own compartment he checked on the beds. A porter had been in and changed the bedding on the blood splattered sheets and had put on new blankets as well.

He settled into the front facing seat and watched the landscape for a while. It was Kansas flat. They would be climbing gradually toward the high plains and then the slope up to the Rocky Mountains. He stared out the window and swore he could see twenty miles to the horizon. What a beautiful, empty country. He wondered if the land would ever be developed.

He had been watching the land for less than five minutes when a knock came on the door. He unlocked it with his six-gun in his right hand and cracked it open. Alexandria stood there.

"May I come in?"

"Yes, of course." He let the hammer down carefully on the revolver and holstered it. She stepped into the compartment and he closed the door.

"I better close it, safety. You understand."

She smiled. "Yes, Spur McCoy, I understand." She sat on the one bunk that had been made into a bed and watched him. "Spur, I want to tell you how grateful I am for what you're doing for me. Most men would have given up and quit the task. I know that you'll see it through, even though you refused to accept the assignment at first."

She patted the bed beside her. "Come and sit so we can talk easier." He hesitated. She was the boss. He sat down on the bed with a foot of space between them.

"When I said I appreciate it, I'm not just talking empty words. I mean it." She moved over beside him until their thighs touched. Alexandria turned toward him, caught his face and pulled it down and kissed him hard on his lips.

She let it last a long time and brushed his lips with her tongue.

When it ended he saw the fire in her eyes.

"Spur, don't think of me as an innocent. When I was fourteen I invited a young boy of 15 to my room and we undressed each other and learned and experimented and he showed me how he could pump himself off. I was fascinated. We didn't make love.

"I told my father about it. My mother is dead. He was furious at first, then he understood. He had a wise woman come and talk with me and instruct me in the art of love making, in how to make a man happy. The last day she was to instruct me, she came with a handsome young man of twenty-one.

"That day I proved to her that I had learned

my lessons well. We made love six times, with my teacher watching from behind the blinds. She didn't have to correct me once.

"We French have a way to prevent the baby. I have made love several times, but only when I wanted to, when I chose. Now I choose you, Spur McCoy. This is the only practical way that I can show you how much I appreciate what you are doing for me."

As she said the last words she opened the front of her dress, which had been unfastened, and shrugged it off her shoulders. It fell to her waist showing her breasts with rosy areolas and nipples already standing tall and pulsating with hot blood.

"Princess. . . ."

"At one time, Mr. McCoy, to refuse a royal order in my country could result in being beheaded." She picked up his hand and placed it over one of her breasts. "We don't want you to lose your head, now, do we?"

Spur chuckled. His hand curved around her breast and he found her other one and both hands caressed the large half moons, warming them even more, making her catch her breath and look up at him quickly.

"Oh, my . . . I understand how Francine is so taken with your charms." He kissed her soft lips again; this time their mouths were open and tongues sparred and then he moved his kisses down her cheek to her neck and on down across her pure white chest to the side of one orb.

"Oh . . . Mr. McCoy . . ."

He kissed up the side of her breast, then licked her throbbing nipple and sucked it into his mouth.

"My, my, but you do know how to please a lady."

"This is just the beginning."

He ministered to both her breasts, then took her hands and put them on his fly. She left them there.

He undid the buttons and she worked one hand inside.

Spur checked her dress, found the clue to how the rest of it came off and helped her out of it. To his surprise, she wore nothing under it.

"Francine's idea," Alexandria admitted.

She knelt before him and undressed him. Each item of his clothing she folded carefully and laid to one side. When he was as naked as she was, she began to kiss his neck and worked down across his hairy chest to the thatch of brownish red hair at his crotch.

His erection was full and pulsating. She kissed it to the roots, then worked back to the tip and took him in her mouth. She let it come out and looked at him.

"I can do you this way if you want. I have some secrets to help you along."

He shook his head and she lay down beside him, dropping one breast into his mouth.

"Do you mind if I talk? Some men don't like it."

He shook his head that he didn't mind.

"Good. There's something about making love that is so far above what people do most of the time that it just can't be compared to anything else. Oh, for a woman having a baby might be as thrilling, I don't know. Will some day, I'm sure."

She moved so she lay on top of him, grinding her hips against his erection.

"That get your interest picking up a bit, Spur? Usually does. You like me to be on top or you want to be up here?"

In answer he rolled her over until he was on top. Then he took her legs and lifted them to his shoulders.

"This is different."

He let her down a little, angled just right and pushed forward.

"Oh, damn! That's what I love. Your big stick poking up into me! I'll never get enough of that. But I can't just go out on the street and call in some young horse of a man. I must be careful. I must be selective. What if I got pregnant? There are a thousand rules I have to follow."

He thrust forward and her knees almost touched her forehead.

"Strange and wild and so good! I've never been done this way I can tell you. Absolutely wonderful."

Then she gasped and moaned and her body spasmed and shook and rattled and she let out a long low growl that built and built as she shook and spasmed time after time. At last she tapered off and opened her eyes.

"Twelve times! Twelve times I climaxed. That's a record for me. Three was the most ever before now. Twelve times!"

She moved her legs off his shoulders and dropped them around his back and locked her ankles together.

"Now, cowboy, ride me on the range."

Spur could hold back no longer. He slammed forward, punching her small body higher on the bed. Again and again he pounded and then he knew it was time. The huge gates behind the dam opened and a billion, billion tons of water and semen cascaded through the long tubes and jolted out with great force as he panted and pawed and dug his toes into the blankets, driving forward a dozen more times before he gave a long, low cry and fell against her, spent, exhausted and totally satisfied.

They lay there a long time. She put her arms around his shoulders strapping them together. He moved first.

"Oh, damn!" the Princess said softly. "I was hoping we could stay this way the rest of the trip to Denver."

Spur laughed softly. "Now that would be a record." He eased away from her and sat on the side of the bed.

The rocking and swaying of the train car became evident again.

"I didn't notice this movement when we were so busy before," he said.

She smiled. "I didn't see or hear anything but you. Strange how that happens, isn't it."

She sat up beside him. "You ever get to Europe?"

"Never been there."

"Any chance you could come?"

"Not much."

"You could be half ruler of the principality of Mantuco. I'll need a consort."

Spur chuckled and kissed her cheek. "Princess, I'm not cut out for a royal court. I'm afraid it wouldn't work out very well. Your daddy wouldn't like me."

"He wouldn't have to." She lifted her brows. "You're right, I'm dreaming again. I'll have to marry some damn prince or duke or somebody like that. I may trade places with Francine. We've talked about it. I'd dye her hair and bleach my own blonde. Then she'd wear all my dresses.

"Her breasts are a little too big, but we could let

the clothes out a little." Alexandria looked at him. "You like her breasts better than mine?"

"No, why should I?"

"Her's are bigger."

"Not that much."

"They are too. We've been comparing our tits for six years now." They both laughed.

"You two are crazy."

Alex shook her head. He bent and kissed both her breasts.

"Again?"

"Better not. We want to have some strength left for dinner in the dining car."

"All right." She began to dress. "Having Francine is the only thing that's kept me anywhere near normal. My father said I had to know who the people were and what they wanted. That's why he sent me to school in London. Nobody knew who I was. I loved it."

"You learned about the common people, like me?"

"Oh, yes. When I take over my country, the first thing I'll do is sell off all of the crown jewels and tear down most of the palace and build housing for everyone. Nobody should be rich, everyone should be equal. We only have thirty thousand people in our whole country. There's no reason everyone can't have a nice house to live in or a good-sized apartment. My father doesn't believe me. But I'll do it."

Spur dressed now as well. He kissed her breasts one last time before she covered them. Alexandria smiled. "Don't look so sad, you'll see the girls again. It's a long trip and we have lots of nights ahead of us."

A half hour later they went into the compartment next door and played cards until it was time for dinner.

Francine had whispered something to Alexandria and both giggled. At the dining room, there were half a dozen empty tables, so they asked for one near the window. They ate as they watched the country flash past. It wouldn't be dark for an hour and a half yet.

Spur was surprised by the menu. It was much larger than it had been just a year ago. He had a platter of fried oysters and a slab of roast beef. The women both ordered chicken baked in a wine sauce they said was better than they expected.

It took almost two hours for dinner and it was starting to get dark when they went back to the compartments. Spur had paid the bill as they left and Francine stared at him.

"Really, we should talk about money. Pierre was funding this expedition."

"He still is," Spur said. "Before we left the train back there he gave me his moneybelt. It has over ten thousand dollars in it in one hundred dollar bills. I doubt if the three of us could eat that much dinner or ride that many trains if we tried."

"We could lose that much easily in the gaming tables of Denver," Alexandria said. "Watch out, Denver, here we come!"

Chapter 12

The train arrived in Denver ten minutes early. Spur got the ladies off and took a rental hack to the hotel where he had made reservations, the Rocky Mountain Manorhouse. It was supposed to be the best one in town.

At their rooms, all in a row on the third floor, Spur aimed a finger at them.

"You go nowhere, you do nothing, unless you check with me or I'm with you. Agreed?"

The woman looked at each other.

"Certainly not in any bedroom without you," Francine said grinning.

"I'm serious. Those two assassins will be in town late this afternoon or tonight sometime. We'll have to be on our guard. We go out the back or side door to the hotel. We don't make a fuss. We stay out of any kind of publicity or limelight. I don't want to have to haul a coffin all the way back to Mantuco."

That sobered them.

"We'll be good, Spur McCoy," Alexandria said. "But we want to have some fun at the same time. What happens first?"

"We have a buggy tour of the city. I've arranged for a guide who knows the town and its history and he'll provide a running commentary for us. We meet him at eleven o'clock. The tour includes a luxurious dinner somewhere of his choice."

"Sounds good. We've never been to Denver. Is it really a mile high? What if we fall off?" The two women broke into laughter.

Spur grinned. "You fall off, I have to catch you. We have a half hour before the tour starts at the side door. Don't wear your best dresses. See you then."

The women went in their rooms and Spur hurried downstairs and to the train station, where he sent a telegram to the Mantuco embassy in Washington.

"Arrived Denver safely. No further problems. Touring Denver and environs, then heading to Cheyenne, Wyoming. No problems. The two dissidents who shot Pierre are still at large. May be following us. All care being taken." He signed it Spur McCoy and paid for it. The clerk said it would go out within ten minutes.

The tour went smoothly. Spur learned some more about Denver's early history and how there used to be two towns, one on each side of Cherry Creek, and how they combined the two and how half of the town was washed away in a flood one spring.

They ate at a "Miner's Cafe." It was set up like the inside of a mine and there was lots of mining equipment around. The waiters all wore head lamps the way the miners did or carried candles in small miner lanterns. The food was fair but nothing to shout about.

The tour ended with a run through the famous gambler's row with more than a dozen large gambling halls.

"Let's stop here," Alexandria said. The tour guide looked at Spur, who nodded. They got out in the middle of a block-long section that sported a big gambling hall in every other building. Spur ushered the women toward the grandest-looking, The El Dorado, and pushed their way inside.

It was half filled with men and women, some Chinese, talking, smoking and gambling.

Spur bought two hundred dollars worth of chips and gave half to each woman.

"Have fun, this is all you get to lose. Stay away from the dice tables. How about some low stakes poker?" Spur found them seats at a dollar limit table and soon both had settled in to the game. There were six players and the pots usually ran about twenty dollars. Francine won the first pot on three of a kind in a five card draw hand.

Alexandria won the next pot when she bluffed out a henna-redheaded woman who snarled when she lost.

An hour later, both the women were still playing. Francine's luck had evaporated and she was down to her last twenty dollars. Alexandria was two hundred dollars ahead.

Spur pulled Francine out of the game and on the next hand, helped Alexandria from the game as well. They cashed in their chips and walked out into the afternoon sunshine.

"What's next?" Alexandria asked.

"We have tickets for the Denver Opera. Not the best in the world, but it should be interesting to see what they do."

"I hate opera, can't we do something else?" Alexandria asked. "I saw a sign about a dog fight. Can we go to the dog fight?"

"Dog fights are illegal in Denver now. We might get arrested. We don't want that. Maybe a play or a concert."

"It all sounds so stuffy," Alexandria said.

Spur frowned. He'd have to come up with something. "It's late, why don't we have supper first and then we'll decide."

"Great idea," Francine whooped. "I'm starved. One of those big Denver steaks would be just right."

They went back to their hotel and to the dining room, which bragged it had the finest cuisine in town. The room was fancy, with white tablecloths, elegant tables, waiters with black coats and white gloves, and a menu in both French and English.

The women read the French side. Both wound up with an inch-thick steak with four side dishes and coffee. Spur had a slab of roast beef with horseradish sauce and four side dishes as well.

They were just starting their main course, when a party of four came into the dining room. It was a dramatic entrance with the star coming in last and a chair held for him. He wore a military uniform but with no insignia. It was a dashing red coat with black leather trim, a high collar shielding a starched white shirt. Black riding breeches ended in black leather boots shined to a gleaming finish.

He sat down two tables away from them and looked directly at Alexandria. She watched him a moment, then went back to her steak. She had it nearly half gone when one of the men from the

172

fancy-dressed man came to the table and gave a small folded note to Alexandria. The man pointed to the man at the table.

Alexandria read the note and smiled. She gave it to Francine.

"You wouldn't!"

"I might."

"Mind letting me in on the secret?" Spur asked.

"The gentleman at the table over there in the red uniform says that he is Don Manuel Del Fortuna. He is an ex-colonel in the Mexican army, now a United States citizen with a large Spanish land grant in California. He's here looking for brood stock for his cattle ranch, and he's invited me to spend a month as his guest on his rancho."

"In California?" Spur asked.

"I would assume so. He can't very well bring several thousand acres of that state here."

Spur stared at the ex-colonel and then looked back at the princess. "It might be best just to ignore him, and the note. We don't have time even to go by train to California. If he has brood stock, he's on horseback, which would take about two months to get down the mountains and into California."

"Good, let's go!"

"You can't go, Alex," Francine said. "You know that. Pierre would tell you that. So since the invitation is open, I think I'll go."

"You can't go if I can't go," Alexandria said. They both laughed and went back to their meal. Now and then Alexandria looked over at the colonel. He was eating but watching her all the time.

They left the dining room half an hour later with no more contact from the tall Spaniard.

They stood in the ornate lobby for a few moments talking.

"There's a play we could see," Spur said. "A traveling troupe the room clerk said was quite good."

"No plays. I get my fill of them at home."

"How about robbing a bank?" Francine suggested. "That would be exciting."

"A little too exciting," Spur said. "Let's sit down over here and figure it out."

Before they could move, the four uniformed Spaniards swept down on them with the colonel in the lead. He shouldered past Spur and bowed low in front of Alexandria.

"Senorita, you did not respond to my invitation, no?" He watched her intently.

"It was not an invitation in good taste, Colonel. You should be chastised. This is not the army camp where you order people around. I'll accept your apology at once, or you may leave."

The Spaniard's eyes went wide, he took a short step backwards, then he chuckled.

"Ah, yes, lots of fire and spirit, I like that. Senorita, it is with my humblest regrets if I have done anything whatsoever to discomfort you or to make you feel slighted or insulted. I apologize profusely." He bowed again, then straightened and looked down at her.

Her frown cracked and she grinned. "Now, Colonel, that's better. Perhaps one of your men would introduce you properly."

One of the aides stepped up quickly.

"Senorita, may I present Don Manuel Del Fortuna. Former colonel in the Spanish and Mexican armies, now retired to his rancho in Southern California."

Francine stepped up. "Colonel, may I present her Royal Highness Princess Alexandria of the House of Mantuco. Heir to the throne of the Principality

174

of Mantuco, Protector of women and small children and princess of the realm."

Colonel Fortuna sucked in a quick breath and went down on one knee and bowed deeply again.

"Rise, Colonel, I'm not here on official business. I'm on a holiday. I understand you have a large rancho in Southern California?"

"Yes, Princess. I apologize again. Had I known of your station, I would not have been so bold as to send you a note, or to approach you this way."

"But you're here now. We were discussing the entertainment for tonight. Is there anything to do in Denver after the sun goes down?"

Colonel Fortuna lifted his brows slightly as he thought for a moment. "There is the opera. I hear it is moderately good. I have seen advertisements for a play. No Shakespeare."

"What about the dog fights?" she asked.

Colonel Fortuna shook his head. "They are not for a lady. They are rough and vulgar. I would not even consider permitting you to go to them."

"The opera it is then, Colonel. My lady and my body guard, Mr. McCoy, will accompany us. Be here in the lobby at eight." She nodded at him, the Colonel bowed again and Princess Alexandria swept away and up the stairs toward her room.

Francine shadowed her and Spur was close behind. On the third floor, outside their rooms, they stopped.

The women whispered together. Spur frowned.

"Now don't be angry, Mr. McCoy," Alexandria said. "He's a truly handsome man, and you did suggest the opera, so you should be happy."

"I'm delirious with joy. This guy represents the biggest danger to you so far. But you gave the royal invitation, so I guess I have to go along with it. I don't want his regiment storming the hotel looking for you at 8:30 tonight."

"Sweet of you, Spur," Francine said. "Don't you know women always swoon over military men?"

"Even this one?"

"He's a Don, he's a colonel, and he must be rich," Francine said with a grin. "What's wrong with that?"

The opera was fair. The colonel came with only one attendant, and the five of them were shown reserved seats in the front row center for the show. The piano was out of tune, but the singers were fair. Spur never did figure out what opera it was.

After the show they went back to the dining room at the hotel and all had desserts. There were bowls of the new ice cream, cream puffs dipped in chocolate, French pastries, dried fruit, a plate of four kinds of cheese and a delicate white wine. All were courtesy of the Colonel, who had ordered it beforehand, and it was spread out for them on their arrival.

"Ice cream! I love it," the princess chirped. She sat beside the colonel and Spur was glad to see both of his hands above the table.

The colonel cleared his throat so everyone would listen. "Princess, now that I know you and have been properly introduced, would this be a good time to invite you to spend the rest of your holiday at my rancho?"

"No, Colonel, it wouldn't be a good time to ask," Francine said. "You can understand how I must protect her. You have your own trouble with young girls clamoring for your attention, no?"

He nodded but frowned. "I must go on a trip into the country tomorrow to look at livestock. Perhaps tomorrow night I can see you again?"

"Perhaps, Colonel. Why don't we decide that tomorrow night?"

They talked for another half hour, then the princess stood and the men leaped to their feet.

"I really have had a full day and must retire," she said. Francine was beside her. They nodded at the men. The Colonel bowed and the women left the dining room and went up the stairs. Spur said good-bye to the Colonel and followed them.

Spur caught them before they went into their rooms.

"Alexandria, what was that all about? You're actually thinking of seeing that phoney again?"

"Yes, I thought he was charming. Of course he's not rich enough for me to marry, but it might be amusing to toy with him for a while."

"Begging your pardon, Alexandria, but Colonel Fortuna doesn't look like the kind of man who you can toy with. What he wants, he wants, and usually he takes. Be extremely careful dealing with him. Let's talk over anything you decide to do tomorrow night."

"If you say so, Spur McCoy." She smiled looking him up and down. "He's not as tall or as well muscled as you are, did you realize that?"

Spur frowned and before his embarrassment faded, the women had laughed lightly and hurried into their rooms.

Spur went to his room. It was the one right beside the Princess. He heard her moving around in it for a time, then it quieted down. She was in bed, he hoped, and sleeping. He needed to have a long serious talk with Francine tomorrow about protecting the princess. The Colonel was used to being obeyed. He'd put on a big show of modesty and obedience and subservience today, but Spur knew that a colonel was always a colonel. He commanded and the troopers obeyed.

In his room, Spur made a list of things they had talked about doing the next day. There was a mine not far out of town. It was worked out, but he had arranged for a tour of the mine. That would start about ten the next morning, giving them plenty of time to get there.

The man said the tour would take two hours, and would not involve any deep shafts, just a level or two down. That was good. Spur didn't want anything to go wrong in a mine tunnel with the princess along.

Dinner and then they had the afternoon. The Princess might want to gamble again. She was two hundred and eighty dollars ahead. He knew she would enjoy it. She must do a lot of gambling on the tables at the casinos in Mantuco. It was world famous for its roulette wheel.

He walked over and stared out the window. It was about midnight and Denver was still rolling along at full throttle. He didn't know when the town slept. He decided it was time for him to get some sleep.

Someone walked by in the hall outside, but they kept going. He pulled off his boots. It should be a quiet night.

The next morning Spur awoke at 6:30 as usual and checked the sky. It would be a bright clear day again. He shaved, washed and put on some clean clothes with a soft gray leather vest and knocked on Francine's door. She mumbled something. A moment later she came to the door.

She squinted at him from one eye. "You up already?"

"I'm a morning, raring to go kind of person. Is the princess awake yet?"

"Haven't heard a thing. Want me to check?"

"Yes, you still have a key?"

Francine put on a robe and waved the key at him, then opened the lock and knocked on the door. There was no response. She opened the panel and looked inside. Then she flung the door open and ran into the room.

Spur followed her.

The princess was not there.

Spur saw the note pinned to the bed which had not been slept in.

"Don't try to find me. I'm going with Colonel Fortuna. Give my regards to Mantuco. Love, Alex."

"Oh, damn!" Spur whispered and ran out the door and down the hall. He had to find her and she already had a seven hour head start!

Chapter 13

Spur McCoy charged to the front desk of the fancy Denver hotel. The clerk looked up with half closed eyes.

"Wake up, damn you! Have you been on duty all night?"

"Y. . . . yes . . . Yes sir."

"The Spaniard, the Colonel. Was he registered here?"

"Yes sir."

"Is he still here?"

"No, sir. He checked out just before midnight. It was a sudden change in plans."

"I bet! Did he say where he was going?"

"I spoke with his second in command who paid the bill. He said nothing about plans."

Spur paused a moment. "Did he have his own horses here? Did he ask you to rent horses for him?"

"Oh, they all had their own mounts, some with fancy silver saddles. I saw them one day."

"Kept them at which stable?"

"The closest one, Armitage Livery, two blocks down one block over."

Spur ran for the front door, blasted through it and charged down the street. The stable was busy when he ran up.

"Where's the night man?" he asked a stable boy. "Where is the man who was on duty at midnight?"

"Huh? Last night? That'd be Charley. He's in the office yet."

Spur ran to the sign that said office and pushed open the door. A small man with a round face and wire framed half glasses perched on the end of his nose looked up from a set of books.

"Yes sir?"

"Last night Colonel Fortuna picked up his stock here. He say where he was heading?"

"Not my business. I just took his money and gave him his an. . . ."

The man stopped when Spur's .44 muzzle pushed upward into the soft flesh under the man's chin. He lifted out of the chair to reduce the pressure on his sensitive flesh.

"Damn! What you doing?"

"Where was he headed? You must have heard something. He must have given some excuse for getting his horses out so late."

"Man said they were leaving unexpectedly. Bought a new mount and saddle and gear. Not much said really. Just something about heading to the Bar K to check out the brood stock he bought the day before."

"Where is the Bar K?" Spur asked, the muzzle pushing a little harder under the man's chin.

"Bar K . . . south about five miles, then to the west two or three miles. Only ranch out in that area. Big devil. Now get that iron out of my jaw."

Spur pulled the weapon down. "You telling me the truth?"

"Every damn word of it. I don't want to get my brains spread all over the ceiling."

"Better be. Man kidnapped a woman. He's in a hell of a big hassle. I need a horse and saddle, a canteen and a repeating rifle, a Spencer if you have one. I need it yesterday, so get moving. Rent the rigs. Cash up front."

Ten minutes later, Spur rode out of Denver to the south. He picked up the south trail toward the village of Colorado Springs. He kicked the mare into a trot and settled her down to six miles an hour. The sun was up. It would be a hot day. It would get hotter the closer he came to Colonel Fortuna.

At the end of an hour he saw the main trail swing slightly east and a turn off to the right marked the Bar K Ranch. He swung that way and was on a slight hill a half hour later looking down at a gentle sloping valley and a sea of cattle, with ranch buildings a mile ahead. No finesse needed. He'd just ride in and find out where the Colonel was.

There were no range guards as he rode up to the outfit. He liked that, which meant there had been no big trouble in the area lately.

He saw some hands at the corral. They waved. He rode toward the ranch house and a tall, thin cowboy with a two day growth of beard came out and waited for him.

"Howdy. I'm Spur McCoy and I need to find that Colonel guy, Colonel Fortuna, a Spanish gent."

"Hello. I'm Johnson. Own this spread. Far as the colonel goes, you missed him by about eight hours or so. He came storming in here last night and said he had to pick up the animals he bought and move them out. Bad news from home he said and he had to get high tailing it."

"You got him moving?"

"Best we could. He bought two hundred head of brood cows and twenty new bulls and headed them out. Then critters don't like to make much of a move at night, but his hands kept them walking. Most of the stock was in the south pasture, about five miles due south of here and a mile or two west. I can have a hand lead you down there so you can pick up their trail. Hard to hide that many cow tracks."

"Be obliged."

"Say, you had any breakfast yet? Cook's got some still cooking, you want a plate."

Spur could smell the bacon and biscuits and home fried potatoes and eggs. The coffee was what got him. He took off 20 minutes and fed his belly and thanked the man and rode out with a hand who looked about 18.

Spur picked up the cattle trail where it started, thanked the cowboy and moved west. The trail ran straight and true for two miles, then slanted to the north where it would angle for a pass that Spur could see in the distance. He wondered if this man knew what he was doing trying to drive a herd of cattle all the way to California. He didn't know if it had been done much. Getting over the Rocky Mountains was the problem.

With the cattle, the Colonel couldn't possibly make more than twelve to fifteen miles a day. Brood cows would be especially slow, taking their time, moving three miles an hour if they were lucky, and wanting to stop at every bit of water they came to. A twelve hour day might get them eighteen miles.

Now that the trail was warm again, Spur let his horse walk and worked on just what he'd do once he got to the herd. He didn't have the fire power to move in on even those five men. The Colonel might have hired another half dozen to help drive the valuable animals to their new range.

So he would be outmanned as well.

Night. He'd have to come at them after dark, check out the situation, and then get the girl and her horse and get away before they knew it. Might be good to take care of the horses at the same time.

He planned as he rode along. Too bad he didn't think in time to get some sticks of dynamite to bring along. It was easy to transport, fairly stable, and would play hob with a remuda in the dark.

By noon he hadn't seen any sign of the herd. The tracks were still moving in a line straight ahead. It was a track as wide as a house and dug into the soft places across the high valley. He hoped that he'd catch them before they hit the mountains.

Then he remembered how easy it was to misjudge distance when it came to the mountains. They might look six or eight miles away but in reality they were 50 miles away through the blue haze.

He found where the drovers had stopped for a meal. Breakfast or dinner, he couldn't figure. The cook back at the ranch had made Spur six big roast beef sandwiches. Cook told him he never did like that Spanish guy.

Spur ate a sandwich while he rode when the sun reached the top of its journey. The trail led up a small rise, then went over a low ridge. When Spur topped the ridge he looked ahead and could see the smudge of a dust cloud ahead kicked up by more than a thousand hooves.

He figured they were four miles ahead of him. He found a small tree and tied his mount and finished the sandwich and took a long pull from his canteen. He didn't want anybody to see him. The Colonel might have enough sense to put out a rear guard the way he would when he was in the army.

He couldn't help but wonder how the princess had fared over the night. They were traveling so there was a good chance the Colonel couldn't have put his hands on her. But you could never tell.

It wouldn't get dark until about eight o'clock. That meant he had some time to kill. He stretched out on the ground, checked for snakes, then put his head on a rock and closed his eyes.

Sometime later, he wasn't sure just how long, Spur heard something and opened his eyes without moving. He stared into the muzzle of a rifle six feet away.

"No move, gringo, or you dead," a heavily accented voice said.

"Yeah? Why would that be? This your private range or something? I'm going to sit up. You think you have to shoot me, you go right ahead. I'm plump cramped up this way."

"Okay, easy."

Spur edged upward, kept his hand away from his gun. He knew he couldn't use the revolver. Not if he wanted to slip up on the trail drive. He twisted his neck to get the kink out of it and then watched the Mexican cowboy with the rifle. He wasn't one of the fancy red coated Spaniards.

"Now, maybe you'll tell me what the hell's going on here. Why the rifle? Am I a threat to you or something."

"You follow the trail."

"Hell yes. Back at the Bar K ranch they told me you might take on another hand. Hey, I'm a damn good cowboy. I can use the work. Besides, I want to get to Californi and this might be my best bet. Ain't got a thin dime to my name."

"Yeah?"

"True. Been riding the grub line trail. Got breakfast back there from that cook with the two front teeth missing. Damn but he cooks up a good batch of *huevos*, right?"

The man with the rifle relaxed a little. He put the rifle down and motioned to the trail. "Why you wait here?"

"Way I look at it, if I go down now and hire on, I'll have to work the rest of the day. Probably get night herding duty as well. But If I wait until they bed the herd down for the night, I won't have to work on the trail today."

The Mexican laughed. "You one lazy gringo."

Spur laughed as well. "Didn't know there were any other kind."

They both laughed. Spur watched him. "How far you supposed to ride back here as rear guard?"

"Colonel say three, four miles. I see you two miles back, wait up in the rocks. You come, stop, watch, then take nap."

"About the size of it. What do you want me to do, go on down now, or should we wait until closer to bedding down time?"

"Maybe better go down now. Colonel is spooky. Like he afraid someone don't like him."

"I had a colonel in the army for a while. Damn sure nobody on the fort liked him. I didn't like him so much I went on a patrol all by myself and never went back to playing soldier at all."

"You vamoose?"

"Sure as hell did." They both laughed again. The Mexican sat down an and Spur stood and stretched. He turned and a moment later, Spur brought his six-gun out of leather and slapped the barrel down hard on the Mexican cowboy's head. He collapsed without a sound.

Spur tied him up hand and foot and then stared at him. This was a complication. The colonel would expect his rear guard to come in and report, but when? Sometime around dark. That cut down his time for the operation. He was hoping he could wait until about midnight. Now it would have to be quickly after dark.

He had to get a reading on the camp they made before he could decide how to do the rescue. If he left the rear guard here afoot and without his boots, it would take him a couple of hours to catch up with the herd.

The Colonel was about four miles ahead now. It was getting on toward three o'clock. They would have to bed down the brood cows soon after four. Another three miles. That put them seven miles out. The Mexican man would take two hours to get the seven miles, if his feet held out.

Another hour to wait. He wanted to take one more nap but he didn't risk it.

Instead he ate another of the roast beef sandwiches. The Mexican came awake swearing.

"Lying gringo!"

"You had the rifle. It was your choice to believe me or not. Don't worry. I'm not going to kill you.

Fact is if you're hungry, I have a roast beef sandwich. Won't be much good tomorrow. You want it?"

The Mexican nodded. Spur put it in the white paper wrapping beside the cowboy. "What's your name?"

"Alhandro."

"Listen, Alhandro. I have no fight with you. You're just doing your job. I do have a problem with the Colonel. I'll untie your hands if you promise not to try to get away or jump me. All right?"

"*Si.*"

Spur cut the rawhide from around his wrists and handed him the sandwich. "When you finish eating that, I want you to take off your boots."

"No boots?"

"You'll walk slower that way, but you'll get there. Where is your horse?"

Alhandro pointed up a narrow split of a canyon.

Two hours before dark, Spur rode up to the rocks, found the rear guard's horse and trailed him on a lead line from his saddle. Then he started riding toward the herd. They had bedded it down two hours before, and now he could see the camp fire smoke as the supper cooked. He was six miles from them, and it would be fully dark by the time he got there.

He needed a little more advantage than that. He swung off the trail and rode along the side of a gentle slope that worked upward into a ridge. Spur lifted the mare to a lope and kept her at it for a mile, then eased off. He needed to get to where he could see the layout of the camp before dark. Coming up along the ridge might put him in some shadows early.

An hour and a half later he lay on a small rise less than a hundred yards from the herd and camp and studied it. Quickly he saw what he needed to know. The remuda of some forty horses had been rope corralled with pickets this side of the herd. There were two tents. One a large one, the other smaller. He watched the smaller one and soon saw a woman step out. She had on pants, and a shirt, and a cowboy hat. She had to be Alexandria.

She went to the chuck wagon, got some food and sat on the ground to eat. Now she was seeing the real West.

The colonel evidently had his food brought to him in the tent. When Alexandria was done with her meal, she left the tin plate on the ground and went back to the tent.

Spur saw no interior guards. There were two men riding herd on the cattle. The rest of the men sat around the fire, or worked on their gear and spread out blankets. He counted eleven men all together.

The former soldiers held to one side and didn't mix with the others he guessed were Mexicans.

A half hour later it was dark. Spur made sure his horse and the rear guard's mount were tied securely; then he worked his way down the dark slope toward the tent where the princess must be. He had not seen her come out of the tent, nor had he seen anyone go into her tent before it grew dark. Spur couldn't even say for sure if the Colonel was with the group below.

He came to within ten yards of the back of the tent, when a Mexican walked straight toward him, turned and urinated into the ground, then went back to the fire.

Spur waited five minutes, then worked ahead again. He came to the back of the small tent. What kind of a reception would he get? He might have to gag the princess to get her out of there quietly. He held his neckerchief in his hand and with his right, he lifted the six-inch knife from his boot. He made a small hole with the point and looked inside the tent. He saw that there was a light on. He enlarged the hole more and saw the woman.

Yes, she was Alexandria!

He widened the hole, then quietly cut a straight slit two feet high down the back of the tent. He pushed his head and shoulders through without a sound, then surged on into the tent and just as Alexandria turned to look at him, he put his hand over her mouth. Her eyes were terrified for a moment, then she must have recognized him. She relaxed in his arms.

"I've come to take you back with me. Do you understand?"

She nodded.

"You have to promise not to scream if I let go of you. Promise?"

Again she nodded.

"Do you want to come back with me?"

Her head bobbed up and down. Slowly, he let his fingers come away from her mouth.

"I'm so glad that you came!" she whispered. "I've been trying to figure out how to get out of here all day. He's such a brute. He wasn't nice at all. He ripped my clothes off and took me like I was a whore. I hate him!"

"Good. Now. We have to get out of here. Will he come and check on you?"

"No, not unless he wants me again."

"Is the flap of your tent tied securely inside?"

191

"You bet!"

"Good. I'll slip out the back, and you come right behind me. Leave the light on, so they'll think you're still here. We'll go straight up the rise and over a small ridge. It's dark enough nobody should see us."

She nodded. "I'm so sorry I ran away like a school girl. I'll be good now, honest."

"The problem now is that we need to get up to that ridge without anyone seeing us. Next I want to spook their horses so they can't just saddle up and chase us down. We don't know how big a start we might have."

She kissed him hard on the lips. Her arms held him tight.

He unwound them. "Yes, later. First we have to get away from here." He went out the slit in the back of the tent. She was right behind him. He walked into the darkness with her two steps to the rear. No one saw them in the darkness as they went to the ridge and scurried over it.

"We're away!" She whispered.

"Yes, but we need those horses to run away." He told her quickly what he was going to do. Then he lifted her into the saddle on the rear guard's horse and told her what to do.

A moment later he was gone again, on foot working downhill. He came to the rope corral and cut the rope in two places. Slowly he worked in among the horses, and pushed and shoved and nudged them out the opening. They wandered away from the camp to the south. He found no saddled horses in the group. He found a likely looking mount and caught her head. He looped his belt around the horse's upper jaw and cinched it tight on the buckle.

Then he vaulted onto the mount's back and herded the rest of the horses out of the remuda. He kicked his horse in the flanks and raced the other horses forward.

"Hey, what's happening with the horses?" someone called. Spur took out his six-gun and fired five times into the air behind the now spooked mounts. They galloped south as fast as they could run.

He angled upward and over the ridge, saw Alexandria waiting for him. He slid off the barebacked horse and quickly mounted his rented nag.

"Come on, it's every horse for itself now. Let's ride. Stay close to me. There'll be about fifty other horses out there."

Most of the horses ran south. They cut to the west, tracing the trail that had brought the animals this far east.

Both rode easily. They galloped the first quarter of a mile. Spur hadn't even thought to ask if the princess could ride. She could. After a quarter of a mile they dropped to a canter. Behind and to the south they heard men shouting. Someone fired a rifle, but no lead came close to them.

It would take the colonel's cowboys all night and half of tomorrow to catch enough of the horses so they could get saddles on them and catch the rest of the horses. The cattle wouldn't move at all tomorrow.

Spur hoped it would give him and Alex time to get away. He hated using his six-gun to spook the horses, but he was afraid they might stop running a hundred yards away. The Colonel's men would discover the rope cut or the princess gone and they would have a lot of horses with which to give chase.

Now the dice had been rolled. They would see how it turned out. He reloaded his six-gun as they rode. He hadn't needed the long gun, at least not yet. That would be for defense if some cowhands chased them tomorrow.

After what Spur guessed was three miles, they eased up on the horses and let them walk east and north. By cutting across they angle they could save several miles.

Alexandria looked at Spur and reached out and touched his shoulder. "I . . . I don't know how to thank you. I did another stupid thing and you rescued me . . . again. I guess I'm just not very grown up yet. Francine is always scolding me about it. I've been held down for so long, the regimen has been so strict . . . I know that's not an excuse."

She touched him again. "Stop, Spur McCoy. If I don't kiss you this minute, I'm going to explode." He stopped and leaned down and they kissed and he stroked her back and she whimpered.

"I know there's not time now, but sometime soon," she said.

Spur nodded and kicked the horses into motion again angling northeast by the stars.

He stopped and motioned for her to be quiet. There were only the prairie sounds. A few birds, some crickets, the scream of a hawk. He could hear no signs of pursuit. Now and again he heard a rifle shot far, far to the rear. The Colonel must still be trying to gather in his horses. Good.

They rode for another hour at a gentle lope and then walked the horses. Somewhere in the distance to the left they saw a few lights, and figured they were the lights from the Bar K ranch. Spur came to a small stream and let the horses drink.

"You want to rest a few minutes?" he asked Alexandria.

She nodded in the soft moonlight and he helped her down. Spur knew she must be tired and sore from riding. It might have been a long time since she'd ridden this far. Still, it would be worth it all if the plan worked.

He and Alexandria sat on the ground and she at once moved over and pulled his arms around her.

"Just hold me tight for a while, all right?"

He did. He heard her catch her breath as if it was the last of a sob, and he looked down but couldn't see any tears.

"I'm sorry," she said. It was a tiny whisper that he almost didn't hear.

"Good," he said. "Francine is going to chew your ears off when we get back to the hotel."

"She should," Alexandria said. "It was a stupid, juvenile, ridiculous thing to do."

Five minutes later, Spur helped her mount the horse again and he eased onto his mount and they moved forward.

It took them another two hours to get to town. They walked the horses all the rest of the way. At last Spur saw the lights to the right and they rode in and put the horses away in the livery.

When they got to the hotel, Spur saw that it was only a little after midnight. He woke up Francine and she flew into Alexandria's arms and the two vanished into Francine's room. Spur wanted a bath to soak away his aches, but he knew it would have to wait until tomorrow. He pushed the dresser in front of the window in his room, set a chair back under the door handle, and fell on his bed. It was all he could do to get his boots off before he slept.

Chapter 14

Spur slept in until nearly eight the next morning. He knocked on Francine's door, but no one answered. She was still asleep or maybe had stayed with the princess for the night. It might take Alexandria a day to recover from her trek into the Colorado outback.

Spur stretched his aching muscles. He hadn't been on a horse that long for some time. He imagined how the princess must feel. Best thing to get him moving was three cups of coffee and a breakfast and a half.

The cafe across the street and four doors down took care of those wants. Now as his body moderated a little, his mind took over and he began to figure out what to do next. Did the assassins get to Denver? Would they even know where the princess was heading?

Wouldn't hurt to check in with the local lawman. He found the courthouse and the sheriff's office. The sheriff himself was there and Spur got to see him in his fancy office with a big polished desk. The cherry wood desk meant that Denver had grown up to the point where the sheriff's office was political and legal more than that of a work-a-day lawman. He'd hire the lawmen he needed.

Sheriff Denton waved Spur to a chair and offered him a cigar. "You the gent who's squiring a princess around my town?"

Spur frowned. "Depends how many princesses you have running loose. My name is Spur McCoy, I'm with the Federal Government's Secret Service." Spur handed him the identification card that had been so handy lately.

The sheriff stared at it. He looked up and a spot of sweat showed on his forehead.

"President's signature and all," he said softly. "I'll be snaked. I got a letter from the State Department in Washington D.C. telling me you would be stopping by here and to offer you any help I might be able to. You want about six of our county officers to escort this princess around?"

"Fact is that's exactly what I don't want, Sheriff Denton. We're here keeping a low profile. We don't want to show on the ridge line and get shot at. There have been three attempts on the life of the princess so far. All have missed, but her associate was severely wounded and sent back to Washington."

"The varmints still after her?"

"Near as I can tell. We left them back in Kansas, but they're probably here in town somewhere. There are still two of them left that we know about, a small woman, about 5-2 or so, and a man near to six feet. Both are armed."

"If them skunks show up here, my boys'll shoot their heads off."

"First we have to identify them, Sheriff. I just wanted to stop by and tell you that we're here and we don't need any special treatment. The princess wants to live the way the average American does out here and learn as much about our country as she can. She speaks fluent English."

"Good, that helps. You taking her on some tours?"

"Yes. We had a mine tour set for yesterday, but we weren't able to get there. We'll try that tomorrow. Now, I better arrange some more things for the princess to do so she doesn't get bored."

"How long you be here, McCoy?"

"Another two days, maybe three. I'll send you a note when we move out. We'll be heading up the tracks to Cheyenne." They shook hands and Spur walked out.

On a hunch, he went back to the hotel and found both ladies up and ready to go on the mine tour.

"Really, Alexandria? You want to go out there after your ordeal of yesterday?"

"It wasn't all that bad, but I am sore from riding a horse so much. Today we'll be in a buggy, right?"

Spur reversed his thinking, rounded up a buggy and by ten o'clock they were rolling westward toward the mountains. Denver isn't in the Rocky Mountains. It sits between the edge of the great sweep of the rising plains that form a high plateau to the east and the mountains to the west.

It took them three hours to ride to the small valley that opened off a two mile drive up a creek. The lush growth of the mountains came right down to the road. The mine had been a silver lode at one time, but it was worked out and now the owner worked the silver himself and made a few dollars giving tours along the dimly lighted tunnel and into some of the cross tunnels and drifts.

They were a day late getting there but the owner waved off Spur's apology.

"Don't get a lot of folks who want to walk around in a dusty old mine," the miner said. His name was Horst Zedicher. He motioned around the site.

"This used to be my mine, well still is, but it used to be a real working silver mine. Feller I know says a man has to own a gold mine so he can afford to have a silver mine. Silver is tougher to mine, more complicated to crush and then get the silver out of the ore.

"Worked this mine for twelve years." He picked up a piece of dry looking bluish muddy dirt. "For a long time we threw this stuff away when we were gold mining. Then somebody had it analyzed and they found it was a lot richer in silver than the ore we were trying to get in gold. So we switched."

"This mine is safe. Ain't never been a cave-in here and no chance that anything can go wrong. Just me and my helper, Old Ruef, are here, but we get by.

"Now, understand you folks want to walk down some tunnels and such. Right over there is the main tunnel for Zedicher Mine number one. Never was more than one, but it sounds good that way. Right near the front we'll each pick up a miner's lantern. Not much different from a regular lantern except they have a reflecting lens to concentrate the coal oil light into one direction. Surprised how much brighter that makes it.

"Let's move along. Right down this way."

"I'll bring up the rear in case we have any sprained ankles or such," Spur said. The old miner nodded.

At the mouth of the tunnel, they saw a variety of tools. The miner picked up each one and talked about it and told what each was used for. The most interesting was the twist drill.

"This is really just an iron bar with some teeth machined in the end of it. One man holds it against the rock or the ore, and another man behind him slams the back end with a ten pound sledge hammer. As soon as it gets hit twice, the man holding the drill turns it, so the teeth will bite into a different part of the rock or ore. By turning it a quarter of a turn every so often, the drill actually pounds or drills a hole into the rock. Then we can use a stick of dynamite and blast a big section of the silver-laden ore out of the end of the tunnel."

"Looks like a lot of work," Alexandria said.

"Indeed it is," Zedicher agreed. "More work than most men want to do if they don't get paid for it. Lots of work and a little danger. The danger comes when the vein of ore goes down. That means you have to sink a shaft straight down in the mountain.

"Go down ten, twelve, fifteen feet and then dig a new tunnel over where the vein vanished, and hope you can find it again. I've seen some veins that run straight down into the mountain. The shaft becomes the ore producer. Don't happen too often. Usual it's on a slant where the mountains got pushed up about a hundred million years ago or so.

"Okay, now we'll walk down number one tunnel here. It's about like two long blocks in Denver.

201

Anybody have trouble walking?"

Nobody spoke up. Zedicher lit the four lanterns and handed one to each of them. "So, right down this way. We'll go about fifty feet and then I'll show you a drift and a room."

Spur moved along behind the women. The tunnel was high enough for him to stand straight and another foot over his head. There were no other lights than the ones they carried. Soon they left the light from the entrance and the darkness closed in around them.

"Don't worry about snakes," Zedicher said. "We have few in here at any time. If one does shows up it usually gets out of the way soon as it hears us coming."

"Wish you hadn't talked about snakes," Francine said. "Not my favorite kind of pet."

They stopped and Zedicher pointed to the left. "Now in here we have a little short tunnel we call a drift. We dig those every so often just to see if there's any ore in there worth while. Come into this drift, but watch your head, it isn't quite as high here."

They went through a low place and then the tunnel expanded into open space.

"This is what we call a room," Zedicher said. "In here they found good ore, so they followed it wherever it went and it went up. We took out a good bunch of rich ore from this room. It was one of the first ones we found and we were really excited about it. The top of the room is up there nearly twenty feet."

"How did you get the ore out?" the princess asked.

"Lots of mines use little rail cars on tracks. I couldn't afford that so I used wide rimmed wheeled carts. Had a donkey pull two at a time out of the tunnel. You can do that as long as it's all on one level."

They went back to the darkness of the main tunnel and walked down another 100 feet. Zedicher came to another room on the other side of the main tunnel.

"This is the dining room. After we dug this one out, the men left their lunch pails and coats or whatever here. Noon time we had our dinner here. We can sit down and rest a bit if you want to. I'm afraid the benches are a mite dusty."

From somewhere out toward the entrance to the tunnel they heard what seemed to be a laugh.

"What was that?" Zedicher asked. "My helper ain't here today."

"I better go check," Spur said. He took his lantern in his left hand and drew his hogleg in his right and ran down the tunnel toward the entrance.

"Die! Die! Die!" a woman's voice screamed from the entrance.

Spur put a shot down the tunnel aiming it at the far speck of light. He had no idea if it would reach the light or not.

When the roaring of the shot inside the cave died down, Spur heard the woman's laugh again.

"Princess. It's all your fault, you and the jailers at Mantuco. They killed my brother, and now you're going to die to avenge his death. Too bad about the rest of you."

Spur could hear it all now clearly. He raced forward. The tunnel had all the makings of a trap, a deadly trap. A hundred angry strides later he was close enough to the entrance to see someone moving. He fired his six-gun again and saw the person drop and move sideways.

"Won't do no good, McCoy. I'm going to seal up this tunnel for good. You won't die for hours yet. But you'll die!"

A hand gun fired from the entrance and Spur heard the lead nicking the rocks along the top of the tunnel. He fired twice more, then reloaded and crept forward. He was still fifty feet from the entrance when the whole end of the tunnel vanished in a gigantic explosion, blasting rocks and dust and sand toward him like sandpaper. He fell away from the blast and covered his head.

The blast loosened rocks over him and a few fell, but missed him. The blast also blew out his lantern. It took what seemed like several seconds for the surge of air and dust to storm past him, then in the partial vacuum it created near the entrance to the tunnel, the dust and sand were sucked back the other way.

He sat up and felt around until he found the lantern. From his pocket he took a plug of waxed matches, tore off one and lit the lantern.

He could see no light at all toward the front of the tunnel. He ran that way now using the light, aware that here and there, there were large rock falls. When he got as far as he could go he figured out that there must be fifteen or twenty feet of rocks blocking the entrance from the floor to the top of the tunnel. They wouldn't dig out that way.

He turned and hurried toward the ladies. They didn't know what had happened to him. He found them trying to light the lanterns which had been blown out.

"Where's Zedicher?"

"He was right near us when the explosion went off, then we didn't hear from him," Francine said. "We've tried calling him but he doesn't answer."

Spur caught the barely suppressed panic in her voice. He took her hands and squeezed them.

"Hey, we've going to be just fine. Nothing to worry about. There must be two or three entrances to a mine like this." He lit the other two lanterns and checked the amount of coal oil. He changed his mind and blew out both of them.

"We better make do with one lantern for a while. Let me find Zedicher."

Spur swept the lantern ahead of him as he moved a few more feet into the tunnel. He saw what he was afraid he would. There had been a sizeable rock fall from the ceiling. Zedicher's feet stuck out from under it and he wasn't moving.

Spur put down the lantern and pulled away rocks and dirt. Nobody could help Zedicher. Two large rocks had battered his face and head.

Spur picked up the lantern and went back to the women.

"You were right. Mr. Zedicher is over there under a couple of tons of rock. He can't help us any. What we need to do is find some other way out of here. We're going to stay together, so don't worry about that. Each of you hang onto those lanterns. Wasn't this the dinning room?"

They nodded in the darkness. "Let's see if we can find anything we can use, torches, more lanterns, rope. We might have a use for some rope if we can find any."

They checked every corner of the dug out room, but there was nothing there except one shovel that might be useful.

"Fine, now we move on into this tunnel and see where it goes. I've heard of some of these that follow a vein of ore and it turns around and comes right back out of the mountain."

They moved past the rock fall and found the tunnel fairly clear beyond it.

"Princess, how are you doing?"

"I'm not afraid of tunnels or closed places, if that's your worry. I don't like this darkness or our situation, but I have confidence that you'll help us find a way out of here."

"Good. Now let's keep moving ahead." They came to a half dozen more drifts and some rooms and one branch tunnel that went for only 50 feet before it ended. They went back and kept on the main tunnel.

Spur stopped. "Do you feel anything?"

Francine shook her head. "Not me."

Alexandria nodded. "Yes, a slight movement of air, a light breeze almost!"

"Right and that means there has to be an opening somewhere ahead. Let's keep going forward."

Spur lit another lantern and let Francine carry it. She sounded a lot more secure with a light of her own. They covered another 100 feet and Spur stopped again.

"Yes, I can feel it now," Francine said, her voice just a level below frantic.

"We're making progress," Spur said. "If air can get out of here, then we can get out, too."

The tunnel made a sharp left turn and seemed to be turning back on itself a little.

"The air movement is getting stronger, it can't be far now."

Another 50 feet. Spur stopped and tried, but he couldn't feel any air movement. Had they passed it? Should they go back? Somehow that didn't seem to be the thing to do. Then a rush of air hit him and he grinned.

"Right this way, I think we're getting close."

They rounded a small curve in the tunnel and ahead they could see light. A moment later a shaft of sunlight streamed down from overhead.

They were in a natural cavern. The sides of the cavern went up 40 or 50 feet to an opening. Spur couldn't be sure how big the opening was, but it had to be big enough for him to get through.

Tears slipped down Francine's cheeks. She moved to Spur and hugged him. Then Alexandria joined them in a three-way hug.

"I was getting worried," Alexandria said. "Now look what you've found for us."

Spur checked the sides of the cavern. It would be easy going up the sides for the first 30 feet. Then it would be tougher, maybe impossible. He checked another way and a moment later found what could only be ancient steps cut in the rock down the far side. They came all the way to the floor and as far as he could see, went right to the top and the burst of sunlight.

He pointed and Alexandria nodded. "Yes, looks like some Indian friends have done us a favor."

Spur went and looked at the steps. They were old. He had no idea what ancient people had cut the steps down from the top. It may have been a burial cave or one for living in the winter or for some ceremonial.

"Stand tight, you two. I'm going to see if those steps really do go all the way to the top."

He put his boots on the first stone steps cut in the rock and began moving upward. There were not only steps but hand holds fashioned along part of the sides as well. In a few moments he was 30 feet up the side of the wall and about half way around. The steps had been cut in a circular pattern so the ascent could be gradual.

Five minutes later he pushed his head out a three foot opening in the top shrouded by grasses and some shrubs.

He lifted out and looked down.

"Hey, palefaces down there. It's easy. Just take one step at a time and don't look down.

"Can't do it," Francine said. "I . . . I can't stand high places."

Spur lifted his brows. He edged into the hole, found the first step and began going down the cut steps. It was much easier coming up.

When he got to the ground, he took Alexandria to the steps and showed her how to work her way up. "Can you do it?"

"Spur McCoy, you don't even need to ask. I can do anything." She grinned, kissed him on the lips and began to move slowly but safely up the wall.

"Take it easy, princess. Slow down just a little. This isn't a race. Make sure of every step."

A short time later Alexandria lifted out the opening. She looked down, "Next!" she called.

Spur had been talking to Francine. "This is the only way out, young lady. I'm not going to leave you here as a sacrifice to some Indian god. I'll be right behind you, a step behind. Now let's give it a try. Don't look down. Always look upward at the next step. Come on."

The first 20 steps were easy, then the route became steeper with more space between the steps. The skirt hampered her. He should have had her take it off.

"I . . . I don't think I can go any farther."

"Why not? You're over the hardest part. From here on it's easier. Just do one step at a time. I'm right here. Neither one of us has fallen off yet, have we?"

She grinned and lifted her brows. He squeezed her hand. She took a deep breath and moved to the next step.

All went fine until they were within six or seven steps of the top. The wall was almost perpendicular here, with no margin for error.

Spur had hurried across this section himself. The Princess had made it. Francine hesitated.

"Hey, sexy lady. I promise you the wildest time in bed you've ever had tonight. But first we have to get out of here. Anything you've ever wanted to do or have done to you, tonight, my room. Deal?"

Francine giggled. Her grin came back and she took one step, then another, then two more and she was past the tough part.

Five minutes later, all three of them lay on the grass near some trees on the side of the mountain. They could see the mining buildings below. The women hugged each other like school girls.

Alexandria cautioned Francine. "Careful, you don't want to wear yourself out before that wild time you've been promised tonight."

They laughed and Spur held up his hand.

"The woman who set off that bomb might be waiting to see if we could dig our way out. Let's not make any more noise. I'll take a run down there and see if they have left. Maybe I can surprise them."

Before he went, he loaded rounds in his six-gun to replace those he had fired. Then he holstered it, nodded at the women and hurried down the slope in the heavy cover of trees and shrubs.

Twenty minutes later he stepped from in back of a tree and said hello to the women. Neither had heard or seen him come.

"Were they there?" Francine asked.

"No, only some tracks showing there had been two horses and some spilled black powder, but nothing else. At least our buggy is still there. Let's get down the hill and into town and report the old miner's death to the sheriff."

Spur helped the women into the rig and soon had it on the road back to town. He had been wondering what the two assassins would do next. What would he do in the same situation? He'd sit beside the road somewhere and wait and see if anyone got out of the mine and headed back to Denver.

As he thought about it, he realized that the princess was just as vulnerable now as she had been. A good rifle shot from ambush somewhere along this twisting road would do the job once and for all.

He asked both the women to slide down in the carriage seat a little so they would not be so easy to see.

"You're wondering if they will wait and watch the road for a while?" Francine asked.

"It did occur to me. So if were just not quite such a good target . . ."

He had only just said the words when a rifle fired and at once the slug ripped past Spur and one of the women behind him cried out in pain. Spur angled the rig off the road on the far side and into a thick stand of evergreen trees giving them cover.

One look in the back seat told the story. Francine had taken the rifle slug high in her left arm. It was bleeding all over the place. Alexandria had Francine on the floor of the carriage and ripped off part of her blouse to make a bandage. She watched Spur a second.

"Go get the devils!" she said.

Chapter 15

As soon as the rifle bullet whammed past him, Spur went into a crouch on the buggy seat and got the rig into the trees. Then he slid out the far side for more cover and ran forward and to the right. The round came from the right side of the road. They had horses and a rifle. He hadn't counted on the rifle.

He worked silently through the brush and trees until he could see the road. On the far side of the trail the brush was just as thick and he couldn't locate the form of a horse. Two must be there somewhere. Or the bushwhacker had been on foot for the shot.

Yes, on foot, then retreated past the brush to a more open space where they left the horses. He had to run across the damn road and expose himself to that rifle's fire.

He didn't stop to think about it. Don't think,

move. He took the road at his sprint speed. Six long strides and he was across and into the cover and concealment of the brush.

No shots came.

He'd guessed right. He worked through the brush and trees and could see it thinning ahead. He checked the area with a sweep of his glance. The black blobs became apparent. Two slightly to the right and farther into the clearing. He worked through the brush keeping low, came up behind a big pine tree and steadied the Colt against it.

Too damn far. A man and a woman stood on the ground next to their horses. They were talking. He sprinted through an open spot with enough brush to cover him. Then stopped behind another pine. This time when he leaned around the tree, the woman had mounted but the man had not. Thirty-five feet.

Spur held the big Colt with both hands, rested it against the pine bark and sighted in. He gave a little loft for the distance and fired, then thumbed back the hammer and got ready for the next shot.

The man was down. The woman pulled the horse away from him. Spur snapped the next shot at the woman on the horse. She must have felt the lead pass her in the air. At once she jerked the reins and the horse's head around and kicked the mount into a gallop directly away from him.

He fired the last three rounds but had no hopes of hitting her.

Slowly, Spur moved out toward the man on the ground. His horse had walked away ten feet and grazed. Spur could see both the assassin's hands. That was a bonus. He got all the way to the body and it didn't move. When he tipped the man over on his back, Spur saw why he had not moved.

The lofted .44 slug had gone a little high, drove through the man's Adam's apple, spewing blood like a river and probably knocking him unconscious. He had bled to death.

Spur threw the body over the saddle, tied the corpse's hands and feet together under the horse's belly and walked the animal back to the carriage. He tied it on a lead line behind the rig.

Francine turned her head away.

Alexandria stared at the man's face. "I don't know him. Why is he trying to kill me?"

"You didn't hear what the woman shouted in the tunnel?"

The princess shook her head.

"The assassin said that you and the guards at the prison in Mantuco had killed her brother. Does that make any sense?"

"I'll be able to check on it. We have a small prison with few prisoners. It's rare for a prisoner to die inside. I'll find out when I get home. So that's why she hates me so. A brother."

"I'm afraid so. Now she's working alone. Her three hired men are dead. I have no idea what she'll try now. She knows that we got out of her tunnel tomb."

"At least she doesn't have the rifle anymore," Spur said. "I think we can drive back to town now and have a doctor take a look at Francine's shoulder."

Francine's shoulder wound wasn't serious. The slug went on through. The doctor bandaged it and told her to have it checked in three days. Then he looked at Spur's shoulder slice from the shotgun slug and rebandaged it. He said it was healing fine.

Spur paid the man and they went on to the sheriff's office. Spur left the horse and the body, spoke with a deputy for a moment and said he'd be back later to fill out the needed papers. They went on to the hotel, in the back door and up to their rooms.

"We're moving to a different hotel," Spur said. "She must know that we're here to have followed us so easily. Please pack up everything. We'll go out the back door, into the carriage and find a hotel a good distance away."

They did. It wasn't as elaborate and the dinner menu wouldn't be so good, but Spur had about decided it was time to move out of Denver.

The morning train left at 8 o'clock for Cheyenne. They would be on it. Cheyenne would be a better town than Denver, he hoped. The assassin was coming too close.

They all had baths that afternoon after the dust storm of the tunnel. They stayed in their rooms that night. Spur went down and brought up trays with their supper on it and they ate in Francine's room.

"That wild night you promised me, Spur," Francine said. "We better postpone that for a few days."

Spur agreed. "What we need to talk about is more serious," he said. "I think it's time to wrap up the tour and head back on the first eastbound train tomorrow in Cheyenne."

"No," Alexandria said. "I haven't been hurt so far. I want it to continue."

"Princess, it might just be time for you to think about somebody else, for a change. I've put up with your antics, up to now. But remember that so far your diplomatic friend has been seriously wounded and is probably still in a hospital. Now your best friend has been shot with a rifle bullet and will have a scar on that upper arm for as long as she lives. Don't you think you're pushing the princess role a little too far?"

"Oh, damn! McCoy. I knew you were going to do this. I knew you were going to appeal to my sense of friendship for Francine and for Pierre. It's just not fair. Not fair to me. I have one chance to see your beautiful country and some crazy woman from France tries to kill me. Not fair at all."

Spur knew when he was ahead. He stood and went to the door. "You think about it, Alexandria. We'll talk more on the way to Cheyenne tomorrow. It isn't a long trip, depending how long we stop at each little town."

They said good night. Spur checked the hallway, stepped outside and went to his room and into it. He didn't think the assassin could have discovered where they had moved, but he had been surprised by her before.

Darlene Benoit lay on her cheap hotel room bed and cried. She cried for her three lost helpers. She cried for Didier, the first to die. She cried because somehow that McCoy man had found a way out of the mine tunnel. It was to have been the perfect tomb for the princess.

Slowly she sat up on the bed. They had moved from the hotel. She figured they would. For three hours she had tramped from one hotel to another, but no one would say that the three people she hunted were in their hotel. They just weren't sure. It was an impossible task.

For a long while she had considered taking the train back to New York and using what money she had left to go home. Darlene hated to admit defeat. All she needed was one lucky shot. Just one. Then she would die happy knowing that Didier had been avenged.

She got up and paced across the room to the window and looked out. It was just getting dark. What would McCoy and his ladies do tomorrow? Did he have another tour planned? A bull and bear fight? No they had been outlawed here in Denver. The opera, a play? What would be Denver to the foreigner? Darlene had always prided herself on being able to figure out people, to know what they were thinking and what they might do next.

Now she had no ideas at all. They could even head back to Kansas City and St. Louis and on to Washington, D.C.

The only other way would be to go on the small railroad spur line up to Cheyenne.

Cheyenne. A town in Wyoming. The name of a fierce Indian tribe. Yes! The sweet princess had not see a real Indian yet. She wouldn't leave this part of the country without seeing at least one Indian. That would be in Cheyenne.

Darlene smiled with a bitter determination. Yes! They would leave Denver in the morning on the train to Cheyenne. She would watch the station, but not take the same train. There was another one at noon. She would be on that. There would be no disguise that would fool McCoy this time. She was sure he would check every woman and young boy on the train tomorrow. Cheyenne was a smaller town. It would be easy to find them. Yes, in Cheyenne she would find a way to kill Princess Alexandria. She knew it.

Darlene pulled off her clothes and lay her thin body down on the bed. She liked to sleep nude. But would the dream come back? She almost didn't care. She had the answer. Soon the princess would be just one more corpse buried in the western soil. Then her father's agony and suffering would start.

Darlene would go to Mantuco and watch the royal palace and laugh at the mourning. She would spit on their mourning!

That night Darlene slept without any dreams. She was up at six, dressed and put on a hat that would disguise her, the best dress she had, and went down the street to find a place near the depot where she could watch the princess and her party get on the coaches for Cheyenne.

Back at Spur McCoy's new hotel the night before, he had prowled the street in front of the building for half an hour, then sat in the lobby watching everyone who came and left. At last he went up the stairs to the third floor and wedged his door open an inch, and moved the straight-backed chair so he could see out down the hall past the princess's door.

He sat on guard there until one o'clock, then gave it up, locked and propped the chair under the door and went to bed.

Morning came at 6:30 as usual for McCoy. He had breakfast alone in the dining room below, then checked on the ladies. They were up and ready when he knocked. The train didn't leave until 8:30 he found out, but he wanted to be there in plenty of time.

They each bought a ticket separately, and sat apart as they waited outside for the train. Spur waited closest to the princess in a nervous state of anticipation. He thought the assassin might find them there and start shooting. The train backed in at the station. He'd told the women to get on board at the first chance and sit opposite each other with one seat back turned around.

He climbed on board when they were safely on, but stayed by a window watching the platform. He saw nothing to spark any worry. McCoy moved into the next car and sat across from the two women making no indications that he knew them. There was no compartment car on this short run.

As soon as the car began to move, Spur went on a survey of the two passenger cars. Only a dozen people had boarded. This time he was certain that the small assassin wasn't on board. Not even a good disguise would have fooled him this time. There was only one small woman, and she was ugly and fat. Two young boys were on board but both had short hair and pimples.

Spur went back to his place across from Francine. She smiled at him and he winked.

The trip to Cheyenne was one long sightseeing excursion. Spur moved over with the women and pointed out some of the wonderful views of the towering Rocky Mountains, the dashing streams and the occasional deer. They spotted one brown bear loping away from the noise of the train and pushing one six month old cub with her.

A half hour before Cheyenne, Spur brought up the idea again.

"Ladies, I still think it would be the smart and proper thing for us to get off this train and go directly to a Central Pacific train heading east. Princess, have you thought about it?"

"She has, but I cast the deciding vote. I told Alex not to worry about me. I'm tough as a London bootblack. I told her that this is her one chance to see America, and she should take it. Say we're half way through. We can stay in Cheyenne for a while and then go on west into the heart of the Rocky Mountains. We haven't seen a buffalo yet and we haven't seen any Indians, and at least a half a hundred other things. We haven't even ridden on a stage coach."

Spur took a long breath before he said anything. "I know I could telegraph the Ambassador and urge him to ask you to come back. I also know that he probably wouldn't do it. I just hope he doesn't wind up getting you and maybe all of us killed before this little adventure is over."

Alexandria frowned and her face worked and she almost cried. She reached out and touched Spur's hand.

"Spur McCoy, I'll always remember you fondly. You and this trip have been the highlight of my life so far. It's going to take a lot to beat this. I pray every night that neither of you, my two good friends, will be hurt. I pray for strength to overcome my bad habits, my quick temper and my unpredictable actions at times. But what can you expect, I'm royalty, the product of a royal marriage, and I've been pampered and spoiled all my life."

McCoy chuckled. Francine laughed. "You're about the most unspoiled princess I've ever known, Alex. Absolutely the most unspoiled."

"You've known hundreds of princesses, right, Spur?"

"One."

They all laughed and were friends again. The train pulled into the station and Spur saw that their bags were taken off; then he caught a hack and it deposited them at the Cheyenne Harrington Hotel. They got rooms as usual on the second floor.

"Mr. McCoy, Francine and I have made out a list of what we want to do out here in the Wild West.

"One, we want to see some real live buffalos. We haven't seen any yet. Two, we want to see some real Indians. You've said there were some town Indians, but they are spoiled. I want to meet and talk with some of these wild redskins."

Spur held up a hand. "Now that one might not be such a good idea. These are not friendly Indians around here. We have Cheyenne and Sioux and a few Arapaho. Not the kind of folks you ask home to Sunday dinner."

"Wild, untamed savages?"

"That's a good start. If a Cheyenne warrior captured you, he could do whatever he wanted to with you. You become his property. He could make you a wife, he could make you his slave, he could sell you for two horses to another warrior. He could torture you and kill you and not a single eye brow in his village would be raised. You were property. It would be like a white man killing a horse. These Cheyenne are not nice to white women, and this is as close as I want you to come to any of them."

"You exaggerate," Alexandria said. "I've heard that they are kind and sensitive, that they live close to the land and worship Mother Earth and Father Sun."

"Oh, that they do. They also live by raiding their Indian enemies, and the white eyes, and wagon trains and settlements. They are warriors, who live to fight and kill and scalp."

"All right, I understand. Now listen to the rest of our list. We want to go on a trail drive, to ride horses and herd cows and sleep under the stars and eat at the chuck wagon."

"That might be a little hard to do, but I'll try."

"Then we really want to see Salt Lake City and the Great Salt Lake. I understand a person can't even swim in it it's so salty. Of course we want to see where the golden spike was pounded in at the meeting of the two railroads to finish the transcontinental railroad."

Spur rubbed the back of his neck. "That's quite a list. You did write it down, didn't you?"

Francine handed him the list. "Figured. Okay, you two can have dinner in the hotel dining room. I'll go see what I can find in good old Cheyenne."

Spur wondered if Town Charlie was still around. He had been a town Sioux who had taken to the saddle making trade. The shop was still there. Spur stepped inside and the wonderful smell of fresh cut leather captured him. He looked around and saw it was about the way he remembered it.

Some stranger stepped in from the back room.

"Yes, sir. Might I be of service to you?"

"Not unless you can tell me where Town Charlie is?"

"Just where he is might be a problem. Army ran him out of here about a year ago. Said he belonged on the reservation. They let him sell the shop. Fact is I gave him twenty dollars for it. Then the army took the twenty dollars away from him."

"You *stole* his saddle business here for twenty dollars?"

"Army said he couldn't own anything in town. So really it wasn't his to start with."

"That's not right. Town Charlie worked hard here."

"I guess. Not much to do about it now."

"One thing I can do," Spur said. When the saddle maker looked up, Spur smashed his fist into the man's chin and dropped him to the floor. The merchant looked up, angry and surprised. Spur turned and walked out of the shop.

He tried the general store and post office next.

"There any Indians out at the fort these days, the scouts?"

The postmistress nodded. "Sure, the old Colonel

221

out there keeps fifteen or twenty Arapahos, the good Indians."

They have their tipis set up the way they used to?"

"Far as I know. I ain't been out that way in six months or so."

Spur thanked the lady, bought a nickel's worth of horehound candy and went down to the livery and rented a buggy. It was slightly after two o'clock when he pulled the rig up in front of the hotel and tied the reins.

Upstairs he found the ladies all dressed and ready to go out for some sightseeing.

"Your carriage awaits, Princess," Spur said and bowed. Alex stuck out her tongue at him.

"I always wanted to do that," she said.

When they were in the buggy, Spur told them about the fort.

"So the army hires friendly Indians to help track down the renegades and the bands that haven't gone to the reservation. The Indians are Arapahos and there are usually about 20 families or so living out by the army fort. They have a small village set up there and their tipis and you can see their way of life.

"This is a close as you'll get to wild Indians. These are the real thing. Probably none of the women will speak any English. Some of the men do for their scouting work."

"Real Indians, not just some people you have dressed up like Indians?" Francine asked.

"Wait until you see them."

It was twenty minutes ride to the fort. Along a small stream that ran past the fort, there were 20 tipis set up. They were old; there were few buffalo around to get new hides from, and their men were always working with the army so they couldn't go hunt for hides.

Spur drove the buggy up within 50 feet of the end tipi and sat there.

"We'll wait and see if they come out to talk," Spur said. "It usually works. This is their home. We can't go in unless they invite us. Some of the women are touchy about this."

After ten minutes, two children came out of the flap of the nearest tipi. It was one of the newer ones. A few minutes later an Indian woman came out carrying a baby in her arms. She and the two children walked slowly toward the buggy.

The children wore only small breechclouts. They were dirty and their eyes ran with some kind of hurt. The Indian woman wore an old dress of soft buckskin. It was tattered but probably the best one she had. She was bare footed. Her hair was long and stringy, her face had a sore on one cheek. For a moment she scowled at the two white eye women. Then she looked at Spur and asked him something.

Spur caught only one word in the plains Indian lingo. It was want. What did they want. He used sign and told her they were visitors from across the big ocean and wished to visit her tipi.

The woman understood. She pushed the two children behind her and scowled. Then a moment later she said something, then signed that they could come.

"She says we can come see her home, so be diplomatic, be nice," Spur said. He helped them from the buggy. "It's customary to give the tipi owner a small gift on leaving. Any clothing you can spare?"

They walked toward the tipi. Spur saw that there

were a number of Indian men around. The army could hire only a few for each mission they had. The others waited. The closer they came to the tipi the better Spur could see that it was in worse repair than he thought. It must be freezing inside during the cold Wyoming winters. The Indian woman stooped and entered through the flap.

"Go inside and wait," Spur said. "Don't touch anything, don't sit down."

Spur had helped the two women into the tipi when a steel tipped lance trailing a row of feathers jolted into the ground a foot from his boots and blocking his entrance to the tipi.

A short, broad shouldered Arapaho warrior came up beside Spur his face flushed and angry. He jerked the lance from the ground and held it at the ready as he stood in front of his tipi.

Spur began to sweat and hoped that he could think of the right signs.

Chapter 16

Spur made the sign for friend, and looked at the Arapaho warrior again. A big grin split the redskin's face. He held out his hand in the white man's style to shake.

"Damn glad see McCoy!" the Indian said.

Spur was so surprised he gawked at the redskin. "Walking Thunder?" Spur blurted, his recognition of the man washing away his concern for his charges.

"Yes, Walking Thunder." He motioned Spur to go inside the tipi. Spur ducked under the flap and stepped in. It was the usual type of conical tipi with ten poles tied at the top and covered with the traditional buffalo skins stitched together.

The two white women were sitting on a buffalo robe near a small cooking fire, and the Indian woman had put something over the fire in an iron pot to cook. The three children they had seen before were nowhere to be seen.

The small Indian woman said something rapidly to the warrior. He only grunted. He pointed to a spot and Spur sat. The stocky Indian sat as well and reached for a white man's corncob pipe. He filled it with tobacco and lit it, then nodded at McCoy.

"Damn long time."

"Five years at least," Spur said. "I was working with the army on something, somebody selling army rifles to the Cheyenne, I think. You were a scout then up by Laramie."

Walking Thunder grunted. "More work here."

Spur pointed at the women. "I'm taking these ladies on a trip through the West. They wanted to see some real Indians. The red man doesn't come any more real than you, Walking Thunder."

"Damn betcha!" the Indian said and both he and Spur laughed.

Spur watched the women. Francine had taken off a light jacket she had been wearing and gave it to the Indian woman. A tear edged out of the Arapaho's face. She scurried around the edges of the tipi looking for something. At last she found it, a beaded head band that she presented to Francine.

At once Francine put on the headband and all three women smiled.

Alexandria had brought a shawl with her. She took it off her shoulders and folded it and presented it to the small Indian woman. Again a tear seeped out and she went and brought back another Indian headband, this one wider and more colorful. She slipped it on Alexandria's head and they all smiled and laughed.

"Women crazy," Walking Thunder said. Spur remembered the last time he had seen Walking

Thunder. They had both been in a shoot out with some gunrunners. The ten man Army patrol had been jumped by the Cheyenne and four of the gun sellers. The scout had tossed Spur a repeating rifle when his other one jammed. It had helped turn the tide of battle.

"Remember those gunrunners up at Laramie?"

"Damn bad."

"Right, but you saved my skin that day with that rifle. Remember?"

The warrior nodded. Spur unbuckled his gun belt, folded it and with his .44 in place, handed it to Walking Thunder.

"Army give Walking Thunder gun," the Indian said.

"This isn't an army gun. This is Walking Thunder's own private revolver. You can keep it and wear it or leave it home. It's yours. It's a debt I owe you. I will be most unhappy if you don't accept it."

Spur could see the gleam in the warrior's eye. The revolvers the scouts got to use were usually the oldest and worst in the armory. Many of them wouldn't work. This one would.

The warrior motioned Spur outside. They stood in the late morning sun a moment and then the Indian led the way toward a small herd of Indian ponies. Spur knew that the Indian felt honor bound to return a gift for such an expensive and desired present. They stopped at the rope corral and Walking Thunder shouted something at a young Indian boy.

The boy walked into the herd of horses and put a halter around a young pinto and brought him to the edge of the herd. He handed the rope to Walking Thunder. They moved a short ways away and Walking Thunder held out the pony's rope.

"To good friend," he said. Spur took the rope and thanked him and the two walked back toward the end tipi. Walking Thunder had the six gun strapped on, the holster flapping against his leg with every step.

Spur led the sleek little pony back to the tipi and asked Walking Thunder to bring out his wife.

The Arapaho at once scowled. "I not trade for wife, just pony," Walking Thunder said and then howled in laughter, slapping his leg as he went into the tipi. A moment later all three of the women came out.

The Indian scout said something softly to his wife and she stood behind him. He stared at Spur for ten seconds, then shrugged. "Good Friend Spur McCoy, my wife, Two Doves."

The Indian woman stepped out and nodded at Spur. He walked forward and gave the rope to her.

"Tell Two Doves that this broken-down nag was forced upon me to settle a wager. I didn't want the horse, I couldn't use him and she would be doing me a great favor if she would take this spavined and sway backed and long of tooth broken down old horse and let me be rid of it."

Walking Bear began to tell his wife what the white eye had said but at the beginning he broke down laughing. Two Doves stared at her husband for a minute, then shrugged and took the pony and tied him to the front of the tent.

"My pony," she said in accented English. Then she laughed and hurried back inside the tipi.

Walking Thunder motioned for the women to follow and the two men went into the tipi first, then Francine and Alexandria ducked inside.

"I have a hundred questions," Alexandria said to Spur. "Can we ask Walking Thunder about his wife?"

Spur looked at Walking Thunder. He nodded.

"Just one wife. Army pay low, so just one wife."

Alexandria nodded. "What do you eat?"

"Army ration to scouts, like soldiers. Scouts also hunt in mountains. Two days ago, deer. Five families ate before spoil."

"Army rations are salt pork and hardtack," Spur said. "Not appetizing but works in the field. At the fort the troopers don't eat much better."

Alexandria nodded and looked at Walking Thunder. "Clothes, does she make your clothes?"

Walking Thunder thought a minute. "Army issue," he said, pointing to his blue cavalry trooper pants and shirt. "Woman use deerskin, rabbit fur, other animal. No buffalo no more."

They talked for a half hour, with both women asking the stout Indian scout questions about the tipi itself, how they lived, what they did in the winter.

"Cut wood, army saw. Stack wood inside tipi. Push snow up on outside of tipi to keep tent warm. Plenty warm."

"If you wear lots of wool clothes and sweaters," Francine said.

Whatever had been cooking over the fire was now done, Two Doves decided. She tasted it, nodded and took the iron pot off the fire and did some cutting and them put the thick soup in three bowls and presented one to each of the white eyes.

Spur knew what was coming. He whispered to the women. "It is considered an insult in an Indian home not to eat what they serve you. You must eat all that she gives you. I'm not sure what it is but it won't harm you."

The women looked at the small crockery bowls that were Two Dove's delight. There were no spoons. Spur took his bowl and lifted it and drank some of the soup. He lowered his bowl and smiled at Two Doves.

"Do it," Spur whispered. The women lifted the bowls and tasted the soup. Francine swallowed a little, blinked and then drank down some more of it.

Alexandria shivered slightly, then forced herself to drink some of the stew.

Spur knew the routine. It did not taste good, but it was acceptable. He lifted the bowl again and drained it of the liquid, then with his fingers lifted out the pieces of meat and parts of a potato and ate them. He put the bowl down but held on to it so she would not give him anything else.

"No sharing," Spur said softly. "This is Two Dove's way of welcoming you. Drink it down, ladies."

It took the women several minutes to drink the liquid. Already Mighty Thunder and Spur were off on another wild story about when Spur had been in Laramie. It concerned a drunk sergeant and his favorite scout and a challenge to shoot a beer bottle off the scout's head.

In the rush to accommodate the challenge, somebody brought out full bottles of beer. It took the sergeant two shots to hit the beer bottle on Mighty Thunder's head. The scout was rewarded with a beer bath and the whole town broke up laughing.

When the women had finished picking out the bits of meat and potato, Two Doves took away the bowls and smiled. Alexandria had more questions for Mighty Thunder.

"Are there any buffalo around here?"

"Buffalo! No, many days' ride north maybe find a few. Hide hunters kill all buffalo."

"I'm sorry. I know that you relied on the buffalo for almost every item you used."

Spur decided it was his move. He stood. "Time for us to go. Don't want to overstay our welcome." Spur went out the tipi door first, followed by Mighty Thunder. The two white eye women came last. Two Doves stayed inside.

Spur held out his hand. "Make them treat you right here, Walking Thunder. You have a good arrangement. Get those rations and dry your own venison if you can."

"Five hunters go tomorrow to mountains, find deer. Cut up there, make jerky there. Then bring back."

"Women's work," Spur said.

Mighty Thunder gave Spur a quick smile. "Yes, but too far for women."

Spur helped the women into the buggy and Walking Thunder lifted the revolver out of the holster and put it back just to get the feel of it. He smiled.

Spur bent and tied the leather thong around the Indian's lower leg. It kept the leather from flapping and anchored it when a quick draw was needed to keep the leather from sliding upward, slowing a draw.

Spur stood and stepped into the buggy.

"Old Friend, be good to yourself. Work for the army for as long as you can. You have the best of both the Indian and the white eye way."

Walking Thunder nodded. He slapped his new six-gun and grinned as Spur whacked the long leather lines on the horse's back and the buggy rolled ahead. They drove around the fort. It

231

was not a palisaded fort, with logs sticking up all the way around it. There were few army forts made that way. This was simply a cluster of buildings arranged around a quarter mile square parade ground with a U.S. flag flying in the center.

They headed back for Cheyenne.

"How did you like the skunk soup?" Spur asked.

"What was that?" Francine asked, her eyes wide.

"That stew that Two Doves fixed for us. Yesterday it was running around with a white stripe down its black back."

Princess Alexandria giggled. "You aren't joking, Spur, are you?"

"Nope, had skunk stew before. Even tried to make it once, but missed getting the scent sack out in time."

They laughed and rode in silence for a while. "Did you notice that the men left the tipi first?" Spur asked.

"I thought it strange," Francine said.

"You wouldn't make a good Indian wife. It's a male oriented society. A warrior society, although the Arapahos weren't as warlike as most plains Indians.

"Oh, guess who takes down and moves the tipi if they have to move it?"

"The women?" Alexandria asked. "That little Two Doves does it all?"

"Correct. The women do most all of the manual work around a village. The men are the hunters and the warriors. During a move the men ride their war ponies around the outside of the village to protect it, even though the closest tribe hostile to them might be 200 miles away.

"The women take down the tipi, use the poles to

make a travois. Fold the heavy tipi cover. Pack all of the family's belongings on the cover and binds it to the travois. Then she hitches the travois up to her horse and is ready to move."

"That's not fair," Francine said.

"Of course not, but it's the Indian way. Had enough Indian culture for a while?"

"Yes, and too much skunk stew," Francine gurgled.

"The hungrier you are, the better it tastes. I've been so hungry a time or two that I ate rattlesnake meat."

"You didn't!" Francine yelped.

"Sure did. Meat is meat when you're half way starving."

Spur let the ladies off at the hotel and took the buggy back to the livery. When he got back to the hotel they were waiting for him in the lobby. He took them upstairs with him as he got the spare .44 Colt, holster and gunbelt from his suitcase and cleaned and loaded the weapon. The two watched him work over the iron with wonder.

"You treat it like it was a treasure," Alexandria said.

"Or like a mistress," Francine added.

"It can be both. More than once my life has depended on a chunk of iron like this. So I respect it, I take care of it, and I keep it handy twenty-four hours a day. Now, where were we?"

"How is that trail drive coming along?" Alexandria asked.

"Are you two dead set on doing that?"

"Right," Francine said.

"I'll go see what I can find out. Not that many trail drives around here. A few bringing in beef to ship on the railroad."

"We could ride out a couple of days, find a herd and see if we could tack on to them," the princess said. "All they'd have to do would be feed us. We might even be some help."

"You ladies take an afternoon beauty nap so I don't have to worry about you, and I'll go out to the loading pens and see who is scheduled to come in soon. Maybe I can find some trail boss who is broad minded and will accept a fifty dollar bribe." He ushered the women to their rooms, then he headed for the stock pens at the edge of town.

Spur found the car loading foreman after a few questions. The man was in his fifties, a railroader through and through. He wore dark blue white striped overalls and a big silver railroad pocket watch on a silver chain. He pushed the Central Pacific visor cap back on his head and scratched the thinking spot on top.

"Yep, should have two herds in a couple of days from now."

"Where are they coming from?" Spur asked. "I have an Easterner who wants to ride out and meet a drive and see what goes on for a couple of days."

"Guy must be plumb loco." The railroader put back on his hat. "I got the Ormley drive should be in here two days from today. That means they're about twenty miles out, or will be by bedding down time. You go straight north up the valley, you should find them. They only have about a thousand head, but that'll put up a dust cloud you can see for ten miles."

"Good, is this Ormley guy easy to get along with? Would he mind a couple of tenderfeet riding along?"

The railroader eyed Spur a minute and nodded. "Yep, figure he'd put up with it. But you sure as hell don't look like no tenderfoot."

Spur thanked him and went down to the livery. He told the man what he wanted and told him to have the horses saddled and ready by six o'clock the next morning.

Now, what about the killer/assassin? Did she figure out they were heading for Cheyenne? He wished that he knew. It wouldn't do any good to talk to the railroad, or to the county sheriff. He'd just have to be watchful.

Spur knew that if he had to, he could kill the woman. If she was shooting at him or at his charges, she was a legitimate target. It had been a few years since he'd killed a woman. But he knew there would be more down the line somewhere. It was that kind of business.

He thought through the cattle drive. He wasn't even sure that Francine could ride. If she could, she'd need a pair of pants to wear. He hurried back toward the hotel so they could get what they needed before the stores closed.

There was no real worry about the woman assassin, just yet. She couldn't get on a second train until noon. Then he frowned. There was need to worry. She could be coming into town any time now. Should he watch the incoming trains from Denver? He thought about it as he walked, and finally decided he wouldn't. Once she arrived it would take her a while to get situated, then she would have to try to find them. He had paid the hotel desk clerk ten dollars to be sure their names did not appear on the sign-in register.

They asked at the desk where women's clothes could be purchased. It was less than a block away. Spur walked ahead of the women watching everyone. Once in the store he stood at the front door prepared to stop any small women who showed up. None did.

The two got pants that would fit them from the surprised shopkeeper. It was a men's and boys' wear shop. Back in the hotel they tried them on and got ready for their adventure the next day.

They ate in the far corner of the hotel dining room and at once after the meal, Spur escorted them back to their rooms.

"Stay inside, don't open the door for anyone but me. The lady from Denver could be in town by now looking for you."

At her door, Francine hesitated. Her big blue eyes looked up at him and she smiled. "Tonight?" she asked.

"I'm worried about tonight. This attacker knows her time is running out. I better watch both your doors most of the night. She could strike at any time."

"Oh, damn."

He grinned. "Ladies shouldn't swear."

"Right now I don't feel like a lady." She reached up and kissed his lips quickly and stepped into her room. He waited until she locked the door and braced the straight chair under the inside door knob, then he walked away.

He stood at the stairs for a moment, but it felt wrong. He didn't want to get trapped in a hallway again and have to face a shotgun.

Spur went back to his own room beyond the princess's and stepped inside. He did as before, opening the door a crack so he could see down the hall. He rested the Colt on his lap and stretched. It could be a long night. About the time he decided he could sample the delicious charms of Francine, that would be when the assassin would show up shooting a shotgun, blowing doors off rooms. He had to watch it carefully. A few more days and he'd convince them that it was time to end the tour. Just a few more days to keep the two of them, no, the three of them, alive.

Chapter 17

Bright and early the next morning, right after a quick breakfast at an early opening cafe across the street from the hotel, the three of them were ready to move. Francine looked at Spur with feigned shock. "Of course I can ride a horse. I used to live on a horse."

Spur walked with the two women to the livery three blocks from the hotel. The attendant had the animals saddled and ready to go. There was a steady bay mare for Francine, a slightly larger black for Alexandria and a sorrel gelding for Spur. On Spur's saddle was the asked-for boot and a Spencer repeating rifle and three extra ammunition tubes loaded and a box of shells as well.

On the back of each horse was a blanket roll and a flour sack with some emergency food. A half gallon water canteen hung from each saddle.

The women wore wide-brimmed Western hats, shirts and the pants they had bought the day before. They didn't have boots but both wore common sense shoes.

"Let's get this cattle drive on the trail," Spur said. He had watched the streets as they walked to the livery but saw nothing suspicious. Either the assassin hadn't followed them or was waiting for a better time to attack them.

They rode from the livery and went north out of town. There was a road of sorts part of the way.

"If we get to the little community of Bosler and haven't seen the herd, either they're late, or we're on the wrong trail," Spur told the women. They walked their mounts out the north trail.

"Let's go faster," Francine said. "We'll never get there this way." She lifted her mount into a canter and Spur saw that someone had taught her how to ride and ride well. They all cantered along for half a mile, then slowed to a walk to let the horses take a short blow.

"Now this is the Wild West," Francine said. "Out in the open, no city, no people, no buggies or shouting merchants. Maybe I'll just stay here, Alex, and send you home alone."

"You wouldn't do that," Alexandria said. "Anyway you don't have the right papers and I'll tell the State Department and get you pitched right into some dank jail."

She looked at Francine sternly and they both broke up laughing.

At ten o'clock, they stopped and took a break. They had been following the Laramie River and now let the horses have a drink and washed faces and arms in the cool water.

Spur spread out a blanket under a tree in some shade and laid out cheese and slices of bread and three big red apples.

"Your dinner is served," he said. Before they were done, all of the food had vanished.

They rode the rest of the morning and most of the afternoon, and then about five o'clock they saw smoke from a town ahead.

"Bosler," Spur said. "Where is that herd of beef?"

A half hour later they rode into the tiny settlement. There was one general store and post office and three houses. Nobody knew anything about a herd of cattle coming through.

The woman who ran the store was a big German-looking lady named Rolanda who insisted that the women sit down in her living room attached to the store and have a cold lemonade.

"Is this the route that the herds take when they are driven down from the north?" Spur asked.

Rolanda nodded. "Couple ranches up there that send down steers to the railroad. None have come through here for a while."

"We were supposed to meet them here," Spur said

"You stay tonight, look for them tomorrow," Rolanda said. "Have two nice rooms you sleep."

Spur said he'd think about it. He went out and studied the sky and the land to the north. He could see no trail of dust in the tall blue sky. It didn't seem right. The yard boss could be off a day or two on the herd, or it might have had some trouble, a lightning storm and a stampede. It could take three days to gather a thousand head of steers running wild in a storm.

Back inside, he talked to the women. They both said the same thing. Move out and try to find the

241

herd before it got dark. If they didn't find it, they'd camp out by the river.

Spur paid for the lemonade and they rode again. The sky was clear, the weather warm but not too hot. Spur knew that Cheyenne was over 7,000 feet high; he had no idea what the altitude was here, but it was higher.

They kept to a northern route and covered another five miles before the light started to fade. They were still beside the river and Spur looked for a good campsite. He found it a quarter of a mile farther along. The river made a small turn and the area was cloistered with brush and trees. They could have a fire that no one from the trail could see.

He tied the horses and Francine gathered dry wood for the fire. Alexandria got the blankets off the horses and put them near the fire, then they looked in the food sacks for something for supper.

Alexandria wanted to cook their supper.

"But you've never cooked a thing in your entire life," Francine said.

"About time I started."

They both helped her. Spur got the fire going, kept it small and surrounded it with dry rocks from near the river. Wet ones could heat up and explode he knew from sad experience.

There was bacon and some potatoes and a small frying pan. Francine did most of the directing.

"We can fry the bacon and save the drippings and then slice the potatoes skins and all in the fry pan and fry them to a golden brown. What else do we have?"

They found a half loaf of bread and more of the cheese and a can of sliced peaches.

Just before dark, Spur took his horse and rode the back trail to a high spot and watched for another ten minutes. Nobody was following them.

The potatoes and bacon were ready when he got back. They had coffee and the peaches and bread and cheese sandwiches and sat around the fire.

"Now this is what I call the real West," Alexandria said. "Life on the frontier, before all the modern stoves and pots and pans and things to make life easier. I don't know if I'd like to live all the time this way, but for now, it's wonderful."

They sat around the fire another hour as Spur told them a few of the cases he had worked in the West.

"Are the Indians really as bad as you say they are?" Francine asked. "Walking Thunder and Two Doves seemed to be quite nice."

"Those are army Indians. They act civilized because they have to. Any problems and the army sends them back to the reservation. Up north of here the Cheyenne still roam around off the reservation they're supposed to be on. They are twice as bad as I told you."

Alexandria picked up her blanket and moved away from the fire. "I'm getting sleepy. I'm going to go over here and curl up and go to sleep. That way I won't hold either of you back. Francine had that look in her eye all afternoon, and she can get like a mean old she cat if she doesn't get some loving real soon." Alexandria grinned. "No, kids, I won't watch, that much I promise."

She chuckled and walked away from the light. They could hear her getting settled. A few moments later he voice came out of the darkness.

"Okay, time to start the action over there, you two, I'm almost asleep."

243

Francine turned to Spur. "You heard the lady. I'm like a real mean old she cat in heat, don't make me get rough with you."

"Might be fun, how mean do you get?"

She moved over beside him in the soft firelight and kissed him.

"Damn mean. I might tear your clothes off."

Spur laughed softly, caught her and rolled her to the ground. They were off the blanket.

"Yes, no blanket, right here on the Wild West ground. I want you to love me right here."

He undressed her gently, slowly, kissing away each item of clothing. Her pants were the hardest. They both laughed before he got them off. She purred softly against his neck, then bit him gently there and he kissed her, long and hard.

Now he could feel the heat from her body as her skin touched his and it blasted through like a furnace.

She broke off the kiss and hurried to undress him. She threw his clothes away from the fire, then put more wood on the small blaze, kneeling in front of it showing a perfect silhouette to him. Her breasts hung down as she moved and he was struck again at the beauty of a woman's upper torso with a flat little tummy and surging, full breasts.

She left the fire and lay on top of his naked form. Her mouth trailed kisses down his face, across his hairy chest and down over his muscled stomach.

She stopped when her lips brushed his pubic hair. Francine caught his erection and pulled it into her mouth. She bobbed on him again and again, then came off and whispered to him. "I want to take you this way, what works best?"

"The same thing you're doing, little darling. The exact same thing."

She moved back down and caught him around the roots of his shaft and then sucked him in and bobbed up and down, putting as much pressure on the living pole as she could.

He felt the fluids building. Spur knew his breath came faster. He fantasized watching her face as he went in and came out of her mouth. Amazing! The pressure on his fluids built and built. He sensed his hips moving now with no direction from him.

The speed increased and he pumped softly toward her. She accepted the deeper penetration and held a moment on each thrust.

It excited him more than anything anyone had done to him in a year.

"Oh damn!," he said softly. "Oh, damn but that feels good!" The pressure built. "Who taught you to do a man that way, that's marvelous."

Then just as it started to taper off, he felt her teeth gently raking up and down his staff of life. The added friction sent him into a spin. He'd never felt anything like it.

The rockets exploded and he felt the juices coming. He thrust hard at her and she held him a moment, then let him continue. He pushed her on her side and he rolled part way to his side and his hips bucked at her that way. She held on to him.

A gentle moan seeped from his lips, then a cry of victory and conquest, and then the game was over and he drove at her a dozen times, each with a holding thrust, planting, planting, planting. At last he sighed and caught her head with his hands and lifted her up and kissed her soft lips and then held her to him until he could manage to talk again.

Spur lay there in a foggy reality, only half alive, wondering what would happen if the assassin showed up right then with her sawed off shotgun. No, she dropped it in the hotel. But she could get another one. He stirred and Francine came awake at once.

"Again?" she asked. He kissed her gentle lips.

"Your turn." He found her breasts and pulled her upwards until he could drop one breast into his mouth. He licked them both and chewed on them and then bit her large nipples until she wailed in desire and rapture.

Her hands worked on his spent tool and before he had her worked to a fever, he was ready again.

"Oh, my yes!" Francine said. "You know I've dreamed of this, of being with a handsome, sexy man on my back in the grass in the middle of the Wild, Wild West. It always got about to this point and then stopped. How can we make it wild!"

"How about standing up."

Francine laughed softly and kissed his nose. "It can't be done standing up. I tried it one night for two hours until we both got out of the mood."

"I can do it with you standing up." His hand darted to her crotch and her legs opened for him and he stroked her wet pussy. She moaned in delight. He worked her higher and higher, then found her node and strummed it like a guitar string.

A moment later Francine wailed like a treed tiger, crying out with a heavy desire and anticipation. Then the wail cut off and she was panting and humping his hand. Her hips pounded a tattoo on him and she spasmed time after time, the tremors shaking her like a mouse in a cat's mouth. Twice, three times, then five, six, seven times she went through the uncontrollable spasms as her body reacted to his caress.

"Stop!" she whispered and pulled away his hand. He held her close as she began to breathe slower and to resupply her body, which had been depleted of oxygen.

She lay there looking up at him, her face in the soft light of the fire showing contentment, radiance.

"Standing up?"

"Absolutely."

He stood, caught her hand and lifted her to her feet. He led her to a sturdy tree at the edge of the water and put her back against it.

"Now, put your hands around my neck and lock your fingers together." She did.

"Good, now lift your legs and lock them around my hips."

"Oh, good lord! I'm standing up, but not standing up."

Spur moved slightly, loosened her legs a little and moved again, then eased forward. Her back remained solidly pressing against the tree.

"Oh, my god! It can be done standing up."

He slid into her gently, then pounded hard and fast. The extreme angle excited him quickly and he burst through and pumped his load off before he wanted to. He gasped and jolted one last time, then leaned against her a moment.

"Now, unfasten your legs and it's done."

Francine giggled as they walked back toward the fire. She put more sticks on it so it blazed up and turned to watch him.

"I want to remember this night, by the fire, in the middle of the wilderness in the Wild, Wild West. It's a picture I'll never forget." She laughed softly. "I'll also never forget the picture of me leaning against that tree back there as well. I won't

247

ask you where you learned that little bit of sexual technique."

"Just as well you don't know." He added some sticks to the fire. "Have you ever watched a fire burn something? That smaller stick there just blazing up. Not a quarter of an inch thick so it burns easily. Starts, burns fiercely for a moment, then the wood is all gone, consumed, turned into heat, ash and light, then it's gone.

"Oh, the energy is still there in the three forms, but the stick itself can't be seen anymore. I love a fire. You can see so much in a campfire.

"Do you know that when an old Indian is about ready to die, some of them will build a small fire and put beside it a pile of sticks. They sit there and their family gathers around. The old person tends his own fire, putting on as much or as little as he wants.

"Then the fire burns lower and lower, but the old Indian doesn't put on anymore sticks. Sometimes he'll start singing. It's his death song. When the song ends, the fire goes out and the old Indian dies."

Francine stared at him. "That really happens?"

"Yes, I saw it happen once, with a band of friendly Indians. Most white men have never seen it."

"I don't want to see it happen. Right now I feel so safe and warm and happy. Are you sure you can't move to Mantuco?"

"I'm sure. Now, It's bed time. We might have to do a lot of riding tomorrow."

They rolled their blankets out side by side with their feet to the fire. Spur kept his .44 close by his right hand.

Francine reached out and touched him. "Hey, you sleeping yet?"

"Yes."

"Good. I . . . I wanted to thank you again for what you're doing here. It's above and beyond and all that. The princess is my best friend, but she also can be a pain in the heart sometimes. She can act spoiled now and then, but the next minute she's the softest, sweetest, dearest person I know.

"McCoy, you'll always be one of my best and closest held memories."

"Thanks, nice lady from Mantuco. I won't be forgetting you for a damn long time, myself." He patted her shoulder through the blanket. "Now, we both better get some sleep."

From the shadows away from the fire a sleepy voice echoed him.

"I'll vote for that, It's about time all three of us get some sleep," the princess of Mantuco said.

Chapter 18

The next morning, they fried the last of the bacon and ate bacon sandwiches and had coffee.

"We'll eat better as soon as we find the trail drive," Spur said. "Otherwise we head back for Cheyenne. What's the vote this morning for moving north to find that herd?"

"You bet!" Alexandria said. "We'll find them today."

Francine's brows furrowed as she thought about it. "If we don't find them by noon, we turn back," she said.

Spur glanced at her with approval. "I vote with the commoner here. This is getting up into hostile country. The ranches are okay, because they have a large group of men. We're not too far from the Laramie Mountains to the north. I know there are still pockets of Cheyenne in there."

Francine looked at Alexandria, but there were no

signs of a veto from the princess.

They rode.

For the past two hours, Spur McCoy had been scanning the horizon for any sign of a dust trail. They had to be out there somewhere. The day had come alive bright and warm, and by ten o'clock it was burning hot. They tapped their canteens again and again as they saw the Laramie River bend to the west.

They cut across the high, dry plateau. Spur could see the mountains in front of them, probably another 50 miles. The cattle herd evidently came from somewhere to the left from the central part of the state.

Spur felt his shoulders tighten and it wasn't from riding. He had been in the rhythm of riding now for a full day and it seemed natural again. Something wasn't as it should be. He could see nothing in front or on the two sides. He knew the river swung back east again. When they came to it the next time he'd call a halt. That would be as far as they went. A half dozen things could have gone wrong with the trail drive. It might not even have left the home range yet.

Small warning signs went off in Spur's senses, but he could see nothing to trigger them. No savages, no sneaking pair of horsemen following them. Nothing but the high dry Wyoming rangeland with no cattle and three lonesome white eyes.

They walked their horses.

A half hour later they came to the green line the river formed through the dry country. Brush and a few trees and a swatch of grass grew along the river and on the low places where the spring runoff produced a flooding and provided deep watering for more grass and brush.

Spur pulled his party under some trees by the river.

"Break time," he said. "Break time and end of the line. This is as far as we go."

"We might see them in another hour or two," Princess Alexandria said. But she didn't demand that they move on.

They washed in the clear, cold water, let the horses drink their fill and then topped off canteens from the sparkling water.

Francine stood and stretched, then without comment walked downstream into the brush. Spur started to follow her, then realized she was relieving herself and stopped.

"Good thinking," Alexandria said. "I'm sorry we didn't find the herd. The trail drive would have been interesting."

"On the way back I'll tell you exactly what happens and how dusty and dirty you get. They you'll know all about it without getting absolutely dust soaked."

Spur had been standing near the princess, now he sat down on the grass. Just as he started to move a rifle cracked from upstream in the brush. If Spur hadn't been moving he knew he'd be dead. The round found only the top of his left shoulder, creasing it, numbing his left arm. He flattened on the ground. It wouldn't do any good to play dead.

They would be Cheyenne on a long-range hunt. The Cheyenne never took male prisoners, and they mutilated the body so the man wouldn't be able to fight as a whole man in the afterlife.

Spur saw six Cheyenne hunters edge through the brush upstream and advance. A bold stance against the Cheyenne sometimes did wonders.

He stood up in one flowing motion and held up

his hand in the peace sign. One of the Indians laughed and lifted his rifle. Another Cheyenne barked something and the rifle lowered.

The six moved forward cautiously.

"Don't move," Spur whispered to Alexandria. "Stay calm. We're not dead yet, we have a chance."

The older brave stepped forward and stopped ten feet from Spur. The warrior carried an army issue Springfield rifle and a bandoleer of rounds. He wore only a breechclout and had on no war paint. Over his back he had slung his bow and a leather quiver of arrows.

At once he pointed to the three horses and two white eyes.

Spur tried to sign but the Cheyenne didn't understand or pretended not to.

"Muerto," Spur said using the Spanish word for dead. He signed that the rider had fallen off and hit her head and died. Five of the Indians had gathered around Alexandria. She paid no attention to them, staring straight ahead where she sat on the grass.

One man touched her long brown hair and she turned and slapped him. The other braves laughed. The embarrassed warrior slapped Alexandria in return.

It was all Spur needed. As soon as the warrior in front of him shifted his glance to the slapping, Spur drew his six-gun and fired. His first round killed the head of the hunting party; he wheeled and fired three more times, hitting two savages. Before any of them could return his fire with their long guns, Spur darted behind one of the horses. He reloaded, dragging out the spent rounds and pushing in new ones until he had all six slots filled.

A rifle barked in front of him and he felt the

round rip through his pant leg near his ankle but miss flesh. He leaned around the heavy rear quarters of the mount. Three Indians were down where they had been. One ran away holding his shoulder.

Alexandria, princess of Mantuco and heir apparent to the royal throne, was not to be seen. Spur grabbed the Spencer rifle from the boot of the saddle. He had to find the princess.

First he had to stay alive. Keeping the horses between him and where he figured the savages had run to, he jolted downstream and sprinted for the brush and large trees 30 feet away.

He had heard nothing from Francine. He prayed she had heard the rifle fire and remained hidden. Two rifle bullets dug up dirt near his feet as he ran and a third whispered past a few feet from his head.

Then he dove behind a fallen log and caught his breath. He had the rifle and two of the extra tubes of rounds. That was 21 shots. He had his six-gun and about 20 rounds in his belt. He was facing three Cheyenne, one of them wounded. They had the advantage—they had Alexandria.

Spur heard a noise behind him and he spun with his Colt out his finger already starting to stroke the trigger. He let off the trigger at once. Francine huddled near the base of a large tree.

He motioned to her and she crawled up to him behind the log. He lifted and looked over it at the battle scene. The three Indians lay where they had fallen. Three to one was lousy odds against the Cheyenne.

He put his arms around Francine and kissed her cheek.

"I . . . I . . . I thought you both were dead. I heard the shots and I couldn't move. I was frozen right there. Then there were some more shots and I heard noises. I figured the Indians were coming after me. But I saw you. Where's Alex?"

"The Cheyenne grabbed her. But not for long. I told them the third rider was dead. So they won't look for you. They have to come back and get their dead. The Cheyenne never leave a body on a battlefield. They must have a proper burial. They'll wait until dark to get them.

"What you have to do is stay here, out of sight and quiet, while I check out these guys. One of them is hit. They must be hunters. They must have horses around here. I'll see what I can find."

There was more brush on the far side of the stream than here. Spur went downstream 20 yards where it turned and the savages couldn't see him, and crossed the water. It was only knee deep here. He took the Spencer with him. Francine had her two shot derringer with her. He had her get it out and hold it, then he kissed her and left.

On the far side of the stream he moved up-current through light brush keeping well out of sight of the Indians. Thirty yards above the attack site, Spur went back to the water and lay in a concealed spot where he could view the other bank and listen.

Soon he heard some chattering. The Indians were arguing among themselves. Good. He moved on upstream until he found a place to cross and then began working downstream behind the Cheyenne.

He had to out stalk a Cheyenne. Spur had done it before. He worked with an Indian friend one summer learning the techniques for walking through the woods and dry brush without making a sound.

Now that training came in handy. He moved silently from tree to tree, paused at each spot watching, listening. Ahead two birds flew up from some trees and Spur turned that way. Something had disturbed them.

He was within 50 feet of the spot. Now Spur moved Indian slow. He moved ahead on his hands and knees inches at a time, careful not to make any grass or brush move to reveal his passing.

Another ten feet took half an hour. He heard a horse nicker to the left. Good, they had horses. That explained them being so far down on the long dry plateau.

Spur edged behind a poplar tree and lifted up to look around its bark side. Through light brush he could see two of the savages. One knelt in front of Alexandria. She was bare to the waist and her hands were tied over her head to a tree. The Indian fondled her breasts. She started to say something, then stopped. Terror enveloped her face.

Spur lifted the rifle and centered his sights on the attacker's back, but slowly he lowered the weapon. He could get only one this way. There would still be two more. He had to be sure of all three.

He moved forward again. Noises to the left stopped him. Through the brush he saw one Indian leading three horses. There was a sharp exchange between the man fondling Alex and a taller brave.

Spur knew he had run out of time. He lifted the Spencer again, targeted the arguing Indian, made sure the round couldn't hurt Alex and fired. The roar brought a scream from the Indian near Alexandria. He jolted away from her; the round had shattered his spinal column and he died moments later.

The other two warriors had vanished. Spur saw the horses. It would do no good to kill them. There were six somewhere. He listened and watched Alexandria, who had stared wide eyed at the dead Indian within inches of her, then her eyes closed and she fainted.

Noise came to the left through heavy brush. Two to one. Not bad odds. Spur moved that way soundlessly. Why were they making noise? Too late he knew why. He crawled back six feet to where he had fired, but Alex was gone from the tree.

They had used a diversion on him.

Noise to the left. Big, defiant, we-don't-care-if-you-hear noise.

Spur jumped up and crashed brush directly away from the river. He broke free and saw two horses galloping hard to the north along the river. For a flash of a second he saw the brown dress Alex wore flapping to the side.

He ran back to the clearing, checked the three Cheyenne. All were dead. He picked up the Springfield and looked it over. It was in good condition; a small buckskin pouch on the warrior's belt held rounds. Spur took the bandoleer off the dead Indian.

"Francine! Francine, it's all right to come back to the horses now. They've left."

Francine ran into the clearing.

"Where is the princess?"

"They took her. We have to go get her back. That presents a problem. Do I leave you here or take you with me? You could ride out south right now and be back to that little town well before night."

"I want to come with you. I can ride, I can shoot a pistol and a rifle. I can help you."

"You could also get your pretty little self killed. These Cheyenne don't play easy."

"Please let me go. It's partly my fault we're out this far. Let me go, please, I will be a help. I can fire that second rifle you have."

"It will cost you a lot more than you've ever imagined if the Cheyenne capture you. Think about that. They brutalize white women, rape them, drag them through cactus patches. They do it for fun once they're through with them. Think it over carefully. I'll be there to protect you, but you'll have to do a lot of the work yourself."

He turned around and threw a rock into the water. When he looked back, her face was white, her eyes wide, but she nodded.

"Yes, Spur. I owe it to the princess. I'm going with you."

They mounted. Spur tied Alexandria's horse on a lead line behind him and they moved out. Spur watched the ground and then began tracking the two unshod Indian ponies north. One was easy to track, it was carrying double and the hooves sank deeper into the ground than the other pony's hooves.

For two hours they tracked the savages north. They held by the river until it turned due east. Then the tracks kept on going north.

"Into the Laramie Mountains," Spur said. "We have to keep after them. They'll stop for the night. Then we'll have a chance to find them. I hope they build a fire."

At dusk they were within sight of the first foothills of the mountains. They paused, checked what was left to eat in their food sacks. Some hard biscuits, a tin of ham and more coffee. They didn't dare build a fire.

"A smoke out here will travel for fifteen miles on a calm day before it dissipates enough so it can't be noticed. A trained nose can whiff a smoke and start tracking it and follow it right back to the source. I hope the Indians make a fire tonight."

"How can we be sure they'll stop?"

"They were on what must have been a hunting party. They lost four of their six men. They have a prize, but at the cost of four braves. They'll want to stop and get their story straight before they try to explain to the chief what happened."

"What about tonight, for Alexandria?"

"It will be the hardest night of her life. Let's hope we can find her before they turn angry with her or get vicious."

"Let's hope. If they just rape her . . . you know, she'll be alright."

Spur knew the warriors would travel fast. At the start, they had galloped the ponies for two miles before they slowed them. He could tell by the look of the hoof prints and how much dirt was thrown away from the mark.

Spur and Francine pushed their horses into a lope now and then, but each time they found some droppings, Spur knew that they had lost a little more ground. He had been unable to see the two riders when they topped any of the rises, but he knew they must not be more than about three hours ahead.

They kept up the pace. The hostiles were making no move to conceal their trail. Probably they didn't figure they would be followed.

Spur hoped for a night stop and a fire. It was the best chance he had. He didn't have a pair of kerosine lanterns to use for night tracking.

They rode straight through to dusk.

Spur looked at Francine. "How does it go?" he asked.

"I'm getting sore again. I'm thankful for the pants."

He pulled up. There was no water anywhere around. At least they had stopped to refill their canteens when the Indians left them at the river. Now they were well away from it.

"Let's take a break here. I'll scout around a little to see—"

"No! Don't leave me here alone. I'll die. I want to go everywhere you go."

He nodded. They did a small circle and found no stream or water and stopped where they had started.

"What now?"

"We wait and hope for some smoke. You might as well spread out a blanket and rest a little. The only chance we have to get her back is at night.

"One of them is wounded. I saw some blood drops back a ways. That's why I think they'll stop and make a fire. Not even an Indian likes to die in the dark."

The Secret Service agent perched on a rock 20 feet up a slight rise from where Francine slept on her blanket. It was a little after ten o'clock. He hadn't smelled any smoke.

Spur swore softly to himself. He had to move to his second plan of attack. They would ride half the night, hope they might still smell a smoke or see a fire. If not they would ride and then hide out, hoping they had followed the line the Indians would still take in the morning. It wasn't the best plan, but it was the only one he could think of.

He kissed Francine twice before she started to wake up, then she returned his kiss passionately before she fully awoke.

"Oh, I was having a dream about you and me."

"Hang on to that thought. I know you're still tired, but we don't have any smoke, so we have

261

to ride hoping we can find them or get ahead of them in the dark and cut them down tomorrow from ambush."

"Bushwhack them?"

"With the Indians, anything is fair. Let's ride."

The stars refused to move that night. It took at least three hours of riding before it was one o'clock by the pointer stars on the Big Dipper where they arrowed to the North Star.

Francine looked at him in the faint light.

"You think we're ahead of them?"

"Maybe. If they rode all night they probably are in their tipis now."

He didn't want to say what was happening to Alexandria if that were true. They rode on. At three o'clock the long valley they had been led into by the last of the Indian tracks came toward a gully and a low pass into the hills beyond. There was no reasonable way to continue. He didn't know which way the Cheyenne would turn.

They found a rise on the edge of the valley carpeted with grass and covered with brush and a few trees. They hid the horses and lay down for some sleep.

Francine drifted off at once. They didn't bother to take off any clothes or boots. This was survival time for all of them.

Spur knew he needed some rest. It had been too long. He nodded off but snapped awake twice. Then he gave in and let his head stay down and he slept.

The next thing he knew someone shook his arm.

"McCoy, wake up. Spur, come on, it's morning."

Spur blinked and sat up. His hand still rested on top of the .44 and the Spencer was beside his left arm.

"McCoy, are you awake? Do you smell what I do? If I'm not mistaken, that's wood smoke I'm taking in."

Spur came fully conscious. He turned his head slowly, "Yes, smoke." He jumped up and walked a slow circle, then turned back until he faced up wind. The smoke came from somewhere behind them, but not far.

"Come on, Francine. You're going to learn how to sneak up on an Indian. If we win, we live. If we lose, all three of us will lose our hair."

Chapter 19

Spur took a long look at the direction from which the smoke came. It was to the right of their position and somewhat behind them. They had passed the savages in the night. He frowned, trying to figure out how to move. The area had more vegetation now, they were in the side of the valley slightly up the slope.

The smoke came from the south and east, in heavier timbered area of the ridge which worked back toward the Laramie Mountains.

He took the Spencer and showed Francine again how to fire and load the army rifle.

"We'll take it along just in case we need it. We better hurry. We don't know how long they'll be there."

"I wonder why they started a fire," Francine said.

"They must be close enough to their summer

camp to feel secure. If we get lucky, I'll only need two shots and it will all be over."

They moved slowly through the trees and low lying growth. Twice they made detours from the line to go around heavy patches of some kind of bramble bush.

Spur stopped often and sniffed, then moved forward. The smoke was stronger, as if they had used it for cooking something before continuing the trip. It seemed a strange activity for two warriors rushing for home. Or were they rushing?

Twice they came up small rises and Spur figured the fire was just on the other side. Both times he was wrong. They had traveled at least two miles. Still the smoke led them on. Spur walked faster now. He figured he'd have plenty of time to react when they got close.

Once he heard a horse ahead of them and he nodded. At least their three animals were too far away to horse talk and give them away.

He went around another outcropping of rock and past some pine trees and then he could see the fire.

The small camp was by a tiny creek. The water was why the Indians had come up here. It surged and chattered for 100 feet, then vanished into the ground again.

Spur dropped to the ground and studied the camp. It was simply the fire with rocks around it, a tin can on the fire, and the two warriors. One worked over his bow. The second one was tending to the fire and the coffee, Spur figured he was brewing.

Where was Alexandria? A cold sweat popped on his forehead, then it warmed as he saw the woman tied to a tree. One arm was fastened to the tree and the other one free. She was 20 feet from the two Cheyenne.

Spur estimated the distance. Still 150 yards. How close could he get without attracting attention? More important, how much time did he have before they moved?

One of the warriors shouted something and the other one laughed. He held his crotch and shook his head. The man at the coffee laughed again and responded. They seemed to be in no rush. With the carbine he should get closer. He told Francine to stay where she was, then he moved stealthily forward. When he turned around, Francine was still right behind him but she hadn't made a sound.

At a hundred yards away from the camp, Spur still had the advantage of altitude, maybe only 50 feet now up the slope. He checked the field of fire. It was open, no brush, no tree limbs, nothing to deflect a shot. He went into a prone position and centered his sights on the man closest to Alexandria.

Do him, work the lever for a new round and get the second one as he started to move. Where would he go? A large tree and a fallen log lay to his left, Spur's right. The second man would try to make it to the log.

Spur moved the sights back to the first warrior. He centered the aim on the man's broad chest and squeezed off the round. He jerked the rifle up, levered down and back up the trigger guard lever and checked for his second target. He saw the Indian dive for the tree and vanish behind it.

Spur motioned for Francine to come up with the rifle. "See where Alexandria is, by that tree? I got one of the Cheyenne but the other one went behind that log to the right. I want you to fire just over the log. Do one round about every thirty seconds."

Spur laid out a dozen rounds for her on the grass and leaves.

"Fire one and let's see you load another."

Francine took the rifle, rested it on the ground and aimed. She fired. The round cut bark over the top of the log. She expelled the old round and put in a fresh one and fired again.

Spur nodded, picked up his Spencer and ran through the trees down the slope aiming just above where the princess sat beside the tree.

He hoped the rounds would convince the Indian that he was safe behind the log. Spur ran, not taking the time to be quiet. He didn't care if the Cheyenne heard him or not. Once at an open space he lifted the Spencer and fired a round at the log from his new angle.

There had been no return fire, which meant the Cheyenne had been so surprised they didn't have their weapons within reach.

Spur slid to a stop behind a pine and looked around. He could see down the length of the old log but there was no Indian there. He fired once down the log, but got no response. Twice more he fired into the area, then changed the empty tube of rounds for a loaded one and began working slowly forward.

When he was 20 yards from Alexandria, Spur saw the Cheyenne brave lift up from a nearby patch of brush and rush at the princess. Spur swung the Spencer around and tracked the savage, led him a shade and fired.

The Indian stumbled, went to his knees. Blood poured from his chest. His right hand went back with the knife ready to throw. Spur drew his six-gun and fired three times so fast they sounded like one continuous roar. All three .44 slugs drilled through the Cheyenne warrior's chest and he slammed backwards into his own unending hunting ground.

Spur stood there a moment looking around.

"Were there any other Indians, or just the two?" he called.

Alexandria didn't answer. She stared at the dead Indian 15 feet from her and the gleaming blade of the knife on the ground beside him.

"Dear God!" she whispered. Spur hurried up to her, knelt beside her and put his arm around her gently. She looked up, seeing him for the first time. A whole symphony of emotions washed over the royal face. Surprise, delight, then wonder and sadness. She looked back at the Indian and began to sob.

He held her as Francine ran down the slope with the heavy rifle. She dropped the weapon and knelt beside the other two, her arms around them both.

"We're here, Alex, we're here. You're all right. You're going to be fine. We're your friends, and we'll protect you and take care of you. We know they hurt you, but that's all over now. All over and we're going to take a ride back to the town where there'll be a hot bath and lots of good food and a big bed that you can rest in for hours and hours."

Spur worked out of the entanglement of arms and stood. "I'll go get the horses," he said. He picked up the army rifle, made sure it was loaded and ready to fire, and leaned it against a tree. Then he went back and with his knife, cut the strip of rawhide that bound Alexandria's wrist to the tree. He untied it from her arm and saw how the tightening rawhide had left a mark. He massaged

269

it and she looked up and thanked him.

Then Spur made sure he had a round ready to fire in the Spencer, brought it to port arms and jogged up the hill through the trees and brush to where they had left their horses.

Spur slowed just before he got to the spot and moved up quietly. There could be visitors there. He had no idea how close he was to some Cheyenne summer camp.

But when he checked around one last tree, he saw the three mounts where he had left them contentedly nibbling on some summer grass under the trees.

Princess Alexandria sat on some grass just on the other side of the big log so she didn't have to look at the dead Indians or their camp. Spur rode up and Francine motioned to him. He rode to her and swung down.

"I don't think we should ride too far at first. Let's get away from here and find some water. Streams always seem to quiet and soothe Alex. She hasn't said much about it yet, but I'm sure both the Indians raped her. The buttons are cut off her pants fly."

Spur nodded and led the horses over to where the princess sat.

"Ready to take a ride, Alexandria?"

She looked up, startled at first, then she relaxed and nodded. She let Spur help her swing up on the horse. Spur led the way, Alexandria came next and Francine brought up the rear.

They rode for two hours before they found a small stream coming down the side of the mountain. Spur stopped there and stepped down and the Princess dismounted by herself. She let the reins drop and hurried to the stream.

An hour later she still sat beside the water. She had made a small dam across the two foot wide stream by using rocks from the bottom. She watched the water and tossed small stones in the pool.

Alexandria dropped in one last stone and stood. "Alright, Mr. McCoy, I'm ready to travel again. You don't have to coddle me, I'm not a china doll. I've talked to women who have sexual intercourse as many as forty times a day. It's a natural bodily function. Now let's get back to civilization. I dearly do need a bath."

Francine grinned at the announcement and called to Spur that the troops were ready to travel.

They rode another two hours, then stopped and investigated their food sacks. They found more tins of peaches, and one of beef stew. They ate both and the rest of the bread and the cheese which was starting to ripen.

After long drinks of fresh water, and filling their canteens, the three mounted and headed for the little village of Bosler.

An hour after they arrived in Bosler, they took rooms with the German lady Rolanda, and soon there was hot water in the bath tub and the princess bathed. The only tub available was a round wash tub type, but the heir to the throne didn't complain and Francine nodded at Spur in the hallway.

"I think she's coming through the shock of it and getting back to normal. Heaven only knows what happened during those hours they held her. We might never find out. But I do think that the experience has changed her. She's more rational, more settled down now than I've ever seen her.

271

"In our country she's known as the Wild, Wild Princess. But that moniker will no longer apply."

"No physical problems, no cuts or slashes?"

"A bruise or two, but you should see the inside of my thighs. I'm black and blue from crotch to knee."

"I'll be glad to look at them any time."

"Not tonight, Spur." They both chuckled.

After both women had baths, they met in the dining room and worked over a roast beef dinner that Rolanda prepared. Her husband and two boys were there as well. None of them said a word while the guests were in the house. That seemed to be the rule laid down by Rolanda.

When the meal was over, the three visitors sat on the front porch of the home and watched the sun go down. Alexandria was quiet, much more reserved than usual. Spur hoped that her ordeal with the Indians hadn't scarred her for life.

They talked of many things with Spur and Francine doing most of the speaking. When the sun was down and it was dark on the front porch, Francine suggested maybe they should go inside.

"No, no let's stay out here," Alexandria said. "I want to tell you some things, talk them out, I guess. Would you mind?"

Both the others murmured and the princess told them what she had been holding inside.

"I was in shock I guess when the first two Indians died. I just sat there with my mouth open. Then there were more shots and the one Indian grabbed my wrist and jerked me to my feet and ran with me, dragging me sometimes into the brush. I kept yelling at him. He hit me once with his hand, and I was so surprised that I kept quiet.

"I didn't know if Spur was dead or alive. I just did

what the Indians showed me to do. I couldn't understand their words and they didn't know English, so we did a lot of pointing."

There was a quiet period then, and the other two didn't say anything, they simply waited for her to begin again.

"Right there at first there was a lot of arguing by the two warriors. One wanted to stay, the other one, who was wounded, seemed to want to get the horses and leave. Do you know why they were arguing?"

"The dead," Spur said softly. "The Cheyenne believe strongly in life after death, and to have the best chance, a dead person must be given a proper burial. Cheyenne almost always take their dead away after a battle with the army. This warrior probably wanted to wait and get the dead before they left."

"Now I see. Anyway, we left and neither of them were happy. The one had a wounded shoulder. I rode in front of the other one, the taller one who wasn't hurt. He indicated several times that I belonged to him. That's when I remembered what you told me about what the Cheyenne did to captive women."

"My timing sometimes isn't any good," Spur said. "Sorry I gave you things to worry about."

"I worried. They rode like lightning, rush, rush, here to there, always watching behind them. Then, after half a day, they didn't look behind them anymore. I guess they decided you had given up any chase."

"We were trying to find you, Alex. Damn but we were trying hard."

"I know now that you were. But that didn't help me any then. That was when I started to cry. The tall one hit me when I cried. But it didn't make me stop. After a while he stopped hitting me and I stopped the crying. I figured I asked for this, I wanted to come up here. If it hadn't been for me we would be back in Cheyenne or Omaha or some strange place like that."

In the darkness, Alexandria gave a little gasp as if she were crying silently. Francine put her arm around the princess, who sniffled twice and then went on.

"We kept riding after dark. I know that's when they figured they would lose you for good. Nobody can track a horse after dark. When we stopped, the big one cut the buttons off my pants and tore my underthings and raped me. He . . . he kept shouting, and calling to the other Indian, but the wounded man was in pain and he lay where he was near the fire, groaning. He did that half the night."

The snuffling came and then stopped. "I don't know how many times he used me, but he got tired after a while and tied me to the tree. Then he went to sleep. The smaller Indian's groaning and yelping with pain kept me awake most of the night.

They didn't get up early. I went to sleep sometime and awoke to smell coffee. They built a fire and brewed coffee before they left. That must come from their time on a reservation somewhere.

"About a half hour after they got the coffee going, they were starting to get ready to travel, when you two rescued me."

She was quiet then. They sat there and listened to a single cricket chirping away looking for a lover.

At last Spur spoke. "Was the last Indian coming after you there at the end, when he had the knife?"

"Oh, yes. He showed me the knife all the time. To prove to me how sharp it was he cut his finger with it. You were right about the Cheyenne being warriors. That's their life. And as white men have proved so often, anything is permitted in war, nothing is wrong, any action is possible and all are excusable."

It was quiet for a moment.

"You've seen your last Cheyenne warrior," Spur said. "The army won't let them come down this far. I still haven't figured out what those six were doing. They weren't hunters, maybe some kind of a delegation. I guess it doesn't matter much."

"What about tomorrow?" Francine asked.

Spur waited for Alexandria to say something. She didn't. "Figure we should be getting back to Cheyenne."

"I've had about all the horseback riding I want for a while," Alexandria said.

"Me too," Francine said. "Suppose there's a buggy around here anywhere?"

"I'll find one," Spur said. "Or I'll make one out of barrels. You ladies won't have to ride the horses to town tomorrow. What happens if we see the trail herd?"

"We wave at them and rush on by to that stretch-out bath tub," Francine said, and all three of them laughed.

Spur stood. "I'm about ready to try out that bed upstairs. We'll be rolling you out bright and early in the morning. The buggy leaves promptly at ten P.M."

Both women cheered.

The next morning at Rolanda's first breakfast at 6:30, Spur arranged for one of the landlady's sons to drive their buggy into town. He had to go anyway to pick up some goods for the store from the train. Spur paid him two dollars to make the drive.

Spur paid Rolanda for the night's lodging and breakfast and dinner the night before. The bill for the three came to six dollars.

"I'll make you a big picnic lunch to eat on the way." Rolanda said. "Twenty miles in a buggy won't be much fun."

"For the ladies, it will be much better than riding their horses," Spur said.

The little troupe moved out at ten-thirty, the three saddle horses trailing along on long lead lines. They made a leisurely pace of it and stopped near the river just after two for their picnic lunch. Rolanda's son was sixteen, all thumbs, elbows and knees. He ate with them and never said a word.

Nothing happened on the way back, for which Spur gave a silent prayer. They went to the side door of the hotel and he reminded them about the French woman.

"If she's coming, she's here by now and wondering where we are. We won't advertise that we're back. We'll meet at eight o'clock tonight in my room to figure out what we're going to do next. The option of heading for St. Louis is still open."

Spur had dropped off the horses and rifles at the livery on the way by and now walked ahead of the women as they entered the hotel and hurried up the steps to the second floor. Their rooms were the way they had left them.

As soon as the women were safely in their rooms, Spur went down stairs and to the railroad depot. He sent a wire to his boss in Washington and one to the Mantuco embassy. He simply said that they were in Cheyenne and there had been no new appearance by the assassin, that there were no plans yet to return, and that he would keep the ambassador advised.

Back in the hotel the two women came right on time for the eight o'clock meeting. They talked about different things they could do the next day. Then the evening was ruptured by the booming sound of a shotgun blast. Spur drew his Colt and edged his door open in time to see a small woman storm out of Alexandria's room and run down the hall.

Spur had time to fire one shot. He hit the woman in the shoulder and she dropped the shotgun and raced down the far stairs and out of sight. Spur tore out of the room and rushed after her. This time he would catch her or else!

Chapter 20

Spur McCoy took the hotel steps three at a time as he stormed down them to the first floor. The clerk pointed to the front door and the Secret Service agent raced out ready to face a fist full of six-gun.

No shots greeted him, only the blackness of night and the usual small town after dark sounds. He stared around him as he walked down the hotel steps and across the boardwalk. To his left a piano banged away in a saloon. To his right two drunks argued on the sidewalk.

Sudden footsteps padded to the left, then turned into the sounds of running. Spur broke and ran down the street to the left. Only two horses stood at rails. He saw a dark shadow scutter around the last horse and head for the alley.

Spur ate up the distance and raced into the alley. The booming roar of six-gun met him, fired from 20 feet away, but the shot went wild. The agent kept running forward. Almost too late, the figure turned and fled.

An open door in the alley materialized in the darkness and the woman darted into it. Spur wanted her alive. Another body wouldn't explain it all. He wanted to know more about why she was doing this. Exactly why.

He stared into the hades-black of the building. Not a glimmer of a light. In one leap he went into the opening at an angle so he showed in the faint outside light only a second. A revolver flashed and roared in the closed room. The lead missed him.

Spur's six-gun came up but he didn't fire at the flash. Alive, he wanted her alive.

They both waited. He could hear her breathe in ragged gasps and pants.

"Ready to give it up and live?" Spur whispered. He moved just after saying the words. Her six-gun roared again firing at where his voice had come from.

That was three. She had two rounds left, no, three. He'd load every chamber on a job like this. He waited. He heard her move to the left. Spur crouched near the floor wishing he could light a match and throw it all in one move. Too dangerous. He heard her patting the walls, touching them, probably looking for a door.

Silently Spur stood. "Over here!" he said. The second he said it he stepped to his right and crouched near the floor. Almost before he went low, the shot came, an automatic response from her. It missed.

Four. She had two left.

Spur moved silently toward the sounds she made. He took a .44 round from his belt and threw it across the room. The six-gun crashed again as the round hit the wall, fell to the floor and bounced twice.

Five.

He eased forward. Did she have another round? Had she reloaded after the alley shot? No way to tell. He nudged something on the floor. He felt with his hands. A chair. He picked it up and threw it hard at the spot where he had seen the last flash.

A scream of pain and fury billowed in the room.

"Bastard!" her voice rasped.

All was quiet after that. Spur listened intently, but she didn't move. He heard her gasp once or twice, but she wasn't crying. He inched forward, moving only when he had a safe foot planted and he knew it would also be quiet. She couldn't be more than six feet away.

In what sounded like desperation, her hands began pounding the walls and she moved to her left away from him. She was hunting a door. What was this place, a storage room? It would have a door. Two, one in leading into the store, one to the alley. He could see the faint gray of the open alley door to the left. She was 15 feet from that one. He heard her cry in joy.

Then a latch fell, squeaky door hinges sounded and her footsteps backed up, then raced ahead.

Spur jolted the same direction, his left hand out sweeping the space in front of him. There was no new light. He hit the door with his hand and held it.

Spur crouched near the floor and felt where the empty space was. Inside he touched the floor. From directly across the room he saw the sliver of light. Another door. It opened spreading yellow light into the room, shocking his eyes. He closed one but forced the other to stay open.

Her dark shadow blotted part of the light as she ran into the next room.

Spur darted for the door. He hit the wall beside it. From inside a shoot crashed and lead zipped through the open doorway.

The agent stepped around the door jamb and into the room. Ten feet away stood the woman, the weapon at her side.

"That was six rounds, Miss. I'd say your stinger is pulled."

The light came from one lamp on a counter. It was the back room of the hardware store. She whirled and ran through a curtain into the main part of the store. There were weapons out there, Spur realized.

He rushed after her. By the time he got to the darker main store, he heard her laugh.

A knife whispered past his shoulder and stuck in the wall. He dropped out of sight.

"You want to be dead in a few minutes, or live to be deported, Miss? I understand you're a French national and you haven't killed anyone that I know of. You'll be charged with attempted murder and expelled from the country."

"No chance of my doing that, Mr. McCoy."

"You want to die, just because your brother died?"

"He was beaten to death in that Mantuco prison! He was just a boy at nineteen. He was not a drug smuggler!"

"So trying to avenge him, you have killed three of your countrymen. Does that make you feel better?"

"No. I weep for them. But they knew the risks. It was for the good of our country as well. Mantuco is a monstrosity, it should be obliterated."

"This isn't the way to do it. You know that. Drop the rest of the knives and stand up and walk back this way. I assure you I won't kill you. I had four chances to do that in the dark room. Don't be stupid and refuse this last chance to live."

Darlene Benoit screamed in French and ran toward where he crouched. She threw three knives at the spot and then swung a hatchet at Spur's torso. The six-gun came down sharply, hit her wrist hard and she cried out in pain. The hatchet fell to the floor.

Spur grabbed her good arm, and put away his Colt.

"That's what those three small triangles were for. Let's see, Liberty, Equality and Justice, is that the French motto?"

"You would know nothing of justice!" She glared at him in the faint light. He held her tightly and they walked back through the two rooms and out the alley door. Someone had left it unlocked tonight.

When he came to the courthouse, he saw a light on in the sheriff's office. A deputy looked at the woman strangely, then at McCoy. The deputy nodded.

"Hey, you're that guy from Washington, D.C., that federal sheriff or something. This your vicious killer?"

Spur nodded. "Matter of fact, she is. I don't know her name yet, but she speaks perfect English and French. She's from somewhere in France and will be your guest until I figure out what to do with her."

"You mean like in one of our cells?"

"Exactly."

"Hey! We ain't never had a woman in jail before." He took the jail keys and walked back to the cells. Two of them were visible from part of the sheriff's office. Spur pushed her in one and saw the way she held her right wrist.

"Is it broken?"

"Yes."

"You also have a bullet in your shoulder. Guess it's time for somebody to go fetch the closest doctor. Tell him it's a bullet wound and a broken wrist. Deputy, I'll hold down the place until you get back."

It was over an hour before Spur returned to the hotel. He had watched the doctor set the woman's arm, then saw him put a heavy cloth bandage on it and over that spread a half inch of plaster of Paris. When it dried the bones wouldn't move.

After that, Spur went to the railroad station and talked to the night telegrapher. Spur sent two wires, one to his boss advising him of the events. The second one went to the Mantuco embassy and reported that the assassin had been captured and was incarcerated in Cheyenne, Wyoming. Spur McCoy was waiting their instructions.

At the hotel, the women waited in the lobby. When he came in they pounced on him. He told them what happened as they went up the stairs and to his room.

"So the woman is in jail. I've wired your embassy for instructions, and I'd say that the assassination threat is over and only a bad memory."

Alexandria hugged Spur and kissed his cheek. "I'm going to have Papa strike a medal for you, a big gold one with a long ribbon."

Francine hugged him and kissed his other cheek. "I'm just ever so glad that pest of a woman is in jail. So now as entertainment director, I want to suggest what we do tomorrow."

"We'll have to wait until we hear from Washington," Spur said.

"That should be before noon," Francine said. "Today I saw a stage coach pull into town. I found out that it runs every day from here to a little town of Twin Mines about twenty miles north east of here. The railroad doesn't go anywhere near it, and it's cut off without the stage. So it's still running. You promised us that we could have a chance to ride on a stagecoach."

"I did? When?"

"I don't remember. Oh, yes, it was one of those nights when things got real personal and intimate . . . and sexy."

"Does it go out and back the same day?" Spur asked.

"That's what the woman said."

"Sounds like a good trip. We'll take along enough food for a picnic for ten, that should feed us. If we can't go tomorrow, we will the next day. When does the stage leave?"

"Not until eight-thirty,"

"Sound good to you, Princess?"

"Yes, I'd love to go. Now, I'm ready for a bed, but my room is a mess."

"The hotel clerk hasn't been up here?" Spur growled. "I'll go down and get you put in another room. Stay here until I get back."

He roared a little at the clerk, got a room just across the hall and went back up and helped Princess Alexandria move her luggage and clothes. Just before Spur left the room, she stopped him.

"Mr. McCoy. I truly think I would have been killed on this trip, except for you. You have . . .

have saved me two or three times now. I don't know how I can repay you. I'll find a way. A commendation to your superiors will be one way. But I'll think of something more. I'm forever in your debt."

Spur nodded and went out. He checked the jail and found the sheriff himself there.

"Understand we have an international criminal with us tonight, Mr. McCoy. She don't look too dangerous to me."

"Three of her friends have died in this try she made to kill the princess. She's used a double barreled sawed off shotgun, a revolver, dynamite, a rifle, and can throw a mean knife. It's all political. You know how emotional these French women get about politics."

The sheriff frowned. "You joshing me, McCoy?"

"Not in the least. Sheriff, have you ever stared in the sawed off barrel of a 10 gauge shotgun and watched the double aught slugs come straight at you? Not pleasant. I was lucky. She was far enough away that they scattered outward enough that only one hit me. I assure you I'm not joshing. I don't want you to let her out of that cell, or let anyone in that cell without my permission. Remember my credentials say they expect your full cooperation."

"Yeah, don't remind me, McCoy."

Spur went back to check on the woman.

She looked up at him. "Your name, Miss?"

"I won't tell you."

"Where are you staying in town?"

"Find out yourself."

Spur nodded. "You need anything?"

"A hacksaw and a shotgun."

"Good luck."

Spur went to the three hotels in town and at the last one found the room clerk who remembered the small woman. She registered as Annie Johnson in room 22. The clerk opened it for Spur and he bundled up her goods in a thin carpet bag. He found her passport: Her name was Darlene Benoit, 28, from Paris. That would be interesting to the Mantuco embassy.

Spur took the carpet bag and her belongings to the jail and left them with the deputy. She was to be given only specific items, not allowed the whole carpet bag. It probably was filled with weapons.

Spur gave it up for the night and went to the hotel. He had just dropped on the bed when a knock sounded on his door. He opened it and found Francine standing there looking forlorn.

"I can't get to sleep," she said.

He pulled her inside and pushed her against the wall and kissed her thoroughly, then caught one of her breasts and caressed it through her dress. She opened the buttons and he went inside to her bare flesh and fondled both her breasts until her breathing speeded up to a panting.

Spur opened the door and led her outside and down to her room. She opened the door and stepped inside. He reached in, kissed her once more.

"Now you should be able to go to sleep easily."

"Hey, no fair!"

Spur shook his head. "I'm too tired to pop, so just dream about it while we both get some rest. It's been a damn long day."

She sighed. "I guess you're right. How is our jail bird?"

"Furious, but I think in a way she's glad it's over. She's hurting right now, but that'll pass."

"Will she be put on trial?"

287

"No, I doubt it. Probably charged and the judge will expel her from the country, deport her and ship her back to Paris."

He waved and closed the door.

Five minutes later, he slept soundly. That night he didn't even bother putting a chair under the door.

Chapter 21

Spur checked with the telegraph office at seven o'clock the next morning but there was nothing for him. He had breakfast, talked with the ladies as they came in the hotel dining room when he was about finished.

"No word yet from Washington, so we can't go on the stagecoach ride today," Spur told them.

"Oh damn," Francine said softly and Spur grinned. She was still mad about last night.

"You ladies can see how the pioneer women did their shopping. Look around the general store and you'll see how they live. Wash tubs, lye soap, sad irons, iron cooking pots. Learn a lot in a general store."

He left them and checked with the sheriff. He looked like he hadn't had much sleep.

"Damn fool woman screeched and yelled all night. The deputy came and got me and I damn near threw a bucket of cold water on her. Damn woman. When are you taking her out of here?"

"Not sure. Have to wait until I hear from Washington."

"Better not be long or I'm sure she's going to be shot while trying to escape."

"Don't try it, Sheriff. The State Department wants to talk with her. The Justice Department will be charging her, and I'm sure that the Principality of Mantuco will have a lot to say. I thought you said she didn't look dangerous last night."

"Not me. That witch tried to hang herself last night. Either that or it was a ruse to escape. Three of us went into her cell without our guns and got the stocking off her throat and off the overhead bunk. She was getting blue."

"I'll have a talk with her."

"Don't talk, get her out of here."

"Just as soon as Washington tells me to." Spur gave the lawman a stern look and went back to the cell. She had on a blouse and a skirt that she had asked for from her carpet bag. She sat on the bunk and glared at him.

"How's the arm this morning?"

"It hurts, what do you expect. I demand to see the French counsel."

Spur chuckled. "He's in New York or Washington. Might take him a day or two to get here. I'm going to charge you with attempted murder, four counts, three counts of murder since three of your men died in your criminal acts, another for the mine owner you killed, and a few other bits and pieces of English type common law. Do you want to spend the rest of your life in a United States Federal prison?"

She glared at him but said nothing.

"Miss Benoit, you're in serious trouble. I wouldn't try to escape again the way you did last night. The next time it might work—up to a point. One of the deputies happens to leave your cell door unlocked. Even the rear door is open. You go through it on a dead run and ten yards down the alley two deputies unlimber their shotguns and blow you into half a dozen chunks. That's what's known as killed while trying to escape."

"They wouldn't do that."

"After the fuss you raised last night, they are tremendously close to doing it. You want to live, you stay inside that cell."

She looked at him. Crossed her arms over her chest and scowled. Then she took a long breath and shivered.

"A little cooperation here will mean you'll get fed and treated like a lady. Otherwise, it's hard to say what could happen. The choice is up to you."

Spur turned and walked away. He heard her stand but he didn't look back.

There were still no telegrams for him at the office when he checked just before noon.

As the three of them ate dinner in a cafe down the street from the hotel, Francine was puzzled.

"What are they doing in Washington? They've had six or eight hours now, at least."

Spur laughed. "First the Justice Department tells the State Department about the case and they see how it might affect their negotiations with Mantuco. Then Mantuco calls on the State Department and they call in the French on it as well and they all three talk.

"Then Justice asks State what they should do, and State says wait until the conference is over. So we wait."

291

"And wait, and wait, and wait," Alexandria said. "Most diplomacy is waiting. I've learned that."

"We should hear something today," Spur said. "If not I'll fire off another round of telegrams."

They finished eating and Spur paid the tab. "Any plans for this afternoon," he asked the two.

"A nap I think first," Alexandria said. "Then maybe try some more shopping. Oh, I'll need some money for that."

Spur peeled off a hundred dollar bill for her and she put it in her small reticule.

"Enjoy yourselves. I'm going to sit in that telegraph office for a spell and see if I can rush those wires. Can't hurt, and I don't figure nothing better I should be at."

The women went toward the general store, and Spur headed for the telegraph key man.

In the Laramie County jail, things had slowed down. The sheriff had gone home for a couple of hours. There was only one prisoner and one deputy had ridden the train to Laramie to bring back a prisoner.

Deputy Silas Retland eyed the prisoner from the front office. She had asked for soap and a basin and water. She had washed herself and seemed like taken half a bath, but he didn't see anything. She used a comb from her reticule and now she called him.

"Silas, you busy?"

"No ma'am." He walked back to the cell area and stayed back from the bars. She had combed her hair, put some rouge on her cheeks and was right near pretty.

"You married, Silas?"

"No, Miss. Not a'tall."

"Strange, so handsome a young man. Bet you

turn the girls' heads at the dances."

"I don't dance too good, Miss."

"Some girl will show you about dancing soon, I bet." She stood and began to dance in the cell. Her hips swayed and her torso worked back and forth.

Silas had never seen a dance like that before. It made him think all sorts of un-pure thoughts. He was amazed the way her breasts bounced. Like she wore nothing under that thin blouse. Oh, damn, he was starting to get a boner. Not now. Not here!

"Silas, come on over here and I'll show you a downright fun dance."

"Really, I should stay in the office."

"Just a minute. You won't get a chance like this often. I mean a grown woman showing a young man what she can do. Come on, what's it going to hurt?"

He walked closer and stopped three feet from the bars. He stared at her chest. Yes! By damn! He could see her nipples pushing out from her breasts through the cloth. Oh, damn!

Darlene grinned. "See anything you like, Silas? I mean just the two of us here. I won't tell anybody if you want to touch anything. The dance. It's called the dirty Gertie. Goes like this."

She thrust her hips out and pulled them back, then thrust them out the way he'd seen some whores do in the windows. Like they was . . . fucking! He watched her hips with fascination. She rubbed one breast with her hand, then undid the three buttons holding the blouse together.

"Silas, you want to see this?" She flipped the cloth away from one breast and then pushed it back. Silas's jaw dropped open and his eyes went wide. He didn't realize he did it, but one hand reached down to where the hardness formed in back of his fly.

"You like that, Silas. Once more." She flipped the cloth away and this time left it open to reveal one breast. Silas gave a soft moan. His hand rubbed his hardness now.

"Silas, just you and me here. I can't do nothing. But I could show you something else, let you touch, if'n' you want to that is."

Silas took a step toward the bars. "Y . . . yes. Sure. What you show me?"

Darlene let the blouse slip off her shoulders and fall to the floor. "Oh, goodness, look what I did."

Silas let a dribble of saliva slip out of his mouth and run down his chin. "Oh, my god!"

"Tits, Silas. You like my naked tits?"

He nodded and took half a step toward her.

"You be real good and you can touch them. You want to touch my titties, Silas?"

"Oh, yes!"

"Then come up here and feel them. Just reach through and grab a handful. You won't hurt them. Tits are tough. Men don't understand that. Come on, Silas. How can a pair of bare tits hurt a great big guy like you?"

He hesitated, looked at the hall to the front. He ran to the door and closed the hall door shutting off the front and came back. He walked up to the bars. She was a little farther away now.

"Just reach in and touch them, Silas. Play with them. Look, I'll keep my hands behind my back."

She did and Silas reached through with his right hand and touched her breast, then he rubbed it and caught it in his hand. A minute later both his hands were through the bars and he petted both her breasts.

"Want to kiss one, Silas? I'll come closer and push up to the bars." She did and Silas bent and pushed his face against the bars as she pressed one breast into his mouth. Silas moaned. One hand rubbed his fly hard now.

As he chewed on her breast, Darlene reached through the bars on both sides of his head and the moment he let off her breast and backed a few inches from the bars, she grabbed his head and pounded it once, twice, three times against the steel rods.

Silas gave a sigh and slid down the bars unconscious. She pulled his legs over to the bars and went through his pockets. No key. She pulled his six-gun from his belt and skidded it between the bars. This jail lock couldn't be that complicated.

She used the butt of the six-gun and slammed it down on Silas's head once for protection. Then she aimed the muzzle of the revolver into the key hole, slanted it at the latch side, and fired. The lead slug penetrated the lock face and splattered among the mechanism inside. Enough of it hit the flange and turned it. The cell door swung open.

She pulled the big body into the cell, stripped down his pants and his shorts, tied his hands and feet. Then she buttoned up her blouse, picked up her carpet bag, and walked to the front of the jail. She cracked the door and looked out. Two men sauntered past. When they were gone, she came out of the jail, holding the carpet bag in front of her shielding the revolver.

Nobody paid any attention to her. She went to the street, down to the alley and quickly moved into the least busy part of town.

What now? The Princess was still in town if McCoy was. Staying at the same hotel. She could go there and wait for her to come back, then kill her. Only McCoy might be there and she knew that the other woman carried a derringer.

Given a second chance she wanted to kill the princess, but she also wanted to come out of it alive. Suddenly life seemed more precious to her than it had a few days ago.

A disguise. She needed something so she wouldn't be so identifiable.

She reversed her direction and went into a women's wear shop. It was the only one she had seen in town. Darlene still had some money. They had left it with her other things in her carpetbag.

She bought a blonde wig, a hat that sat high on her head and made her appear taller. She bought a typical Western jacket so she could blend in better with the locals.

She asked the sales lady to help her pin the wig on and then pin the hat to the wig. When it was done she paid for the purchases and went outside.

When? Supper at the hotel dining room. That would be good. But by then McCoy would know that she had escaped. It had to be sooner. Now! When better.

She walked straight to the hotel, left her carpet bag near a chair in the lobby and walked up to the second floor. The princess would have moved out of the shot up room. Next door? She tried that room, but no one answered. A skeleton key opened the door. No one was renting the room.

She moved across the hall and knocked. There was no response. Then she heard movement. A muffled sound came from the room, then a voice.

"Just a minute."

Darlene lifted the revolver from below the jacket and aimed it at the door.

Two men came up the stairs and walked toward her. She looked that way just as she heard a key in the lock.

One of the men stared. "My god, she's got a gun!" the man bellowed. One of the men fumbled in his jacket evidently to draw a weapon of his own. The first one knelt and seemed to be aiming at her.

"All right, Miss, just drop the gun and nobody gets hurt. Why are you aiming that big six-gun at that door?"

Darlene whirled, fired a shot toward the two without aiming and ran to the end of the hall. She knew there was a fire escape there, wooden stairs built down from the widow. She unlocked the window and stepped through. One of the men was down holding his leg. The other lifted a gun. Darlene hurried out of sight down the stairway. She was out of the alley before the man got to the window to look out.

When the man who ran to the hall window got back to his partner, the two stared at each other.

"I guess we got here just in time," one said. "That must have been the assassin Mr. McCoy told us about."

The man on the floor grunted. He had never been shot before. The round went through the fleshy part of his leg and he was surprised how much it hurt.

"Am I gonna bleed to death here, or can you get something to stop the bleeding?" They used both their large white handkerchiefs to stop the flow.

"Mr. McCoy said he'd check in with us regularly to be sure everything is all right. I just hope that it is all right."

A half hour later Spur ran up the steps and looked

297

at his men. "Somebody say they heard a shot from up here. Any problems?"

He listened tight lipped as the men told him what had happened.

"What did the woman look like?"

"Not real tall, a blonde with a hat on. It was a six-gun she had. We could have been killed."

Spur sent the one man limping to the doctor to get his wound bandaged and told him to come back. He could sit in a chair and be a guard just as well.

The Secret Service Agent slammed his hand against the wall. Darlene Benoit was as slippery as a greased pig at a farmer's fair. He had been the first one to enter the sheriff's office after the escape. He left the deputy where he was for the sheriff to find and grabbed two men to be guards at the hotel.

Then he ran to the general store thinking the women might still be there. He had to cover all the bases.

The women weren't at the store. That's when he ran flat out for the hotel.

Now he went up to Alexandria's door and knocked.

"Just a minute," a voice called.

Francine opened the door. She had on a new weird hat.

"Was that a shot out here a while ago?" Francine asked.

"It was. Darlene Benoit escaped from the jail and came calling."

"Not again."

"I have two guards outside. I doubt that she'll try to come back tonight. Even so, I want the princess to stay with you in your room today and tonight."

"We'll move over there right now."

"Good. I have to go send some more telegrams. Ones I don't want to send to the embassy and to my boss."

At the telegraph office there were three just received telegrams for Spur. He opened them one by one. They were detailed instructions what to do with the prisoner. He tucked them away in his pocket and sent the new wires.

He worded them carefully but they still said the same thing. Darlene Benoit had escaped from the Cheyenne sheriff's jail.

Spur left the train depot and prowled the town. The guard said the woman had on a tall hat and a blonde wig. By now she may have discarded that. There was a train east about three o'clock but he didn't figure that Benoit would be on it. She'd try again to kill the princess.

He wanted to scream and yell and swear at that sheriff's deputy, but that wouldn't do any good. It was plain to see how she had made her escape. She had enticed the deputy close enough to knock him out and get his gun, then shoot open the lock. She probably stripped for him and made wild promises to the young deputy.

Spur patrolled the business section, moving up one side of the street and down the other, looking in every store, and cafe along the way. He didn't find Darlene or anyone who even looked like the blonde wigged one.

He kept looking until supper time. His one hope was that if she saw him out watching for her, she'd stay in hiding and make no new try on the princess. It worked.

When he got back to the hotel just at six, Spur told the ladies he would bring their supper upstairs to them. He ordered and had the hotel dining room put it all on a pair of trays and had them taken to the second floor room.

He let the guards go down and eat in shifts. Then he told them they were on duty all night.

They grumbled but remembered he was paying them three dollars a day—three times what they could make doing anything else.

Spur made one final check with the women, then opened his door and inch and set his .44 close to hand and put the chair in a spot so he could see down the hall to the stairs. He'd be on duty all night as well.

Chapter 22

It was a long night. Spur stayed up until three A.M., then checked his two guards and told one of them he could sleep until morning. He'd be on day watch.

Spur watched the guard, made sure the second one stayed awake and turned in himself.

He slept until seven, got up and had a big breakfast at a cafe down the block, then checked with the stage coach people. The stage would leave promptly at 8:30 for the small town of Twin Mines. He instructed the day guard to make sure no one went in any of their three rooms.

They were safely on board the coach and out of town by 8:35 and Spur relaxed. There had been no sign of Darlene Benoit. He knew she would be back to try again. The only problem was when would she strike? The three of them made up the whole load for the small town outside of some freight and the mail sack.

Spur was surprised when a big Concord Stage Coach pulled in to pick them up. The Concord was the best stage ever made. It had big wheels, sturdy construction, and a suspension of two "through braces" from front to back that let the coach itself ride without taking each jolt and jar of the solid wheels. The braces were made of heavy strips of leather sewn together until they were three inches thick. They served as shock absorbers for the jolts of the road.

Some veteran stage coach riders said the leather springs gave the stage a feeling of being on a ship at sea.

"Ladies, this is a Concord coach, the finest ever built and a veteran of the toughest routes in the country. Most of these are retired now because of the transcontinental and dozens of other railroads. At one time you could take passage in a coach like this from Atchison, Kansas, all the way to Placerville in California for $600. That's a lot of money.

"The trip took 17 days and was more than a thousand nine hundred miles in length. Passengers were limited to baggage of only 25 pounds with a high charge for anything over that weight."

"People sat on these thinly padded wooden benches that far?" Francine asked.

"They did. Nine passengers inside, and two or three on the roof if they wanted to ride there at a slightly lower charge. You might think this rig is short and stubby, and indeed it is. Only eight feet long and five feet wide, but it took the roughest routes the West could throw at it.

"Consider the fine leather upholstery, wood paneling, and leather curtains to let down to keep out the sun, the rain and a little of the dust."

"People went such long distances in these, what did they eat?" Alexandria asked.

"Every 12 miles there was a swing station, where the horses would be unhitched from the stage and a fresh set of four or six put on. The passengers usually weren't allowed to get off at these places because it's a fast switch. Every forty or fifty miles there was a stop for food a home station."

"What about hotels?"

"The stage coach ran day and night. No overnight stops. Passengers slept sitting up if they slept at all. It was not a pleasant way to travel."

The coach hit a deep hole in the road and the three passengers bounced sharply.

Francine scowled. "You mean nine people could ride in here? Three on the front seat and three on the back. That means three have to sit in the middle bench with no backrest?"

Spur chuckled. "About right. There are the straps from the roof to hold on to, but your arm soon got tired doing that."

"At least we get to go on a stage coach before they all get replaced by steam engines," Alexandria said. "I can mark that off my list of things I want to do in America."

They came to a swing station, the only one on the twenty mile run, and they trooped out of the stage to watch the procedure. Four horses had already been harnessed and stood waiting.

The snaps were opened and the traces came off and a moment later the horses that brought them here were walked away without the stage. The new animals were brought into place, the harness hooked up and the driver took a long look at his only three passengers, who still watched.

"In the old days I would have left you standing there," he told them as they hurried on board. Then they were off and rolling again.

"Average speed on a stage coach is about eight miles an hour. That's why they can't afford to lose any time at the way stations. Doesn't seem fast by today's steam engine time tables, but twenty years ago the speed was just the same. That mean a stage could cover almost two hundred miles in a 24 hour period. That is it could if nothing went wrong, and no bridges or roads were washed out, or the snow wasn't too deep or if the rig didn't get struck in the mud somewhere."

About an hour later, they rolled into Twin Mines. The town held three stores, almost 20 houses and two coal mines. There had been talk of running the tracks through Twin Mines so they could utilize the coal, but fresh deposits on down the right of way stopped that move. Now the miners hauled their coal to the tracks to sell it.

"This must be it," Spur said, helping the ladies down from the coach. He grabbed the big picnic basket the hotel had packed for them and they stood in the shade of the overhang of the Twin Mines General Store.

"I'm hungry," Francine said. "Let's find someplace for our picnic."

A small stream wandered down one side of the single street. They walked up the flow a hundred yards and found some trees and a little grass where they spread out the blanket and investigated the lunch.

"Fried chicken!" Alexandria crowed. "Any picnic has to have fried chicken."

Spur had checked before they left the store. The return stage would be leaving at two-thirty.

"Want to go tour a coal mine?" Spur asked.

Both women threw chicken bones at him. He laughed and cleaned up the bones.

"We can always try the general store," Spur said. The women frowned.

"How about a hike?" Alexandria asked. "We haven't been on a good hike yet."

Francine nodded. "See that little hill over there?" Spur pointed to a peak on the horizon. "How far away to you think it is?"

"Two kilometers," Francine guessed.

"Not that far," Alexandria said. "Maybe a kilometer and a half."

"Let's walk over there," Spur said. They began by working across the little stream and into a meadow brightened by a few wild flowers and then up a slope toward the mountain.

When they had hiked for a half mile, Spur called a halt. "Look back at the town," he told them.

"So far away!"

"We've come that far? Look at the mountain. It isn't a bit closer."

"We've walked about half a kilometer. That mountain we're looking at is probably more like twenty kilometers over there."

"You did this to teach us something," Alexandria said.

"True. Distances in wide open spaces such as this, and especially with mountains, are always much more than you suspect. Always figure long when estimating distances in the mountains."

"Let's go back and find a cold drink somewhere," Francine suggested. The princess nodded so they turned around.

They found some cold ginger beer in the general store. There wasn't a saloon in town, so the store served a double purpose. The ice to keep the drinks cold came from the community ice house. Ice cut from a pond in the winter was packed down with straw in an ice house, then more straw put on top and more ice. The frozen chunks of ice would last all summer that way.

All three were ready for the stage to leave when it pulled up in front of the store a half hour later.

"So, you've had your stage coach ride, what's next?" Spur asked the ladies.

"It's not over yet, maybe we'll have a breakdown or a flood or something before it's over," Francine said.

An hour later they bounced away along the road. Nothing had happened to slow down the rig. They got the swing station team on and headed out again.

They were talked out and sat and looked at the mountains, or closed their eyes for small naps.

Spur's eyes snapped open abruptly when he heard a rife shot. He looked out the window and saw two masked men on horses in the roadway ahead. One held the rifle, the other a shotgun. The driver swore so loud they could hear him in the coach and pulled the rig to a stop.

The masked men came up on each side of the coach.

"Jump down, driver!" one of the masked men snarled.

"Got nothing worth stealing," the driver said. But he got to the ground.

Spur had out his six-gun but had no chance to get both of them. He concentrated on the shotgunner. When the man turned and stared at the coach, Spur shot him. The round slapped into his shoulder and tore him out of the saddle and he dropped the scatter gun.

Spur slid out of the off side of the coach away from the man with the rifle.

"What the hell? Who shot Will?"

The man with the rifle aimed it at the driver.

"You're a dead man. Don't know how you hit Will."

"I didn't shoot him. You see me with a weapon?"

"Must have done it. We saw two women back at the swing."

Before the man could get out another word, Spur came around the back of the coach.

"Drop the rifle or you're dead," Spur growled.

The man shook his head and started to swing the long gun to aim it at Spur. The Secret Service Agent fired twice. The first round hit the rifleman in the side and spun him around. He kept the rifle and turned to aim again.

Spur's second round hit the big man in the chest and slammed him backward into the roadway.

Spur ran to the first man he had shot. He was crawling away into the light brush along the road.

"Hold it!"

The man swore and sat down. Tears streamed down his face.

"Hell, we was just out for a little fun. You didn't have to go and shoot us."

"You'll have a long time to think about what your little fun cost you. I'd say five to ten years in the Wyoming Territorial Prison. Now let me tie up that shoulder so you don't bleed to death and cheat the judge who'll sentence you."

The driver had thrown up by the lead team.

"Damn, you killed the son of a bitch," he said, his eyes wide. "We ain't never had a hold up on this run. Everybody knows we don't carry nothing worth stealing."

Spur checked the rifleman. He was dead. Spur scouted around in the small patch of woods until he found the two horses. He led them out, tied the dead man over the saddle on one horse and tied lead lines on both animals to the rear of the coach.

Spur tied the wounded man's wrists together and pushed him inside. He cowered in the far side of the back seat.

"Ladies, meet a hardened Wild West Outlaw. This one will spent ten years in prison. He's so dumb he didn't think to cover the passengers in a coach while he was trying to rob it. Dumb doesn't count in a court of law. The only thing smart he did was not try to get off a shot at me after he got wounded."

Francine stared at the man, her eyes wide with wonder and a touch of fascination.

Alexandria frowned at him. "Men like him should be put in prison," she said. "His kind have no place in a civilized society."

"Couldn't agree with you more, Alexandria. That's exactly where he's going to go."

Nothing else happened on the last half hour of the trip back to town. Spur hurried the two women into their rooms at the hotel. The second guard was on duty now with the day man guarding the three rooms. They both were in place and looked alert.

Spur paid them for two days each and watched as they grinned and put the six dollars in their pockets. He figured that pay as you go always made the help a lot more efficient.

Spur went over to the sheriff's office and saw that the stage driver had already delivered the prisoner. He wasn't making any trouble. The sheriff looked at the dead man and his brows lifted.

"Seen this one before. Drifted in a couple of weeks ago. Had him in jail once overnight for disorderly. Said he was a cowboy out of work."

"He won't need much employment now," Spur said.

Spur arranged to give a deposition with a local lawyer about exactly what happened on the stage run. That and the testimony of the driver would be plenty to convict the other robber.

"McCoy, that deputy I had who let the woman get away. I fired him. He just wasn't old enough to do the work here."

"Don't be too hard on him, Sheriff. Half the men in town probably would have fallen for her tricks. Remember, she's French and used sex as a weapon."

Spur got back to the hotel and checked on the women. They both had taken baths, and were anxious to eat somewhere besides the hotel dining room.

Spur left one of the guards to watch their rooms and took the other one along. They ate at a small restaurant next to the bank. It had white table cloths and leaded glass drinking glasses.

The place also had good food. Spur was ready for a fine meal.

The guard prowled the sidewalk in front of the eatery. Nothing happened. They got back to their rooms safe and sound and Spur held a small conference.

"Ladies, are you ready to start back to Washington?"

"No," they both said at once.

"I want to go to Rock Springs, Wyoming," Princess Alexandria said.

Francine shrugged. "I wanted San Francisco, but it's too far away, I guess. I told Alex Rock Springs probably looks a lot like Cheyenne and it's even smaller."

"I like the sound of the name. I want to go to Rock Springs."

Spur nodded. "Fine, ladies. tomorrow we'll go to Rock Springs. I'll find out when the morning train comes through here. I better do that right now. There'll be two guards outside. I'll let you know when I come back."

He was back in 30 minutes. The Westbound left the station at 10:30. They had tickets.

Spur told the women he was back, then went into his room ready for a long summer's nap. He had pulled off his boots and his shirt when a knock sounded on the door.

Spur wondered where the guards were. He pulled his six-gun from the holster on the chair and opened the door a crack. Francine looked in.

"We need to talk," she said pushing the door open and slipping inside. She wore a robe over something soft and filmy and carried a package. Spur knew he'd see soon exactly what the negligee looked like on Francine and off her.

"Talk about what?"

"Things. Like how strong are you tonight, and can you be an extraordinarily great lover tonight."

She kissed him hard and wanting. Her arms came around his neck and welded his lips to hers. Gently she nudged him toward the bed and he walked backwards. When his legs hit the bed he put his arms around her and twisted and they both fell on the bed gently so they wouldn't knock out the bed boards.

She squirmed under him, got her lips free and stared at him.

"I want you to tell me exactly how you felt when you killed that robber today. Were you all excited and thrilled and wild, or were you nervous and tentative and worried about taking another life?"

He watched her a moment. "You don't understand. It was business. I had to kill him or he would have killed me and probably all four of us. That way there would be no witnesses to testify against him."

Francine's eyes went wild, she breathed fast and hard through her mouth. Then her eyes closed to slits. "But how did you feel?"

"I don't get emotional about killing a man. I can't afford to. I hate the idea of killing, but in some cases like today, it has to be done."

She pushed him off her and ripped open the robe; the filmy, soft silk came off her and she lay there writhing, her breath a panting, her eyes intense, almost screaming at him.

"McCoy, damn you, fuck me right now so hard I scream in pain. I need it now!"

She pulled open his fly and pushed down his pants and underwear, pulling him on top of her spread legs.

"McCoy, I've never seen a man killed before. It just got me going and I couldn't stop. I've been wanting to jump you since the second you got back in the stage coach this afternoon. Right now, McCoy! Don't waste another damn second!"

Spur had seen the after-shock of a killing affect people before, but never quite in this way. He did as she asked, taking her at once and without his

311

pants off, mashing her breasts as he caressed them, pounding hard and fast and dry so it almost burned with each stroke. That made him come sooner.

She pounded upward with each stroke, her eyes wide open, that too-brightness still bothering her. He had to flame it out.

"More, McCoy! Deeper, deeper. God but you're good. Yes, Yes! Oh, god, oh god. Here I go! Christ! What a feeling. Almost there . . ." Then she moaned once and a high keening came from her. Her body spasmed again and again, trailed off only to start again. The vibrations flamed through her body time after time, and her hips pounded against him all the time, wanting more of him, urging him on.

The keening gave way to a soft moan and then a high piercing scream that ended with another climax as her hips surged again and again and her whole body writhed in the multiple spasms that they brought on.

Without any tapering off, she stopped. She lay there like she was unconscious, her breathing gave her away, still boiling with a need for more and more air. She gasped in air as fast as she could. In a few minutes even that slowed and she unlaced her hands from in back of his neck and kissed his cheek and her head rolled to one side.

She tried to say something, but the words didn't come out right. Francine sighed then and took one long deep breath. Then her eyes popped open.

"Oh . . . fuck! But that was good. I was on fire. I've never felt that way before. Not the wanting to be fucked so much. Do you know why?"

"You're a healthy young girl animal."

"Right, but I've been that way for years. This was more, something more." Her eyes went wide. "Oh, god." She looked at him and then closed her eyes.

They stayed shut. "Do you think it's some kind of a reaction to watching that robber get shot and then die today?"

"Yes, I think so."

"Is that unusual?"

"Not anything to be worried about. You are reacting to a shock to your mentality. You've never seen a man shot and die before. Everyone reacts differently. I've seen men start singing when they kill someone. Lots of men cry. I know one young outlaw who always wet his pants everytime he gunned down someone. If anybody laughed at his lack of control, he'd kill the laugher, too."

"Then you don't think I'm strange or weird or unbalanced or anything?"

"Absolutely not. You're the most balanced, and the sexiest little woman I've ever seen."

She grinned. "Really?"

"Damn right. Of course I haven't seen all of the women yet naked and fucking the way you are."

She pretended to hit him.

"You didn't get your turn."

"Next time." They sat side by side on the bed their hands still on each other.

"Oh, I brought some snacks. I get hungry at times like this. Do you?"

"Young men get hungry after sex, old men get sleepy. I think I'll have a nap."

She grinned and hit him with the sack. Inside he found an assortment of hard candy, some home made cookies, a slab of cheese and a smaller sack filled with crackers and two big, red apples.

"Let's eat," she said.

He bent and began chewing on one of her still-flushed breasts.

"Not me, silly. You can eat all of me you want later. Right now the cheese and crackers."

Later they made love again. Francine wasn't quite as wild this time, and when they were through, he saw that the too-bright flames in her eyes had burned out and she was back to the normal, sexy, Francine.

They finished off the cheese and the cookies, and came together once more before they decided a little rest was in order. She stayed in his room that night, sleeping with one arm over his shoulder.

Spur grinned and bent and kissed her soft lips once more as she slept. She nearly roused, then whispered something he couldn't understand. He didn't need to. She smiled a gentle, satisfied way.

McCoy went to sleep.

Chapter 23

Rock Springs had changed in the two years since Spur had seen it. They arrived there without incident just before supper the next day. Spur hoped they had eluded the assassin. He toured the two train passenger cars but saw no one who could possibly be the small woman.

They checked in at the hotel and planned a two day stay. Spur was not sure what they would do. The first night in town they held a street dance. The main avenue had been blocked off with freight wagons, shocks of hay stacked along one end and that area strung with a hundred lanterns on ropes across the street.

An orchestra that played often in the area was on hand, sawing and plunking, and they even rolled out the Black Hole Saloon piano to add to the music making. There were three fiddles, two banjos and a guitar.

They had supper at the Railroad Cafe, which turned out to be the best eatery in town, then walked along the boardwalk and watched the dancers out in the street. For the occasion the street had been sprinkled and rolled hard by a pair of sweating young men. Their work had turned the usually inch-thick dusty street into a firmly packed dance floor.

The rollers were nothing more than flat barrels filled with concrete and with handles attached.

"Looks like the locals are having fun," Francine said. The dance was a Virginia Reel with the squared off dancers going through the routines with a flourish. That ended and it was stomping time with each couple on its own.

Francine poked Spur in the side and pointed to Alexandria and the dance floor. She frowned at him and nodded vigorously.

"Princess, would you care to dance?" Spur asked.

Alexandria looked up, pleased. "Why yes, that might be interesting. I'm not sure if I know those steps."

"I might not either, but it doesn't matter. We'll improvise with the beat."

They went past the piles of hay and to the edge of the floor. Spur held out his arms and she flowed into them in a formal pose and they danced away. It was a two step of some sort and Spur did his best to follow it. He was best at waltzes, but he was sure this group wouldn't play one.

After a time or two around the floor they fell into a workable pattern and the princess looked up and smiled.

"My, but this is nice. I think I could learn to enjoy this kind of dancing. The music is a bit different from what I've known."

"It's certainly loud. At least out here we can dance half a block away from them."

The music stopped and some of the couples left the floor but most waited for the new set. After the next three numbers, Spur and Alexandria went back to the boardwalk.

Francine wasn't where they had left her.

Many of the stores were still open and lanterns were hung by the outside doors to attract customers. Spur checked in three of the nearby stores, but Francine wasn't there.

"Maybe she walked down the street a ways," Spur said. They moved that direction to the end of the dance area, but didn't find her.

"Strange," Spur said. They stood looking at the dancers, and Alexandria pointed.

"There she is, she's dancing. That girl does love to dance."

It was Francine. She was laughing and dancing and holding out her skirt and having a wonderful time. Spur and Alexandria went back where they had left Francine. She didn't come back at the end of the second set of numbers.

"Let's dance out there and find her," Spur said. They made two circuits of the big dance floor before they found her. Spur danced up beside her and touched her arm.

She looked up and grinned.

"Hi there, cowboy!" Francine said. "This gentleman is Hale Grover." They stopped dancing and shook hands. Grover was about five-eight, with a tanned face and a cowboy hat on. He was lean and well built and had a full moustache but no beard.

"Howdy," Grover said. They all were introduced and then Francine smiled.

"Well, we're gonna dance. I'll find you later back

over there by that hardware store."

They two-stepped off. Spur and Alexandria continued as well and Spur saw his charge looking troubled.

"Princess, I really don't think you need to worry. The young man looks tame enough. He's in town for a good time, but my bet is that Francine can more than handle him."

"I hope so. I don't want that girl getting hurt."

"I'll see to it."

Alexandria smiled up at him. "You like our Francine, Don't you, Spur?"

"A charming lady, pretty as a new born foal, perky, smart and can speak her mind. Yes, I like her."

"And last night?"

"I loved her."

"Good, so often she gets left out."

"Looks like tonight she won't get left out."

They waited at the hardware store through the next two sets and at the end of the last one, Francine and Hale hurried up.

"We're going to the cafe for some of that new iced cream, you want to come?"

All four of them found a seat at the crowded cafe and the iced cream was delicious.

Francine was full of nervous talk. "Hale owns his own ranch about ten miles out of town. It isn't real big but it's growing, and he got two hired hands. It's about the best ranch around."

Hale grinned. "Well, not quite that good, but hope to make it into a bigger spread with a little luck and some more heifer calves on the spring drop."

"How many head do you have now?" Spur asked not really caring.

"About a hundred head of brood cows and first crop of steers. So it'll be three years before I can sell any to market. 'Tween now and then is the tough time."

"What's your brand?" Spur asked.

"The Bar H. Simple enough but hard to use a running iron on."

The ice cream and cookies were gone. Spur stood up and so did Hale. "Well, good meeting you, Hale. Think we'll get back to the dance."

"Me and Hale are going to dance some more, too," Francine said.

They walked away first, and Alexandria caught Spur's arm.

"Now, don't be jealous. Give the girl a little bit of freedom here. Besides, I'm ready to dance again, myself."

After three more sets they found a vacant bench near the hardware and sat down. From time to time they saw the pair on the dance floor. Spur had to admit that Francine looked like she was having a good time.

Spur was danced out. It was getting late. The dance was posted as lasting from dusk to midnight. It was then almost eleven.

"Is she going to dance all night?" Spur asked.

Alexandria touched his arm. "You are a bit jealous, aren't you, Spur McCoy?"

"Yes, I guess so. But she's also part of my responsibility, diplomatically speaking of course."

They waited until almost midnight and then Francine hurried up to them. She sat between them and took a hand of each one.

"I am really impressed by this young man. Holt is a true gentleman and he makes me laugh. I. . . ." She hesitated. "Damnit, Spur don't look at me that way. He asked if he can come to my hotel room, and I said he could." Spur stiffened and scowled at her.

"Now, don't go getting jealous. I like this man and I want him, and I don't want you bursting in with your six-gun ready to shoot. I'm a grown woman and can do what I want to do. Unless Princess Alexandria tells me not to, I'm going to be with Holt tonight."

Spur growled.

Alexandria caught both of Francine's hands. "You sure that you'll be all right? Are you sure this man won't hurt you?"

"I'll be fine. And I'm sure Spur won't sleep soundly, if at all, and he's right next door in the hotel. If I need help, I'll scream and you can come rescue me. But I won't. Hale is a dream of a gentleman."

"Have you kissed him?"

Francine nodded. She looked at Spur. "Promise you won't come barging in?"

"Like you say, you're a grown woman. I won't budge unless you call for some help."

"Good!" She leaned over and kissed Spur on the lips then jumped up. "You're both such dears!" She hurried away and met Hale and they drifted down the street toward the hotel.

Spur shifted on the bench.

Alexandria looked at him and smiled. "That was a good thing you did, Spur McCoy. I know you like the girl. But sometimes she needs a little fling like this. A new face. You understand."

He nodded. "Shall we head back to the hotel as well?"

A short time later he left the princess at her door, paused as he passed Francine's door and then went on to his. He tried not to listen to the sounds from the middle room, but when he heard the high keening voice he knew exactly what was happening.

He sat and smoked a rare long black cigar and stared out the window. Then he snuffed the smoke and went out and locked his door.

He knocked softly on the princess's door. She opened it. She hadn't undressed either.

"I've been waiting for you, Spur McCoy. Come in. Maybe we can comfort each other."

She closed the door and locked it, then fell into his arms and reached up for his kiss. Spur picked her up and carried her to the bed and lay her down gently. He stretched out beside her and kissed her with lips barely touching hers. She rolled toward him and kissed him hard pushing her big breasts against his chest. When it ended she looked at him in the soft glow of the kerosene lamp.

"Even a princess needs a fling once in a while, too."

They made love gently the first time, then hard and fast and furiously the second time. After that they lost track. Spur spent the whole night in the bedroom of the Princess of Mantuco.

They slept in until eight. Spur got up and dressed and said he had a small errand to run before breakfast. He went to the General Store and talked with the postmistress. She was most helpful and told him what he wanted to know. His face had a grim set to it as he knocked on the princess's door and took her down to breakfast.

Francine and Hale sat across the room. When they were done with breakfast, they stopped by Spur's table.

"What's our schedule for today?" Francine asked.

"No special plans yet," Spur said.

"Good. Hale has some business to do, and then he and I are going to have a picnic out along the river someplace."

"I'm going to do some shopping," Alexandria said. "Maybe this afternoon we could go on a buggy ride in the mountains."

Francine beamed. "Good. We'll be back here at the lobby at, say two o'clock?"

Alexandria nodded and Francine grabbed the cowboy's arm and they walked out of the restaurant.

"I just hope she doesn't get hurt," Spur said.

Alexandria looked at him quickly. "This morning before breakfast you went somewhere to ask about Hale Grover. What did you find out?"

"He's what he says he is, a rancher out north of town with a small spread. Has a good reputation in town, pays his bills, doesn't get in trouble, doesn't drink too much and never gambles at all."

"A good report."

"Right, so I was a little disappointed."

She touched his hand. "I know you're concerned for her, but so far we're doing all we can. If she makes a mistake, that's the way we learn. Now, let's get back up to the room. Maybe Francine is there and we can do some woman talk."

Spur left the two women talking in Francine's room and toured the town again. This time he checked with the sheriff's office but they gave Grover a good report as well. As a last resort he had a haircut, a light trim and a neck shave, but the barber had no bad news either.

"Grover? Yep, young rancher out north aways. Solid citizen far as I can see. He don't come to the Baptist church on a Sunday, but there's lots of good folks who don't."

Spur paid the cutter and went back to his room not feeling much better. He tried to think of something to do in the small town, but there wasn't much. It had begun as a railroad town as the rails were pushed out to the west.

Every 50 miles or so the railroad established a work camp, and most of them prospered and grew into towns. Cheyenne and Laramie were two others that made the grade from rail construction boom town to respectability.

But Rock Springs, Wyoming, was not a delight for the traveler or a tourist with some spare time.

On a bulletin board next to the general store he saw a sign:

"THE PLAY'S THE THING! Shakespeare tonight at the Masonic Hall. Featuring *Hamlet*. Come see professional thespians perform the story of the moody Dane."

Spur shrugged. Better than nothing. He went back to the hotel and cleaned and oiled his .44 and made sure it was working perfectly. Never could tell. He went back down to the block long town and walked it, watching for anyone who could be Darlene Benoit in disguise. He knew the French woman had not given up. Even with a broken wrist and a shot shoulder, she would try to even the score for her jailed and dead brother.

If they were lucky, Benoit was still in Cheyenne looking for them. It was about time they had some good luck for a change.

He knocked on Alexandria's door. It opened.

"Spur. Good. Francine left about ten minutes ago with Grover for their picnic. Would you mind taking me shopping. I'm looking for anything native and original, even something Indian."

They shopped, they had dinner at a small restaurant, then shopped some more.

At two o'clock they waited in the lobby, but Francine didn't come. She at last showed up at three. Her blouse was mis-buttoned but Spur said nothing about it.

Francine was so happy she was glowing. He had seen her that way before. Grover wasn't with her. Francine said he had some more business but would meet them all for supper.

The buggy ride in the foothills around Rock Springs should have been one of the highlights of the trip. There were still some spring wildflowers in bloom. Alexandria gathered some. Francine sat in the buggy and stared at the clouds.

The slope of the mountains and the blue sky made a pretty picture as they rolled along in the buggy. They stopped and watched a doe and her newborn hurry across the trail. The fawn turned and looked at them with innocent curiosity.

The doe stared at the buggy, then nosed her fawn away from them, turned him around and hustled him into a patch of brush and out of sight.

"Delightful!" Alexandria said. "Did you see how protective of her fawn that beautiful doe was?"

Francine's eyes were glazed. She nodded, said something that didn't make any sense to the situation.

Spur drove on. It had been a bad idea to come to Rock Springs. Now he wished that they had stayed in Cheyenne.

The tour continued with the same results. By the time they got back to the hotel, Francine had almost come back to normal. She smiled at Spur and he said they'd go for supper at 5:30 and then to a play that night. She nodded.

Francine went into her room first at the hotel

and Alexandria waited for Spur.

"I think it's best that we head back to Cheyenne tomorrow morning," she said. "I don't like the way Francine is responding to this man. Earlier today she asked me how hard it would be for the embassy to get her a permanent visa to stay here."

"She serious about this guy?"

"It looks so. I've never seen her so wrapped up in a man before. Yes, she's serious."

Spur almost told the princess then. He decided to wait. He'd have a talk with Grover tonight and get rid of him.

The supper was a disaster. Francine talked only to Grover. It was as if they were dining alone. When it was over, Spur took Grover aside.

"You know Francine is here only temporarily. She's on a diplomatic passport and will be going home tomorrow."

"No, no. It can't be. She said she can stay as long as she wants to."

"Not true. She's escorting the princess. That's her job. She can't leave the princess until she's safely back in Mantuco."

"No, you're wrong, McCoy. You're wrong." Grover surged away from Spur and back to Francine.

Francine pleaded a headache and said she couldn't sit through *Hamlet* again by some third rate players. She insisted that the princess and Spur attend.

"It is my favorite Shakespeare play," Alexandria said.

So they attended.

When they got back to the hotel about eleven o'clock, Spur knocked on Francine's door. There was no response. He knocked again. Alexandria looked concerned. Spur tried the door knob. It was unlocked. He knocked again, then opened the door calling her name.

She wasn't there. The room had been cleaned up and all of Francine's personal items were gone. So was her carpetbag and all of her clothes.

"Grover, that son-of-a-bitch. He's run away with her."

"Oh, dear, I was afraid of this."

"That's only half the bad news," Spur said. "Grover is already married. The fact is he's a Mormon and already has two wives out on that ranch of his. Now he wants three!"

Chapter 24

Twenty minutes later, Spur had rented a horse from the sleepy livery stable man.

"Yeah, I rented Grover a horse tonight," the stable hand said. "Strange, he always has his own animals. Came in long about eight o'clock or so and left right away. Saddle and all. Nice little painted pony."

Spur got a Springfield rifle from the livery and a box of shells and then asked how he could find the Grover ranch. He got explicit directions.

Ten miles, two hours. Would they ride straight to the ranch or bed down along a stream somewhere? Spur guessed it would be the stream. He moved out along the route slowly, walking his animal. Grover probably figured they wouldn't miss Francine until morning. By then he could be at his ranch and hide Francine.

Spur walked his horse so if they were near they wouldn't hear him coming. How would Francine react? She must have come with the man willingly. She knew she couldn't do that. Not with the passport she carried.

Love conquers all—but not this time.

Every quarter of a mile he stopped and sniffed the air. A love nest like this would need a small fire. That would make it so much easier.

A mile on he smelled a smoke, but soon found it came from a small house near the stream. A scratch farm showed there, mostly where the river overflowed in the spring.

Another mile later the trail went right along the stream and continued north. Not a lot up here.

Two more miles and he smelled smoke again. No houses or buildings. He moved up slowly on the smoke, trailed it to the stream and then saw a small glow of the fire itself.

He was still casting about for a way to get Francine to *want* to come back with him. He could drag her along, but that wouldn't last for long. There had to be a better way.

He left his horse and moved up on the fire as silently as a Sioux. Soon he could hear voices and then laughter. Another move forward and he saw them sitting on a saddle blanket near small fire. Both were naked on top at least.

What would set her off?

A long walk to the ranch. Yes, the horses. He circled until he found where the two horses were tied in some grass 40 yards from the fire. This Grover sure was confident. He untied the two horses and led them a half mile back down the creek and tied them in thick brush.

Then he jogged back to the scene. They were

laughing and playing. He moved closer.

"Let's splash in the water," Francine said.

"It's wet and cold," Grover said.

"So we can dry off and get warm by the fire." Without waiting for him she stood and ran toward the small stream. It was no more than two feet deep and ten feet wide. She shrieked and sat down in the water.

Grover reluctantly headed for the water.

Spur grinned and slipped up in the darkness to where their clothes lay. He picked up everything, shoes to underwear, and hauled it all away, back well into the brush again a quarter of a mile downstream near the horses.

He had planned to scatter the fire and make it go out as well, but by the time he got back, they were huddled around the fire.

"It's cold, Grover, build up the fire."

Spur listened. There had been a bit of irritation sounding in her voice. A moment later Spur could tell the fire burned higher.

"Sweetheart, where did you leave my blouse?"

"Right over there where we threw it. You were fantastic tonight, do you know that? I'll get your blouse. Not that I don't like looking at you all bare assed that way."

Spur watched the man searching in the grass and low growth behind the fire.

"Where the hell is it?"

"What, Hale?"

"I can't find your blouse. I can't find any of our clothes."

"Hale, don't make jokes. Our clothes have to be right there where we left them."

"I know that!" Hale said sharply. "You come find them."

"I guess I'll just have to do that. We put them right over...."

"Not here, are they? Maybe we threw them on the other side, away from the creek."

Spur saw the two naked bodies searching another area. He moved back just a little.

"Damnit, where the hell are our clothes!"

"I've heard of squirrels running off with clothes in the woods, but not every single piece," Francine said. "Now even our shoes and boots are gone."

"Oh, damn. I know there are some grubline riders around. They might have heard us, seen our clothes and run off with them. Most of them jaspers don't have much. I had some cash in my wallet. They'd steal the whole mess just for the wallet."

"Oh, dear! Hale, what can we do now?"

"At least it's dark." They both sat near the fire a minute, not touching each other.

"I guess I could get my horse and ride on to the ranch, get us some clothes and come back."

"I'd look silly in men's clothes."

"Not for long. We'll buy you all new ones."

"That would mean.... I'd have to be here alone, while you rode on to the ranch got the clothes and came back. What if those outlaws came back?"

"They aren't outlaws, just men down on their luck riding from one ranch to another looking for work."

"But seeing me this way.... I mean a man might want to have his way with me."

"You've been fucked lots of times."

"Hale! I hate to hear that word. Please never use it around me."

He laughed softly. "High and mighty. Damn. The very first hour I meet you, you let me touch your tits. Then two hours later you invite me up to your hotel and fuck me good all night. Now you don't even like to *hear the word?*"

"It's different now. Why can't I ride along with you?"

"You ever ridden a saddle without any clothes on?"

"Oh, I see. No I haven't. Have you?"

"If one of us goes I could use the saddle blanket."

"Let's both go. I'll gladly walk. How far is it?"

"About five miles."

"Five. . . . that's seven kilometers!"

"Not any other way I can see to do it."

"Oh, damn. Go get the horses, Hale."

The man stood. "One more thing, Francine. I don't ever want you telling me what to do again. It ain't a woman's right to order a man around. Now you remember that."

He slipped off in the darkness toward where he left the horses.

Five minutes later, Spur heard a bellow. "I can't find the damn horses."

"Maybe your saddle bums stole them, too," Francine screeched.

A minute later, Hale showed up at the fire. He shook his head and stared at her. "Something mighty damn funny is going on here. I want to get to the bottom of it." He turned to the darkness.

"All right, you've made your point, whoever you are out there. You had your fun. enough is enough. You come in and bring our clothes and our horses, or somebody is gonna get his ass whipped damn bad. You hear me?"

Only silence answered him.

"Well, you certainly took care of that!" Francine snapped.

"As well as you did. What's your idea of what to do?"

"You walk to your dumb old ranch. Get two horses and clothes and ride back here and rescue me before it gets daylight. No, no, don't walk to your ranch. Run, run all the way because I'm getting a chill. And build up the fire more."

"Any other orders? Francine, you have a sharp tongue. We'll work that out of you in a little while. Now get on your feet. We'll both walk back to the ranch. Be faster that way. Then I'll get a horse and come back here and find our two mounts and our clothes and we'll be laughing about this tomorrow."

"I thought you said we'd get married tomorrow."

"We will, Francine. Just soon as I can get the right man out to the ranch."

"A preacher. It's got to be a religious man of the cloth. Should be at least Episcopal."

"Likely can't do that last one, but it'll be legal and binding and in the eyes of the church. Now, let's walk."

"No. I told you, Hale. I'm not walking seven kilometers to your little ranch. You want me, you walk out there and bring back some clothes for me."

Spur could see Hale standing near her. He had his hands on his hips. Slowly he shook his head.

"You're not near as nice as you were back at the dance. You're a real bitch now, aren't you. Nasty and mean, and wanting your own way. Hell, I don't need no more of that kind of talk at home."

Spur saw Francine stand. She turned to face Hale and the fire silhouetted her side view.

"And just what the hell does that mean, Mr. Hale Grover?"

"You know fucking well what it means. No matter how good a woman is in bed, no matter how big her tits and how hot her little pussy is, if she's a bitch at heart and demands things and orders a man around, she's about as easy to live with as a rattlesnake and a coyote all rolled into one."

"Well, pardon me! Here I didn't know I was talking with Jesus Christ himself, the perfect man. Sure, you're good in bed, but I've never tried a man who wasn't. Hale, let's say you were only *average to fair* in bed. But you're a real bastard when it comes to treating women with respect."

"That does it, bitch. Your big mouth just talked your way right out of a wonderful marriage. You can sit here and rot, or charge the bums who ride by here a quarter a fuck for all I care. I'm going home. I don't give a shit what you do or where you go."

Spur watched as Grover stared hard at her a moment; then she tried to slap him, but he ducked the blow and ran into the darkness.

"Grover, you come back here!"

There was a period of silence.

"Hale Grover you come back here, you can't treat me this way after I been so good to you. I gave you everything."

Another black period of quiet.

"Grooooooooooovvvvvveeeerrrrrr!" The long drawn out scream echoed up and down the stream.

The next thing Spur heard was crying. He wanted to go get the clothes and the horses, but he figured he might lose her in the darkness.

He called out in the darkness.

"Helloooooooooo. Is anybody there?"

It was quiet for a minute.

"Yes. Over here. Who are you?"

Spur moved toward her. "I'm hunting a lost lady. I think somebody kidnapped her tonight. Have you seen Francine Miller?"

A moment passed. "Spur McCoy! Is that really you?"

He moved faster through the brush toward her. "Francine?"

He rushed into the fire light and she threw her arms around him.

"Oh, God! McCoy. I've never been so glad to see anyone in all of my life. I'll be your slave for the rest of the century. I can't start to tell you how dumb I've been."

He held her and looked down at her body.

"Hey, you aren't wearing too much."

"It's a long story. Can you sneak me back to town?"

"I can do even better than that."

He grinned at her naked body, rubbed one breast a moment, then kicked dirt over the fire and stomped it out. He caught her hand.

"Let's walk along the riverbank, it should be easier on your feet that way."

"You must have a horse. Do we have to walk all the way back to town?"

"Not quite."

He walked her most of the way. The last 50 yards through the brush he carried her.

"Hey, this is nice. I've never carried a gorgeous, naked lady this far before."

"I'm thanking you, any way you want, I'm thanking you. Now or later."

He set her on her feet and pulled her clothes out of a pile in the brush.

"How about some clothes I found along the road.

Should fit you pretty good."

She looked at the blouse in the pale moonlight. Her mouth came open, then she laughed softly.

"You bastard, McCoy. You chased us, you found us, you stole our clothes and our horses and you got us into a drag out fight. You are a real bastard, and I love you for it." She kissed him three times before he could edge away.

"I've got some more news for you, just as soon as you get dressed so I don't wind up raping you here against that tree."

"Standing up?" she asked with a grin.

Five minutes later she was dressed. They left the rancher's clothes where they were. He led the rancher's horse over and tied him near the clothes.

Then the two of them mounted the horses and headed for town.

"Oh, I have another bit of news for you. I take it that the man promised to marry you."

"He sure did, and I believed him."

"Oh, he probably would have married you. I found out a little about him in town. Grover is a Mormon. Follows the teachings of the church."

She looked at him. "So?"

"You don't know about the Mormons. They believe in a whole bunch of strange things, including the practice of a man having more than one wife."

"I wouldn't let him marry a second wife. I'd put my foot down."

"Seemed like Grover didn't like it when you ordered him about, when you told him what to do."

"McCoy! You were listening to us fight. You heard the whole thing!"

"True. The interesting part is that Hale Grover

already has two wives out at his ranch. He wanted you for number three."

There was a silence as their horses walked back toward Rock Springs.

"You're not just saying that to make me feel worse, are you, McCoy?"

"To feel better, I hope. You didn't know about Mormon customs."

"The bastard is raising cattle and children!" Francine shouted. "He probably wants four wives with ten kids from each wife. The bastard!"

"Strange customs we Colonials have, wouldn't you say?"

"Oh, damn. Not all of your customs are strange. Like your custom of letting a lady make an absolute ass of herself before you rescue her from a philandering polygamist."

"It was the only way I could figure out to make you want to come back. I could have killed him, and then you would have loved him forever. Or I could have let you get to the ranch and be humiliated in front of his other two wives.

"I figured if I saw you make a fool of yourself, that was a big enough audience. Anyway, I didn't know how many guns he had out at his ranch."

"Oh, damn."

"You said that already. You going to tell the princess about all this tonight? I figured you would want to tell her. Confession is good for the soul."

"But I was so stupid."

"What about the princess going out to the ranch with that widower? She's done some dumb things on this trip as well."

"Yeah. But she's got a title. Maybe we are a pretty good matched pair after all."

"Not at all, your breasts are bigger."

Francine Miller laughed. She wiped tears from her eyes and rode close to him.

"Hey, McCoy. Give me a kiss. I owe you."

The kiss was strong and hard and potent. After it ended she sighed.

"McCoy, I still owe you. You collect anytime you want to. Except tonight. I want a bath first."

They got back into town a little before midnight and turned in the rented horses and the rifle and shells.

Francine looked at the rifle with surprise.

"Hey, you came expecting a battle. I'm impressed."

"Damn right, Francine. You're worth it."

Back at the hotel they knocked on Alexandria's door. She was still up and dressed. She hugged Francine and they both started to cry and Spur chuckled and closed the door.

He loved them, these women, but there wasn't a chance in hell that he'd ever understand their mental goings on. He wondered if they were still set to start on the trip back tomorrow.

Breakfast would be plenty of time to decide. Spur went into his room, closed the door, slipped the chair under the knob and fell into bed.

Chapter 25

The next morning the three travelers took the east-bound out of Rock Springs at 8:12 and were due to arrive in Cheyenne that afternoon. An unscheduled stop for a prairie fire that stormed across the tracks for half an hour held up their progress. Then the tracks and ties had to be inspected by a walking crew and at last the train inched across the fire-scarred area at a walk.

Once on the other side they got up to speed again.

Spur glanced out the windows and shouted at the women. "Look, some buffalo!"

There not 50 yards from the tracks a dozen buffalo grazed contentedly, refusing to let the roaring metal monster upset them.

"They're so big," Alexandria said.

"And shaggy, does all that hair come off in

patches and bunches that way?" Francine asked.

They watched the shaggy beasts as long as they could, then they were out of sight.

Alexandria sighed. "Well, now we can say that we saw buffalo wild and free on the American plains."

"Why are we stopping in Cheyenne?" Francine asked.

"I'm sure there are some telegrams there for me. I also want to take one last look for our little hellcat. I'd like to catch her again and not be worried about her all the way back to St. Louis."

"And it will give us time for one last look in that wonderful general store," Alexandria said.

"We'll register for one night at the hotel and see what I can do about finding our Miss Benoit."

As soon as they registered at the hotel, Spur went to the telegraph office. He had two wires, one from his boss in Washington and one from the Mantuco embassy. He looked at the one from General Halleck first.

"Shocked by loss of prisoner. Hope for recapture. Big controversy still on here about the French addition to the puzzle. Mantuco embassy may be contacting you. Take care. W. D. Halleck, General, U.S. Army."

Spur hesitated before he opened the second wire. The company at least sealed them in envelopes now. That was progress.

"Mr. Spur McCoy. Disappointed about loss of prisoner. Please recapture her as soon as possible. Pierre Dupont out of hospital and doing well. Keep our Princess safe!"

Spur went to see the Laramie County sheriff. The man read the wires and shrugged. "Nobody has reported seeing the woman since she vanished from the jail. She might have taken an east bound the next morning.

"Speaking of trains, I'd just as soon you get that princess out of my county as soon as possible."

"Thanks for the hospitality, Sheriff. I'll make a note of it."

Spur left the office and checked with the four hotels in town. Only one of the room clerks remembered anyone the size and sex of the small woman.

"Yeah, with a little foreign flavor to her English. Not pretty, didn't try to be. Short, maybe thirty. She was here for two days, then left, then came back. She's not here now."

He tried four of the board and room houses but none of the women could remember the small woman. He checked last at the general store. The woman who ran it nodded.

"Sure, she comes in every two or three days. Buys food mostly. I see her walk out to the north, but can't be certain she lives up that way. Must have rented a house somewhere.

The one "Real Estate and Land Office," in town had no record of renting a house to such a person.

"Not all the houses get rented," the agent said. "Sometimes folks just move away and abandon the place rather than try to sell. Not much of a market here right now. Maybe when those new railroad shops get put in we'll have more folks moving here full time."

Spur knew there could be a dozen empty houses in town. He had no way to check on each one. He could not knock on the door and barge in.

Spur turned and headed for the first saloon. It was the "Ore Car Saloon," and he pushed inside and ordered a cold beer. Cold it costs two cents extra. He tilted the bottle and closed his eyes a moment.

Cold beer, yeah! Somebody at the bar beside him moved in close. Spur let the beer down and saw a large back of a man who had to be over six-six. The man pushed backward again and hit Spur jolting him sideways.

The man turned around. He had a sneer on his face, a full beard, small black eyes and a knife scar through his beard on his left cheek.

"Careful," the huge man growled. "I don't like to get bumped into."

"Then sit at a table!" Spur spat back at him.

The big man's eyes flamed. "Little man, you want to apologize for saying that?"

Spur recognized a set up when he saw it. He looked around. The man was working alone. "Never apologized to a tub of lard as big as you in my life. Don't aim to start now. That upset your tender sensitivities?"

"What the hell you say?"

The big man had turned now and the hogleg on his hip had been tied low. His right hand dangled near it.

"I said you're a horse's ass. Who sent you in here to pick a fight with me?"

"Nobody sent me. I don't like shit heads."

Spur stared at the man. It had to be the French woman. Even now she might be at the hotel. He didn't hire the guards!

The saloon had quieted. Nobody said a word. No poker chips sounded. One chair scraped. The bigger man backed up slowly keeping his hand at his side.

"You want it here or in the street?" the beard asked.

Spur's right hand hovered near his six-gun. "You don't get a choice where you die. It's here and now, unless you tell me where I can find the French woman who hired you."

"Nobody hired me. I fight my own fights."

"Then how has an ugly, no talent, slow draw like you lived so long?"

The big man bellowed in anger, his right hand whipping into a draw. Spur's hand powered up, yanked the weapon out of leather, his fingers closed over the handle and his trigger finger eased into the guard.

As the weapon flashed out of leather, Spur lifted the muzzle and pointed his arm at the other man and fired.

The big man barely had his weapon out of leather.

Spur's round caught the heavy man in the gun hand shoulder, spun him around, slammed the iron from his hand and smashed him through a poker table nearby.

Spur picked up the man's gun and jumped beside him as he started to get up. Spur's boot went on the big man's throat and pressed just enough to cut off his breath.

"Now, dumb-ugly, where can I find the French woman?"

Spur let his boot off and put his boot down on the wounded man's right hand, pinning it to the floor.

"What woman?"

"The small woman who hired you to gun me. Where is she?"

"Don't know."

Spur stepped down on the man's gun hand fingers. The giant howled in pain.

"Where is she?"

"Met her in the alley. Lives in some house."

"Let's go pay her a visit."

"She's not there, just at night. Stays in alley watching."

"Dumb-Ugly. You better get out of town. I see you here again, I'll kill you for sure." Spur tossed the gunman's weapon to the barkeep and hurried out the door. He ran down the middle of the street dodging buggies and wagons. He took the hotel stairs three at a time and knocked on Alexandria's door.

She was there.

"The French woman is still here. Stay in my room until I get back. Chance I can rout out the woman. Have Francine stay with you."

Alexandria nodded that she would, then Spur turned and ran back down the stairs. He reloaded his fired round as he walked into the street. Now he concentrated on the alleys in town. He walked half way down each one that came off Main Street. Then worked those that went behind the Main Street stores.

Nothing. No spot where Darlene Benoit could be hiding. How was he going to dig this woman out? He leaned against a store front and thought about it. It was just beginning to get dark. He hurried down the street to the doctor's office and looked inside. The big man he had shot was just coming through a door. Spur dodged back down the street and waited for the shooter.

He came out and went the other direction. Spur followed him. The big man never looked around. Spur noticed that the giant didn't have on a six-gun.

He walked down to the end of the business

344

area and turned right. Spur hurried forward so he wouldn't lose him. The bandaged man walked down one block, then across the street to what seemed to be an abandoned house. It had no glass in the front windows. Weeds grew in the yard. There was no smoke from the chimney now when supper might be cooking.

The giant went to the rear of the small house and disappeared. Spur moved up on the place cautiously. Did the man live here, or was he reporting back to his employer? The darkness settled in and was complete.

Spur saw a light glow in one of the back rooms. This one had windows but blinds had been pulled. The Secret Service Agent slipped closer but he could see nothing through the window.

A door in back banged and Spur froze in place. Someone walked away from the house, going back toward town. A moment later Spur ran around the house in back and saw the outline of what must be the big man walking down the street.

This must be where Darlene Benoit hid out. Check the house or follow the giant? He chose the house.

Now, should he go get the sheriff and make this official? No. She might slip away, the sheriff might take too long to get here or she could slip away in the confusion.

He tested the rear door over a small step. The screen door that had slammed before opened on oiled hinges. Maybe the place wasn't abandoned? Had to be.

He stepped on the porch and the board held fast, no squeaking or creaking.

The back door to the house was three feet away. Not more than four rooms in the place. Probably she used just the back two, a kitchen and a bedroom.

Spur caught the door handle and turned it as far as it would go, then pressed in slowly on the door. It moved a half inch, caught and then slid on open without a sound.

Spur had his Colt out and cocked. He could see the soft light of what he guessed was a candle in the near room. The far one to the other side was dark. He edged into the room farther. The kitchen. A broken table and a chair sprawled to the left. The candle in a cup without a handle rested on an old wood range.

No one was in the kitchen. He looked at the dark room and hesitated.

"Stop right there!" a voice stabbed at him from the dark room. "I've got a shotgun aimed at you and I can use it."

The voice was of a young woman, fifteen, maybe more.

"Don't know what you want here, but you best git. If Roscoe comes back and finds you here, he'll kill both of us."

"Roscoe, that's the name of the big man?"

"Sure. You knew, why else you come?"

"I'm looking for somebody else, a small, French woman."

"She ain't here. She's been staying in an alley, the one in back of the jail. Nobody looks there."

"Thank you. Now, easy with that shotgun."

"You better go, fast."

"True, yes, I'm going. Don't say nothing to Roscoe about this. Then you won't get in trouble. All right?"

"Yeah, I guess. He was trying to buy some milk."

"I'm gone out of here. Good luck."

"Yeah, big chance of that."

Spur holstered the six-gun and slipped out through the back porch door and into the night.

He might have a shot at finding Darlene. Why did she stay here? She must have heard that they left town? She must have expected them to come back, and they had.

Now, all he had to do was capture one small French woman who had one arm in a cast and a bullet hole in her shoulder. Didn't sound like much of a job. Only he knew better.

Spur made his plans as he walked toward the court house. Now was the ideal time. She would be getting settled down for the night hoping to get rid of him tomorrow, then go for the princess. With the broken arm in a cast she wouldn't be able to work a shotgun anymore. Unless she was tremendously determined.

How would he work this? He could start at the near end of the alley and search through every possible place where a person could sleep for the night. The best bets would be big cartons and old shipping boxes. Maybe under a deck or loading platform. He wasn't sure what was in back of the jail in the alley. About time he found out. She was still armed and he knew how dangerous.

Spur settled his six-gun in leather and walked into the far end of the jail house alley. It was dark as a coal mine at midnight. This was the time he would capture the French woman.

Chapter 26

The first hiding places in the alley were easy. Big cardboard packing boxes that he simply tipped over or emptied. Nothing. He moved down past some vacant areas and came to a ten foot wide loading platform where a wagon could back up and use hand trucks to unload it at the same level as the wagon. He looked under the platform for five minutes, but found nothing.

Ahead was a junk pile of boxes and trash, old fencing, some ruined barrels and a jumble of old roofing, metal slats and rusting metal bins. He didn't know where to start.

He kicked a few of the boxes, threw some of the trash around. What irritated him was that this was the place he would pick to hide if he were in the same situation. He calmed down and started at one side and systematically worked back and forth through the mess.

Twice he scraped his fingers on rusty metal. One time he tripped and went to his knees. It took him 20 minutes to check over the whole pile of trash. Benoit wasn't hiding in it.

He moved on down the alley past the jail's back door. All the noise he made in the trash heap could have scared Benoit away. He hurried through the rest of the alley. Only one more good hiding spot and it was empty. He leaned against the brick wall near the far end and tried to think it through.

Where would she go? It all came down to the hotel. He ran around to Main and down to the hotel. Spur checked the lobby. Nobody suspicious there. Then he worked through the dining room and cleared it.

He went up the steps to the second floor silently. No one lurked at the end of the corridor. He ran down to his room and knocked.

"Yes" a small voice asked through the door.

"McCoy here. You all right?"

The door unlocked a chair moved and the panel swung open. Francine rushed into his arms.

"She was here! We heard her next door. She shot off the door lock and kicked it open. Then we heard her swearing in French. We thought she was coming in here. She went in the other room too, we think."

Spur checked the two rooms. They were shot up and trashed. He went back in his own room and closed the door. He leaned against the back of it, nodded to the princess and tried to reason it out.

"She must be downstairs waiting for you to come back. I'll slip out the fire escape and see if I can get spot her. She's got to be down there."

Spur pulled a second derringer from his bag and gave it to Alexandria.

"Can you use that?"

"Yes, of course. I had firearms training. I can use it. Two shots?"

He nodded, saw Francine with her small gun and slipped out the door. He heard her lock it and push the chair under the handle.

Moments later, Spur stepped off the fire escape stairs at the side of the hotel and walked around near the front. He studied all the hiding places near the steps leading up to the hotel's main door. Two were in deep shadows he couldn't see through. He ran up to them quickly but no one huddled there.

Now Spur looked around the lobby again. It would be logical for her to stay there close by and wait for the women to return. But where was she? He checked the whole lobby again, bothered two women reading a newspaper, but neither of them was the Benoit desperado.

Spur shook his head and sat on the steps leading to the second floor rooms. Where could she be?

A revolver shot from the second floor followed by a muffled scream and then two more shots thundered down the staircase.

Spur had his six-gun in his hand and powered up the steps to the second floor. He paused as his sight line came to the floor level. Down the hall he saw an open door. In the middle of the hall opposite his room stood Darlene Benoit. She fired again into the door, then tried to kick it open.

A muffled sound of a shot came as one of the derringers inside fired and the bullet tore through the thin door hitting Benoit in the right arm. She staggered but kept hold of the six-gun.

Spur bellied out on the steps and steadied his Colt on the floor.

"Give it up, Benoit, One move and you're dead."

She spun and fired at him. The round tore up splinters in front of him and daggered half a dozen into his face. One narrowly missed his eye. He blinked, swiped at the splinters and fired. He had no time to aim. The shot missed.

Spur dropped down two steps, pulled out some of the larger splinters, then wiped his eyes and checked over the top of the steps.

A door had been opened across the hall from Spur's door and he saw the edge of one of Benoit's shoes showing in front of it.

Spur put one round through the door about where she could be crouching. There was no response except the shoe pulled back.

"I have a man below on the fire escape, Benoit. You're in my sights right now. All I have to do is keep firing until I blow you full of holes. You ready to give up and live?"

In reply she fired through the bullet hole in the door and Spur ducked away from more splinters. He lifted up and shot twice into the door, then watched the spot as he reloaded until he had six rounds chambered.

"You give up now and I can get you off of any charges and have you deported as an undesirable alien. Give it up and live."

"Liberty! Fraternity! Equality!" the French woman shouted.

Spur changed his aim and fired twice about chest high on the door and close to the wall side.

When the roaring sound of the two shots faded, a scream stabbed through the short hallway.

"Damn you, McCoy! This was a private matter."

"Murder is never private, Benoit. Throw out your gun and walk this way."

She reached around the door and fired, then the arm yanked back and Spur guessed she was in the room out of danger.

From below, Spur saw two men start up the stairs. One was the sheriff. He turned and whispered to the lawman to put one of his deputies on the fire escape at the north side of the hotel. One of the deputies below ran to cover it.

"Is she down there?" The sheriff asked.

"In a room across from mine with the door open. Wish we had one of those military smoke shells to flush her out."

"Where's your princess?"

"Right across the hall with the door barricaded. The women both have derringers."

"She could sit in there all night," the sheriff said. "No way we can get down that hall without losing a man or two. I ain't about to do that."

Spur nodded. "You won't have to. Just fire a round down the hall every two or three minutes. Can you have one of your men get me fifty feet of half inch rope?"

The sheriff eyed him. "What for?"

"Down from the top, to the window. Catch her by surprise."

The sheriff gave the order and Spur went down to the first floor to wait for it.

Five minutes later he climbed the outside ladder to the top of the hotel and found a spot to anchor the rope. He counted over from the end and picked out the room where Benoit must be. Spur tied the rope off securely, then looped it around his body and let it slip slowly as he eased down the side of the building a small step at a time. He didn't want to make any noise, otherwise she would know he was coming.

He heard a shot from inside the hotel and nodded. That would help cover any noise.

He came down between the windows to the second floor and looked over at the glass on his right. It had to be that one. The window was open. Most were on a hot night like this one. He edged over that way until he could see inside. There was no light on. He could see dim light from the hallway lamps. A figure crouched near the door, a big .45 in one fist.

Spur nodded. He held his .45 in one hand, lowered another foot so where he sat on the rope would clear the raised window. Then he pushed out hard with his feet, swinging ten feet over the street. As he swung back soundlessly, he stretched out his feet and leaned back so he could fit through the open window.

Darlene Benoit left the doorway and retreated to the middle of the room.

At the same time Spur came powering into the room. He let out slack on the rope just as he cleared the window. His feet slammed into the standing Benoit. She screamed and was slammed forward, stumbling and trying to catch herself. She staggered into the hallway and past the door.

Spur heard four shots from down the hall, enveloping the room and hall in a roaring, crashing sound that covered up everything else.

Spur dropped to the floor in a tumble and scurried to stand. By the time he was on his feet the sound had faded and he saw Benoit on the floor in the hall beyond the open door.

She wasn't moving.

"Hold your fire!" Spur bellowed and rushed out to the hall. He found the fallen six-gun and pushed it away. Darlene Benoit wasn't dead. She looked at Spur and her eyelids fluttered open, closed then open.

"Tell Didier I tried to avenge him. Tried the best way I could." Darlene shuddered. Her eyes went wide in terror and she screamed. When the scream ended her eyes stared blankly at Spur and the last breath she would ever take gushed out of her lungs.

"She's dead," Spur called to the sheriff. Spur stood and went across the hall and knocked on his door.

"Alexandria, Francine, it's all over. You can open the door."

He heard the chair removed, the lock open. There were four gunshots holes in the door. The panel opened and both women rushed out and hugged him.

Francine was still shaking. She wouldn't look at the body. Alexandria stared at the dead woman a moment, then shook her head.

"It's too bad she didn't write me a letter. I've intervened many times for Frenchmen in our custody. I'll make an inspection trip when I get home. What happened to her brother will never happen again."

The sheriff came up and looked at the body. He nodded. "Maybe we didn't have to kill her, but she didn't seem a mind to give up." He pointed to two deputies to remove the body.

"Sorry about this, Miss. Just had to be done." He tipped his hat to the princess and turned around and left.

When the deputies had all gone, the room clerk came up to look at the damage. He said he would move the two women into new rooms. Spur said he'd use the one he had.

The clerk left to get the new numbers and Spur and the two women sat on the bed. He held his arm around Francine, who was still shaking and sniffling through the last of her crying. Alexandria held Francine on the other side.

"It's over," Spur said at last. "I'm sorry it ended this way."

"You didn't kill her, Spur," Alexandria said. "You had some chances. I don't know if the sheriff had to or not, but he did and it's done and over with. The tour of the West is over. We'll start back tomorrow. But first I have some shopping to do. I hope it's an afternoon train."

The three of them sat huddled together that way for an hour. At last Francine stopped shivering. She kissed Spur on the cheek, then kissed Alexandria on the forehead.

"I think it's time I get to bed now," she said. Alexandria stood as well and helped her to her new room down the hall.

Spur checked to see where the bullets went that had come through his door. One was in the floor. One in the wall. A third hit his carpet bag and came to rest in a pair of socks. The last one he never did find.

Spur shrugged, locked his door and fell to sleep as soon as he took his boots off. There probably was no need but his six-gun lay ready and waiting beside his right hand.

Chapter 27

At breakfast the next morning, Princess Alexandria reminded Spur that she and Francine were going shopping.

"We'll need two hundred dollars to spend," she said sweetly watching him closely.

Spur frowned, then took out his wallet and took two of the $100 bills from the roll and handed them to the brown haired woman.

"It's Mantuco money, but that seems like a lot to spend on a last day shopping splurge. There's going to be a train through here east at two-fifteen this afternoon. We have tickets and should be on it."

"Plenty of time," Alexandria said. She looked at Francine and they both grinned.

"Oh, we also want you to meet us at ten o'clock with a buggy, a rather large one."

His brows went up. "A buggy, and you're not telling me what this is all about?"

"Not a chance, McCoy," Francine said. The old sparkle was back in her eyes and he nodded.

"Buggy at ten o'clock. Where?"

"At the general store, that should be a central point," Alexandria said.

Spur finished his meal, bid the women good-bye and went down to the sheriff's office for the last time. He wrote out a statement about the death of Darlene Benoit and signed it. Then he made a copy of the statement for his own use and asked the sheriff if his report was ready.

The sheriff growled and gave Spur what he and his deputies had readied. Spur read it over, had them add the date and the town and state, then had the sheriff sign it. He folded that report plus his own in his shirt pocket and gave the sheriff a copy of his own report on the death and a crisp new ten dollar bill.

"That's for cost of burial. I assume that you can have the matter taken care of."

The sheriff said he could. They parted without shaking hands. The man would never be one of Spur's best friends.

Spur's next stop was the telegraph office. He spent a half hour writing and rewriting his telegrams. They would go to his boss and to the Mantuco embassy. Both said about the same thing.

"Darlene Benoit, 28, native of Paris, France, was killed by the sheriff of Laramie County, Wyoming, on Tuesday, June 24. She was shot by the sheriff and deputies while resisting arrest after being cornered in a hotel room as she was attempting to kill Princess Alexandria of Mantuco, and her traveling companion, Miss Francine Miller.

"Both the later were unharmed.

"The body was buried in Cheyenne, Wyoming, in a public burial ground and the grave marked.

"Substantiating documents will be sent by U.S. Mail today to the Mantuco embassy in Washington, D.C.

"The Western trip is over. The Princess and Miss Miller will be returning by rail, leaving today. Agent Spur McCoy will accompany them as far as St. Louis, Missouri, where some representative of the Mantuco Principality is requested to be on hand to meet them and take responsibility.

"A complete financial report will be included to justify expenses from the $10,000 (U.S.) turned over to McCoy by Pierre Dupont when he was returned for medical attention. All unspent funds will be returned to your representative in St. Louis, Missouri."

He signed it Spur McCoy, U.S. Secret Service Agent.

He sent both wires and wrote down the expense, then went back to his room and began an hour-long session to remember where and how much money they had spent since Dupont left them.

He was surprised how little they had spent. Mostly in travel and hotel bills. He had over $9,000 left.

Spur checked the time, then hurried down to the livery and hired a buggy to carry six and drove to the general store. The two women stood on the board walk waiting for him. Two steamer trucks sat near them.

Two employees came from the store to help Spur load the trunks in the carriage. Then there was barely room for the rest of them.

"I'd guess you want these taken to the train station," Spur said.

The women giggled.

"Absolutely not," Francine said.

"You may drive us out to the fort," Alexandria said.

"The army fort?"

"Quite right," Francine said.

Spur lifted his brows, whacked the reins on the back of the pair of grays and they drove toward the fort.

As he neared the gate about 20 minutes later, Francine motioned to him.

"Drive us down to Mighty Thunder's tipi," she said.

"You didn't," Spur said.

"Just a few things for Two Doves, and some other things she can share with the Indian women. They have so little."

By the time the carriage came to a stop outside Mighty Thunder's tipi, there were half a dozen Indian children around them. Spur jumped down and Mighty Thunder appeared at the side of his home.

"Women's work," Spur said. He and Mighty Thunder wrestled the steamer trunks off the buggy, then sat in the shade of the tipi and smoked as the women opened the trunk and began giving away the items they brought.

There were pots and pans for cooking, towels, blankets, women's clothes, pants, and a hundred other items.

Two Doves' eyes went wide, then she sat down amid her treasures and began to cry.

Mighty Thunder shouted at her, but Spur touched the Indian's arm.

"It's just women's sweat," Spur said and he and the Arapaho laughed loud and long.

It was an hour later that the goods were all given out, and the steamer trunks left for the Indians as well. The three got on the buggy, waved good-bye and hurried back to town. They had only a little time before the train would leave.

They had a quick dinner and still made it to the train on time.

They had a pair of compartments, and all three settled down in the women's room and watched out the window.

"It's been a wonderful tour of the Wild, Wild West," Alexandria said. "I'm glad Pierre is recovering. At least he got to see some of your amazingly large country."

"So many things happened I'll never forget," Francine said. "Including how I almost became the third wife of a Mormon rancher!"

They reminisced for 50 miles and then it was time for supper. The dining car was adequate and after they ate they went back to the women's compartment.

Alexandria, Princess of the Principality of Mantuco, looked at McCoy and wiggled a finger at him.

"Now, Spur McCoy, Francine and I have agreed that there are a certain amount of accounts that need to be balanced, some comparisons made, and debts to be paid so they are met with fairness and honesty."

"I totally agree, Secret Service Agent Spur McCoy. Some things and some debts can be paid in only one way, and Princess Alexandria and I have come to total agreement."

Spur frowned and looked from one to the other. "Debts, I don't understand."

"Like when you saved me from that gambler's

361

bedroom on the riverboat," Alexandria said.

"And when you came after me and rescued me in the wilds of Wyoming when I was naked and alone and it was dark and I was so terrified I thought I was going to die," Francine said.

As she said it, she began to open the buttons down the front of her dress.

Spur furrowed his forehead and looked at Alexandria, who had her dress opened to the waist and shrugged it off her shoulders.

"We want to have one last fling all the way to St. Louis," Alexandria said.

"Share and share alike, Spur McCoy, with no arguments who is first, or who is best, or who had the biggest titties, or the best pair of legs," Francine said, followed by a wild whoop.

Francine pushed the top of her dress off her shoulders and took off the chemise that covered her breasts.

Spur laughed softly. "Then one thing I suggest is that we close the window blind so we don't entertain the whole Wild West with three naked people."

It wasn't a race exactly, but Alexandria had the last of her clothes off first, and she knelt beside Spur and began to take his vest off.

Francine kicked off the pink bloomers she wore and stood and stretched, luxuriantly naked and free.

"Like anything you see, cowboy?" she asked.

Spur McCoy chuckled as he grabbed her and dropped her on the bed and then it was a gentle tangle as the three of them sought to satisfy each other in every way that any of them could think of.

Spur came up for a long breath and laughed softly. What a perfect ending to a job that he turned down three times. Next call for an escort for a princess around the West, he would be first in line for the job.

Two wonderful days, and three long and amazing nights later, the train pulled into St. Louis. A tired and startlingly satisfied looking Spur McCoy turned the two ladies over to a Colonel in the Mantuco army and gently kissed them both on the cheek goodbye.

He watched them off on the afternoon train for Washington, D.C. Now all he needed was to report by wire to General Halleck that he was ready for a new assignment.

He took two steps toward a hotel and revised his plans. After two days of resting up, he would send a wire to General Halleck. Spur smiled as he walked on to the hotel and a much needed two days of rest.